T5-CWL-546
ST. MARY'S COLLEGE OF MARYLAND
ST. MARY'S CITY, MARYLAND

THE BRICK MOON
AND OTHER STORIES

Thirty Years' Home, Roxbury

The Brick Moon

and

Other Stories

BY

EDWARD EVERETT HALE

Short Story Index Reprint Series

BOOKS FOR LIBRARIES PRESS
FREEPORT, NEW YORK

First Published 1899
Reprinted 1970

STANDARD BOOK NUMBER:
8369-3512-8

LIBRARY OF CONGRESS CATALOG CARD NUMBER:
73-121555

PRINTED IN THE UNITED STATES OF AMERICA

Preface

TO read these stories again, thirty and more years after they were written, is to recall many memories, sad or glad, with which this reader need not be interrupted. But I have to make sure that they are intelligible to readers of a generation later than that for which they were written.

The story of The Brick Moon was begun in my dear brother Nathan's working-room in Union College, Schenectady, in the year 1870, when he was professor of the English language there. The account of the first plan of the moon is a sketch, as accurate as was needed, of the old chat and dreams, plans and jokes, of our college days, before he left Cambridge in 1838. As I learned almost everything I know through his care and love and help, directly or indirectly, it is a pleasure to say this here. The story was published in the "Atlantic Monthly," in 1870 and 1871. It was the last story I wrote for that magazine, before assuming the charge of "Old and New," a magazine which I edited from 1870 to 1876, and for which I wrote "Ten Times One is Ten," which has been printed in the third volume of this series.

Among the kind references to "The Brick Moon" which I have received from sympathetic friends, I now recall with the greatest pleasure one sent me by Mr. Asaph Hall, the distinguished astronomer of the National Observatory. In sending me the ephemeris of the two moons of Mars, which he revealed to this world of ours, he wrote, "The smaller of these moons is the veritable Brick Moon." That, in the moment of triumph for the greatest astronomical discovery of a generation, Dr. Hall should have time or thought to give to my little parable, — this was praise indeed.

Writing in 1870, I said, as the reader will see on page 66, that George Orcutt did not tell how he used a magnifying power of 700. Nor did I choose to tell then, hoping that in some fortunate winter I might be able myself to repeat his process, greatly to the convenience of astronomers who have not Alvan Clark's resources at hand, or who have to satisfy themselves with glass lenses of fifteen inches, or even thirty, in diameter. But no such winter has come round to me, and I will now give Orcutt's invention to the world. He had unlimited freezing power. So have we now, as we had not then. With this power he made an ice lens, ten feet in diameter, which was easily rubbed, by the delicate hands of the careful women around him, to precisely the surface which he needed. Let me hope that before next winter passes some countryman or countrywoman of mine will have equalled his success, and with an ice lens will surpass all the successes of the glasses of our time.

The plan of "Crusoe in New York" was made when I was enjoying the princely hospitality of Henry Whitney Bellows in New York. The parsonage in that city commanded a view of a "lot" not built on, which would have given for many years a happy home to any disciple of Mayor Pingree, if a somewhat complicated social order had permitted. The story was first published in Frank Leslie's illustrated paper. In reading it in 1899, I am afraid that the readers of a hard-money generation may not know that "scrip" was in the sixties the name for small change.

I regard a knowledge of every detail of the original Robinson Crusoe as well-nigh a necessity in education. Girls may occasionally be excused, but never boys. It ought to be unnecessary, therefore, to say that some of the narrative passages of Crusoe in New York are taken, word for word, from the text of Defoe. If I do state this for the benefit of a few unfortunate ladies who are not familiar with that text, it is because I think no one among many courteous critics has observed it.

"The Survivor's Story" is one of eight short stories which were published in the first Christmas number of "Old and New."

Of the other stories I think no explanation is needed, but such as was given at the time of their publication and is reprinted with each of them here.

EDWARD E. HALE.

ROXBURY, July 6, 1899.

CONTENTS

VOLUME IV

PAGE

The Brick Moon 3
Crusoe in New York 103
Bread on the Waters 169
The Lost Palace 241
99 Linwood Street 267
Ideals 289
Thanksgiving at the Polls 327
The Survivor's Story 349

THE BRICK MOON

THE BRICK MOON

[From the papers of Captain FREDERIC INGHAM.]

I

PREPARATION

I HAVE no sort of objection now to telling the whole story. The subscribers, of course, have a right to know what became of their money. The astronomers may as well know all about it, before they announce any more asteroids with an enormous movement in declination. And experimenters on the longitude may as well know, so that they may act advisedly in attempting another brick moon or in refusing to do so.

It all began more than thirty years ago, when we were in college; as most good things begin. We were studying in the book which has gray sides and a green back, and is called "Cambridge Astronomy" because it is translated from the French. We came across this business of the longitude, and, as we talked, in the gloom and glamour of the old South Middle dining-hall, we had going the usual number of students' stories about rewards offered by the Board of Longitude for discoveries in that matter, — stories, all of which, so far as I know, are lies. Like all boys, we had tried our hands at perpetual motion. For me, I was sure I could square the circle, if they would give me chalk enough. But as to this business of the longitude, it was reserved for Q.[1] to make the happy hit and to explain it to the rest of us.

I wonder if I can explain it to an unlearned world, which has not studied the book with gray sides and a green cambric back. Let us try.

You know then, dear world, that when you look at the North Star, it always appears to you at just the same height above the horizon or what is between you and the horizon: say the Dwight School-house, or the houses in Concord Street; or to me, just now, North College. You know also that, if you were to travel to the North Pole, the North Star would be just over your head. And, if you were to travel to the equator, it would be just on your horizon, if you could see it at all through the red, dusty, hazy mist in the north, — as you could not. If you were just half-way between pole and equator, on the line between us and Canada, the North Star would be half-way up, or 45° from the horizon. So you would know there that you were 45° from the equator. Then in Boston, you would find it was 42° 20′ from the horizon. So you know there that you are 42° 20′ from the equator. At Seattle again you would find it was 47° 40′ high, so our friends at Seattle

[1] Wherever Q. is referred to in these pages my brother Nathan is meant. One of his *noms de plume* was Gnat Q. Hale, because G and Q may be silent letters.

know that they are at 47° 40′ from the equator. The latitude of a place, in other words, is found very easily by any observation which shows how high the North Star is; if you do not want to measure the North Star, you may take any star when it is just to north of you, and measure its height; wait twelve hours, and if you can find it, measure its height again. Split the difference, and that is the altitude of the pole, or the latitude of you, the observer.

"Of course we know this," says the graduating world. "Do you suppose that is what we borrow your book for, to have you spell out your miserable elementary astronomy?" At which rebuff I should shrink distressed, but that a chorus of voices an octave higher comes up with, "Dear Mr. Ingham, we are ever so much obliged to you; we did not know it at all before, and you make it perfectly clear."

Thank you, my dear, and you, and you. We will not care what the others say. If you do understand it, or do know it, it is more than Mr. Charles Reade knew, or he would not have made his two lovers on the island guess at their latitude, as they did. If they had either of them been educated at a respectable academy for the Middle Classes, they would have fared better.

Now about the longitude.

The latitude, which you have found, measures your distance north or south from the equator or the pole. To find your longitude, you want to find your distance east or west from the meridian of Greenwich. Now, if any one would build a good tall tower at Greenwich, straight into the sky, — say a hundred miles into the sky, — of course if you and I were east or west of it, and could see it, we could tell how far east or west we were by measuring the apparent height of the tower above our horizon. If we could see so far, when the lantern with a Drummond's light, "ever so bright," on the very top of the tower, appeared to be on our horizon, we should know we were eight hundred and seventy-three miles away from it. The top of the tower would answer for us as the North Star does when we are measuring the latitude. If we were nearer, our horizon would make a longer angle with the line from the top to our place of vision. If we were farther away, we should need a higher tower.

But nobody will build any such tower at Greenwich, or elsewhere on that meridian, or on any meridian. You see that to be of use to the half the world nearest to it, it would have to be so high that the diameter of the world would seem nothing in proportion. And then, for the other half of the world you would have to erect another tower as high on the other side. It was this difficulty that made Q. suggest the expedient of the Brick Moon.

For you see that if, by good luck, there were a ring like Saturn's which stretched round the world, above Greenwich and the meridian of Greenwich, and if it would stay above Greenwich, turning with the world, any one who wanted to measure his longitude or distance from Greenwich would look out of window and see how high this ring was above his horizon. At Greenwich it would be over his head exactly. At New Orleans, which is quarter round the world from Greenwich, it would be just in his horizon. A little west of New Orleans you would begin to look for the other half of the ring on the west instead of the east; and if you went a little west of the Feejee Islands the ring would be over your head again. So if we only had a ring like that, not round the equator of the world, — as Saturn's ring is around Saturn, — but vertical to the plane of the equator, as the brass ring of an artificial globe goes, only far higher in proportion, — "from that ring," said Q., pensively, "we could calculate the longitude."

Failing that, after various propositions, he suggested the Brick Moon. The plan was this: If from the surface of the earth, by a gigantic pea-shooter, you could shoot a pea upward from Greenwich, aimed northward as well as upward; if you drove it so fast and far that when its power of ascent was exhausted, and it began to fall, it should clear the earth, and pass outside the North Pole; if you had given it sufficient power to get it half round the earth without touching, that pea would clear the earth forever. It would continue to rotate above the North Pole, above the Feejee Island place, above the South Pole and Greenwich, forever, with the impulse with which it had first cleared our atmosphere and attraction. If only we could see that pea as it revolved in that convenient orbit, then we could measure the longitude from that, as soon as we knew how high the orbit was, as well as if it were the ring of Saturn.

"But a pea is so small!"

"Yes," said Q., "but we must make a large pea." Then we fell to work on plans for making the pea very large and very light. Large, — that it might be seen far away by storm-tossed navigators: light, — that it might be the easier blown four thousand and odd miles into the air; lest it should fall on the heads of the Greenlanders or the Patagonians; lest they should be injured and the world lose its new moon. But, of course, all this lath-and-plaster had to be given up. For the motion through the air would set fire to this moon just as it does to other aerolites, and all your lath-and-plaster would gather into a few white drops, which no Rosse telescope even could discern. "No," said Q. bravely, "at the least it must be very substantial. It must stand fire well, very well. Iron will not answer. It must be brick; we must have a Brick Moon."

Then we had to calculate its size. You can see, on the old moon, an edifice two hundred feet long with any of the fine refractors of our day. But no such refractors as those can be carried by the poor little fishermen whom we wanted to befriend, the bones of whose ships lie white on so many cliffs, their names unreported at any Lloyd's or by any Ross,

> Themselves the owners and their sons the crew.

On the other hand, we did not want our moon two hundred and fifty thousand miles away, as the old moon is, which I will call the Thornbush moon, for distinction. We did not care how near it was, indeed, if it were only far enough away to be seen, in practice, from almost the whole world. There must be a little strip where they could not see it from the surface, unless we threw it infinitely high. "But they need not look from the surface," said Q.; "they might climb to the mast-head. And if they did not see it at all, they would know that they were ninety degrees from the meridian."

This difficulty about what we call "the strip," however, led to an improvement in the plan, which made it better in every way. It was clear that even if "the strip" were quite wide, the moon would have to be a good way off, and, in proportion, hard to see. If, however, we would satisfy ourselves with a moon four thousand miles away, *that* could be seen on the earth's surface for three or four thousand miles on each side; and twice three thousand, or six thousand, is one fourth of the largest circumference of the earth. We did not dare have it nearer than four thousand miles, since even at that distance it would be eclipsed three hours out of every night; and we wanted it bright and distinct, and not of that lurid, copper, eclipse color. But at four thousand miles' distance the moon could be seen by a belt of observers six or eight thousand miles in diameter. "Start, then, two moons," — this was my contribution to the plan. "Suppose one over the meridian of Greenwich, and the other over that of New Orleans. Take care that there is a little difference in the radii of their orbits, lest they 'collide' some foul day. Then, in most places, one or other, perhaps two will come in sight. So much the less risk of clouds: and everywhere there may be one, except when it is cloudy. Neither need be more than four thousand miles off; so much the larger and more beautiful will they be. If on the old Thornbush moon old Herschel with his reflector could see a town-house two hundred feet long, on the Brick Moon young Herschel will be able to see a dab of mortar a foot and a half long, if he wants to. And people without the reflector, with their opera-glasses, will be able to see sufficiently well." And to this they agreed: that eventually there must be two Brick Moons. Indeed, it were better that there should be four, as each must be below the horizon half the time. That is only as many as Jupiter has. But it was also agreed that we might begin with one.

Why we settled on two hundred feet of diameter I hardly know. I think it was from the statement of dear John Farrar's about the impossibility of there being a state house two hundred feet long not yet discovered, on the sunny side of old Thornbush. That, somehow, made two hundred our fixed point. Besides, a moon of two hundred feet diameter did not seem quite unmanageable. Yet it was evident that a smaller moon would be of no use, unless we meant to have them near the world, when there would be so many that they would be confusing, and eclipsed most of the time. And four thousand miles is a good way off to see a moon even two hundred feet in diameter.

Small though we made them on paper, these two-hundred-foot moons were still too much for us. Of course we meant to build them hollow. But even if hollow there must be some thickness, and the quantity of brick would at best be enormous. Then, to get them up! The pea-shooter, of course, was only an illustration. It was long after that time that Rodman and other guns sent iron balls five or six miles in distance, — say two miles, more or less, in height.

Iron is much heavier than hollow brick, but you can build no gun with a bore of two hundred feet now, — far less could you then. No.

Q. again suggested the method of shooting ofi the moon. It was not to be by any of your sudden explosions. It was to be done as all great things are done, — by the gradual and silent accumulation of power. You all know that a fly-wheel — heavy, very heavy on the circumference, light, very light within it — was made to save up power, from the time when it was produced to the time when it was wanted. Yes? Then, before we began even to build the moon, before we even began to make the brick, we would build two gigantic fly-wheels, the diameter of each should be "ever so great," the circumference heavy beyond all precedent, and thundering strong, so that no temptation might burst it. They should revolve, their edges nearly touching, in opposite directions, for years, if it were necessary, to accumulate power, driven by some waterfall now wasted to the world. One should be a little heavier than the other. When the Brick Moon was finished, and all was ready, IT should be gently rolled down a gigantic groove provided for it, till it lighted on the edge of both wheels at the same instant. Of course it would not rest there, not the ten-thousandth part of a second. It would be snapped upward, as a drop of water from a grindstone. Upward and upward; but the heavier wheel would have deflected it a little from the vertical. Upward and northward it would rise, therefore, till it had passed the axis of the world. It would, of course, feel the world's attraction all the time, which would bend its flight gently, but still it would leave the world more and more behind. Upward still, but now southward, till it had traversed more than one hundred and eighty degrees of a circle. Little resistance, indeed, after it had cleared the forty or fifty miles of visible atmosphere. "Now let it fall," said Q., inspired with the vision. "Let it fall, and the sooner the better! The curve it is now on will forever clear the world; and over the meridian of that lonely waterfall,—if only we have rightly adjusted the gigantic flies,—will forever revolve, in its obedient orbit, the—

BRICK MOON,

the blessing of all seamen,—as constant in all change as its older sister has been fickle, and the second cynosure of all lovers upon the waves, and of all girls left behind them." "Amen," we cried, and then we sat in silence till the clock struck ten; then shook each other gravely by the hand, and left the South Middle dining-hall.

Of waterfalls there were plenty that we knew.

Fly-wheels could be built of oak and pine, and hooped with iron. Fly-wheels did not discourage us.

But brick? One brick is, say, sixty-four cubic inches only. This moon,—though we made it hollow,—see,—it must take twelve million brick.

The brick alone will cost sixty thousand dollars!

The brick alone would cost sixty thousand dollars. There the scheme of the Brick Moon hung, an airy vision, for seventeen years,—the years that changed us from young men into men. The brick alone, sixty thousand dollars! For, to boys who have still left a few of their college bills unpaid, who cannot think of buying that lovely little Elzevir which Smith has for sale at auction, of which Smith does not dream of the value, sixty thousand dollars seems as intangible as sixty million sestertia. Clarke, second, how much are sixty million sestertia stated in cowries? How much in currency, gold being at 1.37¼? Right; go up. Stop, I forget myself!

So, to resume, the project of the Brick Moon hung in the ideal, an airy vision, a vision as lovely and as distant as the Brick Moon itself, at this calm moment of midnight when I write, as it poises itself over the shoulder of Orion, in my southern horizon. Stop! I anticipate. Let me keep — as we say in Beadle's Dime Series — to the even current of my story.

Seventeen years passed by, we were no longer boys, though we felt so. For myself, to this hour, I never enter board meeting, committee meeting, or synod, without the queer question, what would happen should any one discover that this bearded man was only a big boy disguised? that the frock-coat and the round hat are none of mine, and that, if I should be spurned from the assembly, as an interloper, a judicious public, learning all the facts, would give a verdict, "Served him right." This consideration helps me through many bored meetings which would be else so dismal. What did my old copy say? —

"*Boards are made of wood, they are long and narrow.*"

But we do not get on!

Seventeen years after, I say, or should have said, dear Orcutt entered my room at Naguadavick again. I had not seen him since the Commencement day when we parted at Cambridge. He looked the same, and yet not the same. His smile was the same, his voice, his tender look of sympathy when I spoke to him of a great sorrow, his childlike love of fun. His waistband was different, his pantaloons were different, his smooth chin was buried in a full beard, and he weighed two hundred pounds if he weighed a gramme. O, the good time we had, so like the times of old! Those were happy days for me in Naguadavick. At that moment my double was at work for me at a meeting of the publishing committee of the Sandemanian Review, so I called Orcutt up to my own snuggery, and we talked over old times; talked till tea was ready. Polly came up through the orchard and made tea for us herself there. We talked on and on, till nine, ten at night, and then it was that dear Orcutt asked me if I remembered the Brick Moon. Remember it? of course I did. And without leaving my chair I opened the drawer of my writing-desk, and handed him a portfolio full of working-drawings on which I had engaged myself for my "third"[1] all that winter. Orcutt was delighted. He turned them over hastily but intelligently, and said: "I am so glad. I could not think you had forgotten. And I have seen Brannan, and Brannan has not forgotten." "Now do you know," said he, "in all this railroading of mine, I have not forgotten. When I built the great tunnel

1 "Every man," says Dr. Peabody, "should have a vocation and an avocation." To which I add, "A third."

for the Cattawissa and Opelousas, by which we got rid of the old inclined planes, there was never a stone bigger than a peach-stone within two hundred miles of us. I baked the brick of that tunnel on the line with my own kilns. Ingham, I have made more brick, I believe, than any man living in the world!"

"You are the providential man," said I.

"Am I not, Fred? More than that," said he; "I have succeeded in things the world counts worth more than brick. I have made brick, and I have made money!"

"One of us make money?" asked I, amazed.

"Even so," said dear Orcutt; "one of us has made money." And he proceeded to tell me how. It was not in building tunnels, nor in making brick. No! It was by buying up the original stock of the Cattawissa and Opelousas, at a moment when that stock had hardly a nominal price in the market. There were the first mortgage bonds, and the second mortgage bonds, and the third, and I know not how much floating debt; and worse than all, the reputation of the road lost, and deservedly lost. Every locomotive it had was asthmatic. Every car it had bore the marks of unprecedented accidents, for which no one was to blame. Rival lines, I know not how many, were cutting each other's throats for its legitimate business. At this juncture dear George invested all his earnings as a contractor, in the despised original stock, — he actually bought it for 3¼ per cent, — good shares that had cost a round hundred to every wretch who had subscribed. Six thousand eight hundred dollars — every cent he had — did George thus invest. Then he went himself to the trustees of the first mortgage, to the trustees of the second, and to the trustees of the third, and told them what he had done.

Now it is personal presence that moves the world. Dear Orcutt has found that out since, if he did not know it before. The trustees who would have sniffed had George written to them, turned round from their desks, and begged him to take a chair, when he came to talk with them. Had he put every penny he was worth into that stock? Then it was worth something which they did not know of, for George Orcutt was no fool about railroads. The man who bridged the Lower Rapidan when a freshet was running was no fool.

"What were his plans?"

George did not tell — no, not to lordly trustees — what his plans were. He had plans, but he kept them to himself. All he told them was that he had plans. On those plans he had staked his all. Now, would they or would they not agree to put him in charge of the running of that road, for twelve months, on a nominal salary? The superintendent they had had was a rascal. He had proved that by running away. They knew that George was not a rascal. He knew that he could make this road pay expenses, pay bond-holders, and pay a dividend, — a thing no one else had dreamed of for twenty years. Could they do better than try him?

Of course they could not, and they knew they could not. Of course they sniffed and talked, and waited, and pretended they did not know, and that they must consult, and so forth and so on. But of course they all did try him, on his own terms. He was put in charge of the running of that road.

In one week he showed he should redeem it. In three months he did redeem it!

He advertised boldly the first day: "*Infant children at treble price.*"

The novelty attracted instant remark. And it showed many things. First, it showed he was a humane man, who wished to save human life. He would leave these innocents in their cradles, where they belonged.

Second, and chiefly, the world of travellers saw that the Crichton, the Amadis, the perfect chevalier of the future, had arisen, — a railroad manager caring for the comfort of his passengers!

The first week the number of the C. and O.'s passengers was doubled: in a week or two more freight began to come in, in driblets, on the line which its owners had gone over. As soon as the shops could turn them out, some cars were put on, with arms on which travellers could rest their elbows, with head-rests where they could take naps if they were weary. These excited so much curiosity that one was exhibited in the museum at Cattawissa and another at Opelousas. It may not be generally known that the received car of the American roads was devised to secure a premium offered by the Pawtucket and Podunk Company. Their receipts were growing so large that they feared they should forfeit their charter. They advertised, therefore, for a car in which no man could sleep at night or rest by day, — in which the backs should be straight, the heads of passengers unsupported, the feet entangled in a vice, the elbows always knocked by the passing conductor. The pattern was produced which immediately came into use on all the American roads. But on the Cattawissa and Opelousas this time-honored pattern was set aside.

Of course you see the result. Men went hundreds of miles out of their way to ride on the C. and O. The third mortgage was paid off; a reserve fund was piled up for the second; the trustees of the first lived in dread of being paid; and George's stock, which he bought at 3¼, rose to 147 before two years had gone by! So was it that, as we sat together in the snuggery, George was worth wellnigh three hundred thousand dollars. Some of his eggs were in the basket where they were laid; some he had taken out and placed in other baskets; some in nests where various hens were brooding over them. Sound eggs they were, wherever placed; and such was the victory of which George had come to tell.

One of us had made money!

On his way he had seen Brannan. Brannan, the pure-minded, right-minded, shifty man of tact, man of brain, man of heart, and man of word, who held New Altona in the hollow of his hand. Brannan had made no money. Not he, nor ever will. But Brannan could do much what he pleased in this world, without money. For whenever Brannan studied the rights and the wrongs of any enterprise, all men knew that what Brannan decided about it was wellnigh the eternal truth; and therefore all men of sense were accustomed to place great confidence in his prophecies. But, more than this, and better, Brannan was an unconscious dog, who believed in the people. So, when he knew what was the right and what was the wrong, he could stand up before two or three thousand people and tell them what was right and what was wrong, and tell them with the same simplicity and freshness with which he would talk to little Horace on his knee. Of the thousands who heard him there would not be one in a hundred who knew that this was eloquence. They were fain to say, as they sat in their shops, talking, that Brannan was not eloquent. Nay, they went so far as to regret that Brannan was not eloquent! If he were only as eloquent as Carker was or as Barker was, how excellent he would be! But when, a month after, it was necessary for them to do anything about the thing he had been speaking of, they did what Brannan had told them to do; forgetting, most likely, that he had ever told them, and fancying that these were their own ideas, which, in fact, had, from his liquid, ponderous, transparent, and invisible common sense, distilled unconsciously into their being. I wonder whether Brannan ever knew that he was eloquent. What I knew, and what dear George knew, was, that he was one of the leaders of men!

Courage, my friends, we are steadily advancing to the Brick Moon!

For George had stopped, and seen Brannan; and Brannan had not forgotten. Seventeen years Brannan had remembered, and not a ship had been lost on a lee-shore because her longitude was wrong, — not a baby had wailed its last as it was ground between wrecked spar and cruel rock, — not a swollen corpse unknown had been flung up upon the sand and been buried with a nameless epitaph, — but Brannan had recollected the Brick Moon, and had, in the memory-chamber which rejected nothing, stored away the story of the horror. And now George was ready to consecrate a round hundred thousand to the building of the Moon; and Brannan was ready, in the thousand ways in which wise men move the people to and fro, to persuade them to give to us a hundred thousand more; and George had come to ask me if I were not ready to undertake with them the final great effort, of which our old calculations were the embryo. For this I was now to contribute the mathematical certainty and the lore borrowed from naval science, which should blossom and bear fruit when the Brick Moon was snapped like a cherry from the ways on which it was built, was launched into the air by power gathered from a thousand freshets, and, poised at last in its own pre-calculated region of the ether, should begin its course of eternal blessings in one unchanging meridian!

Vision of Beneficence and Wonder! Of course I consented.

Oh that you were not so eager for the end! Oh that I might tell you, what now you will never know, — of the great campaign which we then and there inaugurated! How the horrible loss of the Royal Martyr, whose longitude was three degrees awry, startled the whole world, and gave us a point to start from. How I explained to George that he must not subscribe the one hundred thousand dollars in a moment. It must come in bits, when "the cause" needed a stimulus, or the public needed encouragement. How we caught neophyte editors, and explained to them enough to make them think the Moon was well-nigh their own invention and their own thunder. How, beginning in Boston, we sent round to all the men of science, all those of philanthropy, and all those of commerce, three thousand circulars, inviting them to a private meeting at George's parlors at the Revere. How, besides ourselves, and some nice, respectable-looking old gentlemen Brannan had brought over from Podunk with him, paying their fares both ways, there were present only three men, — all adventurers whose projects had failed, — besides the representatives of the press. How, of these representatives, some understood the whole, and some understood nothing. How, the next day, all gave us "first-rate notices." How, a few days after, in the lower Horticultural Hall, we had our first public meeting. How Haliburton brought us fifty people who loved him, — his Bible class, most of them, — to help fill up; how, besides these, there were not three persons whom we had not asked personally, or one who could invent an excuse to stay away. How we had hung the walls with intelligible and unintelligible diagrams. How I opened the meeting. Of that meeting, indeed, I must tell something.

First, I spoke. I did not pretend to unfold the scheme. I did not attempt any rhetoric. But I did not make any apologies. I told them simply of the dangers of lee-shores. I told them when they were most dangerous, — when seamen came upon them unawares. I explained to them that, though the costly chronometer, frequently adjusted, made a delusive guide to the voyager who often made a harbor, still the adjustment was treacherous, the instrument beyond the use of the poor, and that, once astray, its error increased forever. I said that we believed we had a method which, if the means were supplied for the experiment, would give the humblest fisherman the very certainty of sunrise and of sunset in his calculations of his place upon the world. And I said that whenever a man knew his place in this world, it was always likely all would go well. Then I sat down.

Then dear George spoke, — simply, but very briefly. He said he was a stranger to the Boston people, and that those who knew him at all knew he was not a talking man. He was a civil engineer, and his business was to calculate and to build, and not to talk. But he had come here to say that he had studied this new plan for the longitude from the Top to the Bottom, and that he believed in it through and through. There was his opinion, if that was worth anything to anybody. If that meeting resolved to go forward with the enterprise, or if anybody proposed to, he should offer his services in any capacity, and without any pay, for its success. If he might only work as a bricklayer, he would work as a bricklayer. For he believed, on his soul, that the success of this enterprise promised more for mankind than any enterprise which was ever likely to call for the devotion of his life. "And to the good of mankind," he said, very simply, "my life is devoted." Then he sat down.

Then Brannan got up. Up to this time, excepting that George had dropped this hint about bricklaying, nobody had said a word about the Moon, far less hinted what it was to be made of. So Ben had the whole to open. He did it as if he had been talking to a bright boy of ten years old. He made those people think that he respected them as his equals. But, in fact, he chose every word, as if not one of them knew anything. He explained, as if it were rather more simple to explain than to take for granted. But he explained as if, were they talking, they might be explaining to him. He led them from point to point, — oh! so much more clearly than I have been leading you, — till, as their mouths dropped a little open in their eager interest, and their lids forgot to wink in their gaze upon his face, and so their eyebrows seemed a little lifted in curiosity, — till, I say, each man felt as if he were himself the inventor, who had bridged difficulty after difficulty; as if, indeed, the whole were too simple to be called difficult or complicated. The only wonder was that the Board of Longitude, or the Emperor Napoleon, or the Smithsonian, or somebody, had not sent this little planet on its voyage of blessing long before. Not a syllable that you would have called rhetoric, not a word that you would have thought prepared; and then Brannan sat down.

That was Ben Brannan's way. For my part, I like it better than eloquence.

Then I got up again. We would answer any questions, I said. We represented people who were eager to go forward with this work. (Alas! except Q., all of those represented were on the stage.) We could not go forward without the general assistance of the community. It was not an enterprise which the government could be asked to favor. It was not an enterprise which would yield one penny of profit to any human being. We had therefore, purely on the ground of its benefit to mankind, brought it before an assembly of Boston men and women.

Then there was a pause, and we could hear our watches tick, and our hearts beat. Dear George asked me in a whisper if he should say anything more, but I thought not. The pause became painful, and then Tom Coram, prince of merchants, rose. Had any calculation been made of the probable cost of the experiment of one moon?

I said the calculations were on the table. The brick alone would cost $60,000. Mr. Orcutt had computed that $214,729 would complete two fly-wheels and one moon. This made no allowance for whitewashing the moon, which was not strictly necessary. The fly-wheels and water-power would be equally valuable for the succeeding moons, if any were attempted, and therefore the second moon could be turned off, it was hoped, for $159,732.

Thomas Coram had been standing all the time I spoke, and in an instant he said: "I am no mathematician. But I have had a ship ground to pieces under me on the Laccadives because our chronometer was wrong. You need $250,000 to build your first moon. I will be one of twenty men to furnish the money; or I will pay $10,000 to-morrow for this purpose, to any person who may be named as treasurer, to be repaid to me if the moon is not finished this day twenty years."

That was as long a speech as Tom Coram ever made. But it was pointed. The small audience tapped applause.

Orcutt looked at me, and I nodded. "I will be another of the twenty men," cried he. "And I another," said an old bluff Englishman, whom nobody had invited; who proved to be a Mr. Robert Boll, a Sheffield man, who came in from curiosity. He stopped after the meeting; said he should leave the country the next week, and I have never seen him since. But his bill of exchange came all the same.

That was all the public subscribing. Enough more than we had hoped for. We tried to make Coram treasurer, but he refused. We had to make Haliburton treasurer, though we should have liked a man better known than he then was. Then we adjourned. Some nice ladies then came up, and gave, one a dollar, and one five dollars, and one fifty, and so on, — and some men who have stuck by ever since. I always, in my own mind, call each of those women Damaris, and each of those men Dionysius. But those are not their real names.

How I am wasting time on an old story! Then some of these ladies came the next day and proposed a fair; and out of that, six months after, grew the great Longitude Fair, that you will all remember, if you went to it, I am sure. And the papers the next day gave us first-rate reports; and then, two by two, with our subscription-books, we went at it. But I must not tell the details of that subscription. There were two or three men who subscribed $5,000 each, because they were perfectly certain the amount would never be raised. They wanted, for once, to get the credit of liberality for nothing. There were many men and many women who subscribed from one dollar up to one thousand, not because they cared a straw for the longitude, nor because they believed in the least in the project; but because they believed in Brannan, in Orcutt, in Q., or in me. Love goes far in this world of ours. Some few men subscribed because others had done it: it was the thing to do, and they must not be out of fashion. And three or four, at least, subscribed because each hour of their lives there came up the memory of the day when the news came that the —— was lost, George, or Harry, or John, in the ——, and they knew that George, or Harry, or John might have been at home, had it been easier than it is to read the courses of the stars!

Fair, subscriptions, and Orcutt's reserve, — we counted up $162,000, or nearly so. There would be a little more when all was paid in.

But we could not use a cent, except Orcutt's and our own little subscriptions, till we had got the whole. And at this point it seemed as if the whole world was sick of us, and that we had gathered every penny that was in store for us. The orange was squeezed dry!

II

HOW WE BUILT IT

THE orange was squeezed dry! And how little any of us knew, — skilful George Orcutt, thoughtful Ben Brannan, loyal Haliburton, ingenious Q., or poor painstaking I, — how little we knew, or any of us, where was another orange, or how we could mix malic acid and tartaric acid, and citric acid and auric acid and sugar and water so as to imitate orange-juice, and fill up the bank-account enough to draw in the conditioned subscriptions, and so begin to build the MOON. How often, as I lay awake at night, have I added up the different subscriptions in some new order, as if that would help the matter: and how steadily they have come out one hundred and sixty-two thousand dollars, or even less, when I must needs, in my sleepiness, forget somebody's name! So Haliburton put into railroad stocks all the money he collected, and the rest of us ground on at our mills, or flew up on our own wings towards Heaven. Thus Orcutt built more tunnels, Q. prepared for more commencements, Haliburton calculated more policies, Ben Brannan created more civilization, and I, as I could, healed the hurt of my people of Naguadavick for the months there were left to me of my stay in that thriving town.

None of us had the wit to see how the problem was to be wrought out further. No. The best things come to us when we have faithfully and well made all the preparation and done our best; but they come in some way that is none of ours. So was it now, that to build the BRICK MOON it was necessary that I should be turned out of Naguadavick ignominiously, and that Jeff. Davis and some seven or eight other bad men should create the Great Rebellion. Hear how it happened.

Dennis Shea, my Double, — otherwise, indeed, called by my name and legally so, — undid me, as my friends supposed, one evening at a public meeting called by poor Isaacs in Naguadavick. Of that transaction I have no occasion here to tell the story. But of that transaction one consequence is that the BRICK MOON now moves in ether. I stop writing, to rest my eye upon it, through a little telescope of Alvan Clark's here, which is always trained near it. It is moving on as placidly as ever.

It came about thus. The morning after poor Dennis, whom I have long since forgiven, made his extraordinary speeches, without any authority from me, in the Town Hall at Naguadavick, I thought, and my wife agreed with me, that we had better both leave town with the children. Auchmuty, our dear friend, thought so too. We left in the seven o'clock Accommodation for Skowhegan, and so came to Township No. 9 in the 3d Range, and there for years we resided. That whole range of townships was set off under a provision admirable in its character, that the first settled minister in each town should receive one hundred acres of land as the "minister's grant," and the first settled schoolmaster eighty. To No. 9, therefore, I came. I constituted a little Sandemanian church. Auchmuty and Delafield came up and installed me, and with these hands I built the cabin in which, with Polly and the little ones, I have since spent many happy nights and days. This is not the place for me to publish a map, which I have by me, of No. 9, nor an account of its many advantages for settlers. Should I ever print my papers called "Stay-at-home Robinsons," it will be easy with them to explain its topography and geography. Suffice it now to say, that, with Alice and Bertha and Polly, I took tramps up and down through the lumbermen's roads, and soon knew the general features of the lay of the land. Nor was it long, of course, before we came out one day upon the curious land-slides, which have more than once averted the flow of the Little Carrotook River, where it has washed the rocks away so far as to let down one section more of the overlying yielding yellow clay.

Think how my eyes flashed, and my wife's, as, struggling though a wilderness of moosewood, we came out one afternoon on this front of yellow clay! Yellow clay of course, when properly treated by fire, is brick! Here we were surrounded by forests, only waiting to be burned; yonder was clay, only waiting to be baked. Polly looked at me, and I looked at her, and with one voice, we cried out, "The MOON!"

For here was this shouting river at our feet, whose power had been running to waste since the day when the Laurentian hills first heaved themselves above the hot Atlantic; and that day, I am informed by Mr. Agassiz, was the first day in the history of this solid world. Here was water-power enough for forty fly-wheels, were it necessary to send heavenward twenty moons. Here was solid timber enough for a hundred dams, yet only one was necessary to give motion to the fly-wheels. Here was retirement, — freedom from criticism, an escape from the journalists, who would not embarrass us by telling of every cracked brick which had to be rejected from the structure. We had lived in No. 9 now for six weeks, and not an "own correspondent" of them all had yet told what Rev. Mr. Ingham had for dinner.

Of course I wrote to George Orcutt at once of our great discovery, and he came up at once to examine the situation. On the whole, it pleased him. He could not take the site I proposed for the dam, because this very clay there made the channel treacherous, and there was danger that the stream would work out a new career. But lower down we found a stony gorge with which George was satisfied; he traced out a line for a railway by which, of their own weight, the brick-cars could run to the centrings; he showed us where, with some excavations, the fly-wheels could be placed exactly above the great mill-wheels, that no power might be wasted, and explained to us how, when the gigantic structure was finished, the BRICK MOON would gently roll down its ways upon the rapid wheels, to be launched instant into the sky!

Shall I ever forget that happy October day of anticipation?

We spent many of those October days in tentative surveys. Alice and Bertha were our chainmen, intelligent and obedient. I drove for George his stakes, or I cut away his brush, or I raised and lowered the shield at which he sighted; and at noon Polly appeared with her baskets, and we would dine *al fresco*, on a pretty point which, not many months after, was wholly covered by the eastern end of the dam. When the field-work was finished we retired to the cabin for days, and calculated and drew, and drew and calculated. Estimates for feeding Irishmen, estimates of hay for mules, — George was sure he could work mules better than oxen, — estimates for cement, estimates for the preliminary saw-mills, estimates for rail for the little brick-road, for wheels, for spikes, and for cutting ties; what did we not estimate for — on a basis almost wholly new, you will observe. For here the brick would cost us less than our old conceptions, — our water-power cost us almost nothing, — but our stores and our wages would cost us much more.

These estimates are now to me very curious, — a monument, indeed, to dear George's memory, that in the result they proved so accurate. I would gladly print them here at length, with some illustrative cuts, but that I know the impatience of the public, and its indifference to detail. If we are ever able to print a proper memorial of George, that, perhaps, will be the fitter place for them. Suffice it to say that with the subtractions thus made from the original estimates, — even with the additions forced upon us by working in a wilderness, — George was satisfied that a money charge of $197,327 would build and start THE MOON. As soon as we had determined the site, we marked off eighty acres, which contained all the essential localities, up and down the little Carrotook River, — I engaged George for the first schoolmaster in No. 9, and he took these eighty acres for the schoolmaster's reservation. Alice and Bertha went to school to him the next day, taking lessons in civil engineering; and I wrote to the Bingham trustees to notify them that I had engaged a teacher, and that he had selected his land.

Of course we remembered, still, that we were near forty thousand dollars short of the new estimates, and also that much of our money would not be paid us but on condition that two hundred and fifty thousand were raised. But George said that his own subscription was wholly unhampered: with that we would go to work on the preliminary work of the dam, and on the flies. Then, if the flies would hold together, — and they should hold if mortise and iron could hold them, — they might be at work summers and winters, days and nights, storing up Power for us. This would encourage the subscribers, it would encourage us; and all this preliminary work would be out of the way when we were really ready to begin upon the MOON.

Brannan, Haliburton, and Q. readily agreed to this when they were consulted. They were the other trustees under an instrument which we had got St. Leger[1] to draw up. George gave up, as soon as he might, his other appointments; and taught me, meanwhile, where and how I was to rig a little saw-mill, to cut some necessary lumber. I engaged a gang of men to cut the timber for the dam, and to have it ready; and, with the next spring, we were well at work on the dam and on the flies! These needed, of course, the most solid foundation. The least irregularity of their movement might send the MOON awry.

Ah me! would I not gladly tell the history of every bar of iron which was bent into the tires of those flies, and of every log which was mortised into its place in the dam, nay, of every curling mass of foam which played in the eddies beneath, when the dam was finished, and the waste water ran so smoothly over? Alas! that one drop should be wasted of water that might move a world, although a small one! I almost dare say that I remember each and all these, — with such hope and happiness did I lend myself, as I could, each

[1] The St. Leger of these stories was Francis Brown Hayes, H. C. 1839.

day to the great enterprise; lending to dear George, who was here and there and everywhere, and was this and that and everybody,—lending to him, I say, such poor help as I could lend, in whatever way. We waked, in the two cabins in those happy days, just before the sun came up, when the birds were in their loudest clamor of morning joy. Wrapped each in a blanket, George and I stepped out from our doors, each trying to call the other, and often meeting on the grass between. We ran to the river and plunged in,—oh, how cold it was!—laughed and screamed like boys, rubbed ourselves aglow, and ran home to build Polly's fire beneath the open chimney which stood beside my cabin. The bread had risen in the night. The water soon boiled above the logs. The children came laughing out upon the grass, barefoot, and fearless of the dew. Then Polly appeared with her gridiron and bear-steak, or with her griddle and eggs, and, in fewer minutes than this page has cost me, the breakfast was ready for Alice to carry, dish by dish, to the white-clad table on the piazza. Not Raphael and Adam more enjoyed their watermelons, fox-grapes, and late blueberries! And, in the long croon of the breakfast, we revenged ourselves for the haste with which it had been prepared.

When we were well at table, a horn from the cabins below sounded the reveille for the drowsier workmen. Soon above the larches rose the blue of their smokes; and when we were at last nodding to the children, to say that they might leave the table, and Polly was folding her napkin as to say she wished we were gone, we would see tall Asaph Langdon, then foreman of the carpenters, sauntering up the valley with a roll of paper, or an adze, or a shingle with some calculations on it,—with something on which he wanted Mr. Orcutt's directions for the day.

An hour of nothings set the carnal machinery of the day agoing. We fed the horses, the cows, the pigs, and the hens. We collected the eggs and cleaned the hen-houses and the barns. We brought in wood enough for the day's fire, and water enough for the day's cooking and cleanliness. These heads describe what I and the children did. Polly's life during that hour was more mysterious. That great first hour of the day is devoted with women to the deepest arcana of the Eleusinian mysteries of the divine science of housekeeping. She who can meet the requisitions of that hour wisely and bravely conquers in the Day's Battle. But what she does in it, let no man try to say! It can be named, but not described, in the comprehensive formula, "Just stepping round."

That hour weli given to chores and to digestion, the children went to Mr. Orcutt's open-air school, and I to my rustic study,—a separate cabin, with a rough square table in it, and some book-boxes equally rude. No man entered it, excepting George and me. Here for two hours I worked undisturbed,

— how happy the world, had it neither postman nor door-bell! — worked upon my Traces of Sandemanianism in the Sixth and Seventh Centuries, and then was ready to render such service to The Cause and to George as the day might demand. Thus I rode to Lincoln or to Foxcroft to order supplies; I took my gun and lay in wait on Chairback for a bear; I transferred to the hewn lumber the angles or bevels from the careful drawings: as best I could, I filled an apostle's part, and became all things to all these men around me. Happy those days! — and thus the dam was built; in such Arcadian simplicity was reared the mighty wheel; thus grew on each side the towers which were to support the flies; and thus, to our delight not unmixed with wonder, at last we saw those mighty flies begin to turn. Not in one day, nor in ten; but in a year or two of happy life, — full of the joy of joys, — the "joy of eventful living."

Yet, for all this, $162,000 was not $197,000, far less was it $250,000; and but for Jeff. Davis and his crew the BRICK MOON would not have been born.

But at last Jeff. Davis was ready. "My preparations being completed," wrote General Beauregard, "I opened fire on Fort Sumter." Little did he know it, — but in that explosion the BRICK MOON also was lifted into the sky!

Little did we know it, when, four weeks after, George came up from the settlements, all excited with the news! The wheels had been turning now for four days, faster of course and faster. George had gone down for money to pay off the men, and he brought us up the news that the Rebellion had begun.

"The last of this happy life," he said; "the last, alas, of our dear MOON." How little he knew and we!

But he paid off the men, and they packed their traps and disappeared, and, before two months were over, were in the lines before the enemy. George packed up, bade us sadly good-by, and before a week had offered his service to Governor Fenton in Albany. For us, it took rather longer; but we were soon packed; Polly took the children to her sister's, and I went on to the Department to offer my service there. No sign of life left in No. 9, but the two gigantic Fly-Wheels, moving faster and faster by day and by night, and accumulating Power till it was needed. If only they would hold together till the moment came!

So we all ground through the first slow year of the war. George in his place, I in mine, Brannan in his, — we lifted as we could. But how heavy the weight seemed! It was in the second year, when the second large loan was placed, that Haliburton wrote to me, — I got the letter, I think, at Hilton Head, — that he had sold out every penny of our railroad stocks, at the high prices which railroad stocks then bore, and had invested the whole fifty-nine thousand in the new Governments.

"I could not call a board meeting," said Haliburton, "for I am here only on leave of absence, and the rest are all away. But the case is clear enough. If the government goes up, the MOON will never go up; and, for one, I do not look beyond the veil." So he wrote to us all, and of course we all approved.

So it was that Jeff. Davis also served. Deep must that man go into the Pit who does not serve, though unconscious. For thus it was that, in the fourth year of the war, when gold was at 290, Haliburton was receiving on his fifty-nine thousand dollars seventeen per cent interest in currency; thus was it that, before the war was over, he had piled up, compounding his interest, more than fifty per cent addition to his capital; thus was it that, as soon as peace came, all his stocks were at a handsome percentage; thus was it that, before I returned from South America, he reported to all the subscribers that the full quarter-million was secured: thus was it that, when I returned after that long cruise of mine in the Florida, I found Polly and the children again at No. 9, George there also, directing a working party of nearly eighty bricklayers and hodmen, the lower centrings wellnigh filled to their diameter, and the BRICK MOON, to the eye, seeming almost half completed.

Here it is that I regret most of all that I cannot print the working-drawings with this paper. If you will cut open the seed-vessel of Spergularia

Rubra, or any other carpel that has a free central placenta, and observe how the circular seeds cling around the circular centre, you will have some idea of the arrangement of a transverse horizontal section of the completed MOON. Lay three croquet-balls on the piazza, and call one or two of the children to help you poise seven in one plane above the three; then let another child place three more above the seven, and you have the *core* of the MOON completely. If you want a more poetical illustration, it was what Mr. Wordsworth calls a mass

> "Of conglobated bubbles undissolved."

Any section through any diameter looked like an immense rose-window, of six circles grouped round a seventh. In truth, each of these sections would reveal the existence of seven chambers in the moon, — each a sphere itself, — whose arches gave solidity to the whole; while yet, of the whole moon, the greater part was air. In all there were thirteen of these moonlets, if I am so to call them; though no one section, of course, would reveal so many. Sustained on each side by their groined arches, the surface of the whole moon was built over them and under them, — simply two domes connected at the bases. The chambers themselves were made lighter by leaving large, round windows or open circles in the parts of their vaults farthest from their points of contact, so that each of them looked not unlike the outer sphere of a

Japanese ivory nest of concentric balls. You see the object was to make a moon, which, when left to its own gravity, should be fitly supported or braced within. Dear George was sure that, by this constant repetition of arches, we should with the least weight unite the greatest strength. I believe it still, and experience has proved that there is strength enough.

When I went up to No. 9, on my return from South America, I found the lower centring up, and half full of the working-bees, — who were really Keltic laborers, — all busy in bringing up the lower half-dome of the shell. This lower centring was of wood, in form exactly like a Roman amphitheatre if the seats of it be circular; on this the lower or inverted brick dome was laid. The whole fabric was on one of the terraces which were heaved up in some old geological cataclysm, when some lake gave way, and the Carrotook River was born. The level was higher than that of the top of the fly-wheels, which, with an awful velocity now, were circling in their wild career in the ravine below. Three of the lowest moonlets, as I have called them, — separate croquet-balls, if you take my other illustration, — had been completed; their centrings had been taken to pieces and drawn out through the holes, and were now set up again with other new centrings for the second story of cells.

I was received with wonder and delight. I had telegraphed my arrival, but the despatches had never been forwarded from Skowhegan. Of course, we all had a deal to tell; and, for me, there was no end to inquiries which I had to make in turn. I was never tired of exploring the various spheres, and the nameless spaces between them. I was never tired of talking with the laborers. All of us, indeed, became skilful bricklayers; and on a pleasant afternoon you might see Alice and Bertha, and George and me, all laying brick together, — Polly sitting in the shade of some wall which had been built high enough, and reading to us from Jean Ingelow or Monte-Cristo or Jane Austen, while little Clara brought to us our mortar. Happily and lightly went by that summer. Haliburton and his wife made us a visit; Ben Brannan brought up his wife and children; Mrs. Haliburton herself put in the keystone to the central chamber, which had always been named G on the plans; and at her suggestion, it was named Grace now, because her mother's name was Hannah. Before winter we had passed the diameter of I, J, and K, the three uppermost cells of all; and the surrounding shell was closing in upon them. On the whole, the funds had held out amazingly well. The wages had been rather higher than we meant; but the men had no chances at liquor or dissipation, and had worked faster than we expected; and, with our new brick-machines, we made brick inconceivably fast, while their quality was so good that dear George said there was never so little waste. We celebrated Thanksgiving of that year together,

— my family and his family. We had paid off all the laborers; and there were left, of that busy village, only Asaph Langdon and his family, Levi Jordan and Levi Ross, Horace Leonard and Seth Whitman with theirs. "Theirs," I say, but Ross had no family. He was a nice young fellow who was there as Haliburton's representative, to take care of the accounts and the pay-roll; Jordan was the head of the brick-kilns; Leonard, of the carpenters; and Whitman, of the commissariat,— and a good commissary Whitman was.

We celebrated Thanksgiving together! Ah me! what a cheerful, pleasant time we had; how happy the children were together! Polly and I and our bairns were to go to Boston the next day. I was to spend the winter in one final effort to get twenty-five thousand dollars more if I could, with which we might paint the MOON, or put on some ground felspathic granite dust, in a sort of paste, which in its hot flight through the air might fuse into a white enamel. All of us who saw the MOON were so delighted with its success that we felt sure "the friends" would not pause about this trifle. The rest of them were to stay there to watch the winter, and to be ready to begin work the moment the snow had gone. Thanksgiving afternoon,— how well I remember it,— that good fellow, Whitman, came and asked Polly and me to visit his family in their new quarters. They had moved for the winter into cells B and E, so lofty, spacious, and warm, and so much drier than their log cabins.

Mrs. Whitman, I remember, was very cheerful and jolly; made my children eat another piece of pie, and stuffed their pockets with raisins; and then with great ceremony and fun we christened room B by the name of Bertha, and E, Ellen, which was Mrs. Whitman's name. And the next day we bade them all good-by, little thinking what we said, and with endless promises of what we would send and bring them in the spring.

Here are the scraps of letters from Orcutt, dear fellow, which tell what more there is left to tell: —

"December 10th.

". . . After you left we were a little blue, and hung round loose for a day or two. Sunday we missed you especially, but Asaph made a good substitute, and Mrs. Leonard led the singing. The next day we moved the Leonards into L and M, which we christened Leonard and Mary (Mary is for your wife). They are pretty dark, but very dry. Leonard has swung hammocks, as Whitman did.

"Asaph came to me Tuesday and said he thought they had better turn to and put a shed over the unfinished circle, and so take occasion of warm days for dry work there. This we have done, and the occupation is good for us. . . ."

"December 25th.

"I have had no chance to write for a fortnight. The truth is, that the weather has been so open that I let Asaph go down to No. 7 and to Wilder's, and engage five-and-twenty of the best of the men, who, we knew, were hanging round there. We have all been at work most of the time since, with very good success. H is now wholly covered in, and the centring is out. The men have named it Haliburton. I is well advanced. J is as you left it. The work has been good for us all, morally."

"February 11th.

". . . We got your mail unexpectedly by some lumbermen on their way to the 9th Range. One of them has cut himself, and takes this down.

"You will be amazed to hear that I and K are both done. We have had splendid weather, and have worked half the time. We had a great jollification when K was closed in, — called it Kilpatrick, for Seth's old general. I wish you could just run up and see us. You must be quick, if you want to put in any of the last licks. . . ."

"March 12th.

"DEAR FRED, — I have but an instant. By all means make your preparations to be here by the end of the month or early in next month. The weather has been faultless, you know. Asaph got in a dozen more men, and we have brought up the surface farther than you could dream. The ways are well forward, and I cannot see why, if the freshet hold off a little, we should not launch her by the 10th or 12th. I do not think it worth while to wait for paint or enamel. Telegraph Brannan that he must be here. You will be amused by our quarters. We, who were the last outsiders, move into A and D to-morrow, for a few weeks. It is much warmer there.

"Ever yours, G. O."

I telegraphed Brannan, and in reply he came with his wife and his children to Boston. I told him that he could not possibly get up there, as the roads then were; but Ben said he would go to Skowhegan, and take his chance there. He would, of course, communicate with me as soon as he got there. Accordingly I got a note from him at Skowhegan, saying he had hired a sleigh to go over to No. 9; and in four days more I got this letter: —

March 27th.

DEAR FRED, — I am most glad I came, and I beg you to bring your wife as soon as possible. The river is very full, the wheels, to which Leonard has added two auxiliaries, are moving as if they could not hold out long, the ways are all but ready, and we think we must not wait. Start with all hands as soon as you can. I had no difficulty in coming over from Skowhegan. We did it in two days.

This note I sent at once to Haliburton; and we got all the children ready for a winter journey, as the spectacle of the launch of the MOON was one to be remembered their life long. But it was clearly impossible to attempt, at that season, to get the subscribers together. Just as we started, this despatch from Skowhegan was brought me, — the last word I got from them: —

Stop for nothing. There is a jam below us in the stream, and we fear back-water.

ORCUTT.

Of course we could not go faster than we could. We missed no connection. At Skowhegan, Haliburton and I took a cutter, leaving the ladies and children to follow at once in larger sleighs. We drove all night, changed horses at Prospect, and kept on all the next day. At No. 7 we had to wait over night. We started early in the morning, and came down the Spoonwood Hill at four in the afternoon, in full sight of our little village.

It was quiet as the grave! Not a smoke, not a man, not an adze-blow, nor the tick of a trowel. Only the gigantic fly-wheels were whirling as I saw them last.

There was the lower Coliseum-like centring, somewhat as I first saw it.

But where was the Brick Dome of the MOON?

"Good Heavens! has it fallen on them all?" cried I.

Haliburton lashed the beast till he fairly ran down that steep hill. We turned a little point, and came out in front of the centring. There was no MOON there! An empty amphitheatre, with not a brick nor a splinter within!

We were speechless. We left the cutter. We ran up the stairways to the terrace. We ran by the familiar paths into the centring. We came out upon the ways, which we had never seen before. These told the story too well! The ground and crushed surface of the timbers, scorched by the rapidity with which the MOON had slid down, told that they had done the duty for which they were built.

It was too clear that in some wild rush of the waters the ground had yielded a trifle. We could not find that the foundations had sunk more than six inches, but that was enough. In that fatal six inches' decline of the centring, the MOON had been launched upon the ways just as George had intended that it should be when he was ready. But it had slid, not rolled, down upon these angry fly-wheels, and in an instant, with all our friends, it had been hurled into the sky!

"They have gone up!" said Haliburton; "She has gone up!" said I; — both in one breath. And with a common instinct, we looked up into the blue.

But of course she was not there.

NOT a shred of letter or any other tidings could we find in any of the shanties. It was indeed six weeks since George and Fanny and their children had moved into Annie and Diamond, — two unoccupied cells of the MOON, — so much more comfortable had the cells proved than the cabins, for winter life. Returning to No. 7, we found there many of the laborers, who were astonished at what we told them. They had been paid off on the 30th, and told to come up again on the 15th of April, to see the launch. One of them, a man named Rob Shea, told me that George kept his cousin Peter to help him move back into his house the beginning of the next week.

And that was the last I knew of any of them for

more than a year. At first I expected, each hour, to hear that they had fallen somewhere. But time passed by, and of such a fall, where man knows the world's surface, there was no tale. I answered, as best I could, the letters of their friends, by saying I did not know where they were, and had not heard from them. My real thought was, that if this fatal MOON did indeed pass our atmosphere, all in it must have been burned to death in the transit. But this I whispered to no one save to Polly and Annie and Haliburton. In this terrible doubt I remained, till I noticed one day in the "Astronomical Record" the memorandum, which you perhaps remember, of the observation, by Dr. Zitta, of a new asteroid, with an enormous movement in declination.

III

FULFILMENT

LOOKING back upon it now, it seems inconceivable that we said as little to each other as we did, of this horrible catastrophe. That night we did not pretend to sleep. We sat in one of the deserted cabins, now talking fast, now sitting and brooding, without speaking, perhaps, for hours. Riding back the next day to meet the women and children, we still brooded, or we discussed this "if," that "if," and yet others. But after we had once opened it all to them, — and when we had once answered the children's horribly naïve questions as best we could, — we very seldom spoke to each other of it again. It was too hateful, all of it, to talk about. I went round to Tom Coram's office one day, and told him all I knew. He saw it was dreadful to me, and, with his eyes full, just squeezed my hand, and never said one word more. We lay awake nights, pondering and wondering, but hardly ever did I to Haliburton or he to me explain our respective notions as they came and went. I believe my general impression was that of which I have spoken, that they were all burned to death on the instant, as the little aerolite fused in its passage through our atmosphere. I believe Haliburton's thought more often was that they were conscious of what had happened, and gasped out their lives in one or two breathless minutes, — so horribly long! — as they shot outside of our atmosphere. But it was all too terrible for words. And that which we could not but think upon, in those dreadful waking nights, we scarcely whispered even to our wives.

Of course I looked and he looked for the miserable thing. But we looked in vain. I returned to the few subscribers the money which I had scraped together towards whitewashing the moon, — "shrouding its guilty face with innocent white" indeed! But we agreed to spend the wretched trifle of the other money, left in the treasury after paying the last bills, for the largest Alvan Clark telescope that we could buy; and we were fortunate in obtaining cheap a second-hand one which came to the hammer when the property of the Shubael Academy was sold by the mortgagees. But we had, of course, scarce a hint whatever as to where the miserable object was to be found. All we could do was to carry the glass to No. 9, to train it there on the meridian of No. 9, and take turns every night in watching the field, in the hope that this child of sorrow might drift across it in its path of ruin. But, though everything else seemed to drift by, from east to west, nothing came from south to north, as we expected. For a whole month of spring, another of autumn, another of summer, and another of winter, did Haliburton and his wife and Polly and I glue our eyes to that eye-glass, from the twilight of evening to the twilight of morning, and the dead hulk never hove in sight. Wherever else it was, it seemed not to be on that meridian, which was where it ought to be and was made to be! Had ever any dead mass of matter wrought such ruin to its makers, and, of its own stupid inertia, so falsified all the prophecies of its birth! Oh, the total depravity of things!

It was more than a year after the fatal night, — if it all happened in the night, as I suppose, — that, as I dreamily read through the "Astronomical Record" in the new reading-room of the College Library at Cambridge, I lighted on this scrap: —

"Professor Karl Zitta of Breslau writes to the *Astronomische Nachrichten* to claim the discovery of a new asteroid observed by him on the night of March 31st.

											(92)
				App. A. R.			App. Decl.			
Bresl. M. T.	h.	m.	s.	h.	m.	s.	°	′	″	Size.
March 31	12	53	51.9	15	39	52.32	—23	50	26.1	12.9
April 1	1	3	2.1	15	39	52.32	—23	9	1.9	12.9

He proposes for the asteroid the name of Phœbe. Dr. Zitta states that in the short period which he had for observing Phœbe, for an hour after midnight, her motion in R. A. seemed slight and her motion in declination very rapid."

After this, however, for months, nay even to this moment, nothing more was heard of Dr. Zitta of Breslau.

But, one morning, before I was up, Haliburton came banging at my door on D Street. The mood had taken him, as he returned from some private theatricals at Cambridge, to take the comfort of the new reading-room at night, and thus express in practice his gratitude to the overseers of the college for keeping it open through all the twenty-four hours. Poor Haliburton, he did not sleep well in those times! Well, as he read away on the *Astronomische Nachrichten* itself, what should he find but this in German, which he copied for me, and then, all on foot in the rain and darkness, tramped over with, to South Boston: —

"The most enlightened head professor Dr. Gmelin writes to the director of the Porpol Astronomik at St. Petersburg, to claim the discovery of an asteroid in a very high southern latitude, of a wider inclination of the orbit, as will be noticed, than any asteroid yet observed.

"Planet's apparent α $21^{h.}$ $20^{m.}$ $51^{s.}.40$. Planet's apparent δ $-39° 31' 11''.9$. Comparison star *a*.

"Dr. Gmelin publishes no separate second observation, but is confident that the declination is diminishing. Dr. Gmelin suggests for the name of this extra-zodiacal planet 'Io,' as appropriate to its wanderings from the accustomed ways of planetary life, and trusts that the very distinguished Herr Peters, the godfather of so many planets, will relinquish this name, already claimed for the asteroid (85) observed by him, September 15, 1865."

I had run down stairs almost as I was, slippers and dressing-gown being the only claims I had on society. But to me, as to Haliburton, this stuff about "extra-zodiacal wandering" blazed out upon the page, and though there was no evidence that the "most enlightened" Gmelin found anything the next night, yet, if his "diminishing" meant anything, there was, with Zitta's observation,— whoever Zitta might be,— something to start upon. We rushed upon some old bound volumes of the Record and spotted the "enlightened Gmelin." He was chief of a college at Taganrog, where perhaps they had a spyglass. This gave us the parallax of his observation. Breslau, of course, we knew, and so we could place Zitta's, and with these poor data I went to work to construct, if I could, an orbit for this Io-Phœbe mass of brick and mortar. Haliburton, not strong in spherical trigonometry, looked out logarithms for me till breakfast, and, as soon as it would do, went over to Mrs. Bowdoin, to borrow her telescope, ours being left at No. 9.

Mrs. Bowdoin was kind, as she always was, and at noon Haliburton appeared in triumph with the boxes on P. Nolan's job-wagon. We always employ P., in memory of dear old Phil. We got the telescope rigged, and waited for night, only, alas! to be disappointed again. Io had wandered somewhere else, and, with all our sweeping back and forth on the tentative curve I had laid out, Io would not appear. We spent that night in vain.

But we were not going to give it up so. Phœbe might have gone round the world twice before she became Io; might have gone three times, four, five, six, — nay, six hundred, — who knew? Nay, who knew how far off Phœb-Io was or Io-Phœbe? We sent over for Annie, and she and Polly and George and I went to work again. We calculated in the next week sixty-seven orbits on the supposition of so many different distances from our surface. I laid out on a paper, which we stuck up on the wall opposite, the formula, and then one woman and one man attacked each set of elements, each having the Logarithmic Tables, and so in a week's working-time the sixty-seven orbits were completed. Seventy-seven possible places for Io-Phœbe to be in on the forthcoming Friday evening. Of these sixty-seven, forty-one were observable above our horizon that night.

She was not in one of the forty-one, nor near it.

But Despair, if Giotto be correct, is the chief of sins. So has he depicted her in the fresco of the Arena in Padua. No sin, that, of ours! After searching all that Friday night, we slept all Saturday (sleeping after sweeping). We all came to the Chapel, Sunday, kept awake there, and taught our Sunday classes special lessons on Perseverance. On Monday we began again, and that week we calculated sixty-seven more orbits. I am sure I do not know why we stopped at sixty-seven. All of these were on the supposition that the revolution of the Brick Moon, or Io-Phœbe, was so fast that it would require either fifteen days to complete its orbit, or sixteen days, or seventeen days, and so on up to eighty-one days. And, with these orbits, on the next Friday we waited for the darkness. As we sat at tea, I asked if I should begin observing at the smallest or at the largest orbit. And there was a great clamor of diverse opinions. But little Bertha said, "Begin in the middle."

"And what is the middle?" said George, chaffing the little girl.

But she was not to be dismayed. She had been in and out all the week, and knew that the first orbit was of fifteen days and the last of eighty-one; and, with true Lincoln School precision, she said,

"The mean of the smallest orbit and the largest orbit is forty-eight days."

"Amen!" said I, as we all laughed. "On forty-eight days we will begin."

Alice ran to the sheets, turned up that number, and read, "R. A. 27° 11′. South declination 34° 49′."

"Convenient place," said George; "good omen, Bertha, my darling! If we find her there, Alice and Bertha and Clara shall all have new dolls."

It was the first word of pleasantry that had been spoken about the horrid thing since Spoonwood Hill!

Night came at last. We trained the glass on the fated spot. I bade Polly take the eye-glass. She did so, shook her head uneasily, screwed the tube northward herself a moment, and then screamed, "It is there! it is there, — a clear disk, — gibbous shape, — and very sharp on the upper edge. Look! look! as big again as Jupiter!"

Polly was right! The Brick Moon was found!

Now we had found it, we never lost it. Zitta and Gmelin, I suppose, had had foggy nights and stormy weather often. But we had some one at the eye-glass all that night, and before morning had very respectable elements, good measurements of angular distance when we got one, from another star in the field of our lowest power. For we could see her even with a good French opera-glass I had, and with a night-glass which I used to carry on the South Atlantic Station. It certainly was an extraordinary illustration of Orcutt's engineering ability, that, flying off as she did, without leave or license, she should have gained so nearly the orbit of our original plan, — nine thousand miles from the earth's centre, five thousand from the surface. He had always stuck to the hope of this, and on his very last tests of the Flies he had said they were almost up to it. But for this accuracy of his, I can hardly suppose we should have found her to this hour, since she had failed, by what cause I then did not know, to take her intended place on the meridian of No. 9. At five thousand miles the MOON appeared as large as the largest satellite of Jupiter appears. And Polly was right in that first observation, when she said she got a good disk with that admirable glass of Mrs. Bowdoin.

The orbit was not on the meridian of No. 9, nor did it remain on any meridian. But it was very nearly South and North, — an enormous motion in declination with a very slight *retrograde* motion in Right Ascension. At five thousand miles the MOON showed as large as a circle two miles and a third in diameter would have shown on old Thornbush, as we always called her older sister. We longed for an eclipse of Thornbush by B. M., but no such lucky chance is on the cards in any place accessible to us for many years. Of course, with a MOON so near us the terrestrial parallax is enormous.

Now, you know, dear reader, that the gigantic

reflector of Lord Rosse, and the exquisite fifteen-inch refractors of the modern observatories, eliminate from the chaotic rubbish-heap of the surface of old Thornbush much smaller objects than such a circle as I have named. If you have read Mr. Locke's amusing Moon Hoax as often as I have, you have those details fresh in your memory. As John Farrar taught us when all this began, — and as I have said already, — if there were a State House in Thornbush two hundred feet long, the first Herschel would have seen it. His magnifying power was 6450; that would have brought this deaf and dumb State House within some forty miles. Go up on Mt. Washington and see white sails eighty miles away, beyond Portland, with your naked eye, and you will find how well he would have seen that State House with his reflector. Lord Rosse's statement is, that with his reflector he can see objects on old Thornbush two hundred and fifty-two feet long. If he can do that he can see on our B. M. objects which are five feet long; and, of course, we were beside ourselves to get control of some instrument which had some approach to such power. Haliburton was for at once building a reflector at No. 9; and perhaps he will do it yet, for Haliburton has been successful in his paper-making and lumbering. But I went to work more promptly.

I remembered, not an apothecary, but an observatory, which had been dormant, as we say of volcanoes, now for ten or a dozen years, — no matter why! The trustees had quarrelled with the director, or the funds had given out, or the director had been shot at the head of his division, — one of those accidents had happened which will happen even in observatories which have fifteen-inch equatorials; and so the equatorial here had been left as useless as a cannon whose metal has been strained or its reputation stained in an experiment. The observatory at Tamworth, dedicated with such enthusiasm, — "another light-house in the skies," — had been, so long as I have said, worthless to the world. To Tamworth, therefore, I travelled. In the neighborhood of the observatory I took lodgings. To the church where worshipped the family which lived in the observatory buildings I repaired; after two Sundays I established acquaintance with John Donald, the head of this family. On the evening of the third, I made acquaintance with his wife in a visit to them. Before three Sundays more he had recommended me to the surviving trustees as his successor as janitor to the buildings. He himself had accepted promotion, and gone, with his household, to keep a store for Haliburton in North Ovid. I sent for Polly and the children, to establish them in the janitor's rooms; and, after writing to her, with trembling eye I waited for the Brick Moon to pass over the field of the fifteen-inch equatorial.

Night came. I was "sole alone"! B. M. came, more than filled the field of vision, of course! but for that I was ready. Heavens! how changed.

Red no longer, but green as a meadow in the spring. Still I could see — black on the green — the large twenty-foot circles which I remembered so well, which broke the concave of the dome; and, on the upper edge — were these palm-trees? They were. No, they were hemlocks, by their shape, and among them were moving to and fro — — — — — flies? Of course, I cannot see flies! But something is moving, — coming, going. One, two, three, ten; there are more than thirty in all! They are men and women and their children!

Could it be possible? It was possible! Orcutt and Brannan and the rest of them had survived that giddy flight through the ether, and were going and coming on the surface of their own little world, bound to it by its own attraction and living by its own laws!

As I watched, I saw one of them leap from that surface. He passed wholly out of my field of vision, but in a minute, more or less, returned. Why not! Of course, the attraction of his world must be very small, while he retained the same power of muscle he had when he was here. They must be horribly crowded, I thought. No. They had three acres of surface, and there were but thirty-seven of them. Not so much crowded as people are in Roxbury, not nearly so much as in Boston; and, besides, these people are living underground, and have the whole of their surface for their exercise.

I watched their every movement as they approached the edge and as they left it. Often they passed beyond it, so that I could see them no more. Often they sheltered themselves from that tropical sun beneath the trees. Think of living on a world where from the vertical heat of the hottest noon of the equator to the twilight of the poles is a walk of only fifty paces! What atmosphere they had, to temper and diffuse those rays, I could not then conjecture.

I knew that at half-past ten they would pass into the inevitable eclipse which struck them every night at this period of their orbit, and must, I thought, be a luxury to them, as recalling old memories of night when they were on this world. As they approached the line of shadow, some fifteen minutes before it was due, I counted on the edge thirty-seven specks arranged evidently in order; and, at one moment, as by one signal, all thirty-seven jumped into the air, — high jumps. Again they did it, and again. Then a low jump; then a high one. I caught the idea in a moment. They were telegraphing to our world, in the hope of an observer. Long leaps and short leaps, — the long and short of Morse's Telegraph Alphabet, — were communicating ideas. My paper and pencil had been of course before me. I jotted down the despatch, whose language I knew perfectly: —

"Show 'I understand' on the Saw-Mill Flat."

"Show 'I understand' on the Saw-Mill Flat."

"Show 'I understand' on the Saw-Mill Flat."

By "I understand" they meant the responsive signal given, in all telegraphy, by an operator who has received and understood a message.

As soon as this exercise had been three times repeated, they proceeded in a solid body — much the most apparent object I had had until now — to Circle No. 3, and then evidently descended into the MOON.

The eclipse soon began, but I knew the MOON'S path now, and followed the dusky, coppery spot without difficulty. At 1.33 it emerged, and in a very few moments I saw the solid column pass from Circle No. 3 again, deploy on the edge again, and repeat three times the signal: —

"Show 'I understand' on the Saw-Mill Flat."

"Show 'I understand' on the Saw-Mill Flat."

"Show 'I understand' on the Saw-Mill Flat."

It was clear that Orcutt had known that the edge of his little world would be most easy of observation, and that he had guessed that the moments of obscuration and of emersion were the moments when observers would be most careful. After this signal they broke up again, and I could not follow them. With daylight I sent off a despatch to Haliburton, and, grateful and happy in comparison, sank into the first sleep not haunted by horrid dreams, which I had known for years.

Haliburton knew that George Orcutt had taken with him a good Dolland's refractor, which he had bought in London, of a two-inch glass. He knew that this would give Orcutt a very considerable power, if he could only adjust it accurately enough to find No. 9 in the 3d Range. Orcutt had chosen well in selecting the "Saw-Mill Flat," a large meadow, easily distinguished by the peculiar shape of the mill-pond which we had made. Eager though Haliburton was to join me, he loyally took moneys, caught the first train to Skowhegan, and, travelling thence, in thirty-six hours more was again descending Spoonwood Hill, for the first time since our futile observations. The snow lay white upon the Flat. With Rob. Shea's help, he rapidly unrolled a piece of black cambric twenty yards long, and pinned it to the crust upon the snow; another by its side, and another. Much cambric had he left. They had carried down with them enough for the funerals of two Presidents. Haliburton showed the symbols for "I understand," but he could not resist also displaying . . — . —, which are the dots and lines to represent O. K., which, he says, is the shortest message of comfort. And not having exhausted the space on the Flat, he and Robert, before night closed in, made a gigantic **O. K.,** fifteen yards from top to bottom, and in marks that were fifteen feet through.

I had telegraphed my great news to Haliburton on Monday night. Tuesday night he was at Skowhegan. Thursday night he was at No. 9. Friday he and Rob. stretched their cambric. Meanwhile, every day I slept. Every night I was glued to the eye-piece. Fifteen minutes before the eclipse every night this weird dance of leaps two hundred feet high, followed by hops of twenty feet high, mingled always in the steady order I have described, spelt out the ghastly message: —

"Show 'I understand' on the Saw-Mill Flat."

And every morning, as the eclipse ended, I saw the column creep along to the horizon, and again, as the duty of opening day, spell out the same: —

"Show 'I understand' on the Saw-Mill Flat."

They had done this twice in every twenty-four hours for nearly two years. For three nights steadily I read these signals twice each night; only these, and nothing more.

But Friday night all was changed. After "Attention," that dreadful "Show" did not come, but this cheerful signal: —

"Hurrah. All well. Air, food, and friends! what more can man require? Hurrah."

How like George! How like Ben Brannan! How like George's wife! How like them all! And they were all well! Yet poor *I* could not answer. Nay, I could only guess what Haliburton had done. But I have never, I believe, been so grateful since I was born.

After a pause, the united line of leapers resumed their jumps and hops. Long and short spelled out: —

"Your O. K. is twice as large as it need be."

Of the meaning of this, lonely *I* had, of course, no idea.

"I have a power of seven hundred," continued George. How did he get that? He has never told us. But this I can see, that all our analogies deceive us, — of views of the sea from Mt. Washington, or of the Boston State House from Wachusett. For in these views we look through forty or eighty miles of dense terrestrial atmosphere. But Orcutt was looking nearly vertically through an atmosphere which was, most of it, rare indeed, and pure indeed, compared with its lowest stratum.

In the record-book of my observations these despatches are entered as 12 and 13. Of course it was impossible for me to reply. All I could do was to telegraph these in the morning to Skowhegan, sending them to the care of the Moores, that they might forward them. But the next night showed that this had not been necessary.

Friday night George and the others went on for a quarter of an hour. Then they would rest, saying, "two," "three," or whatever their next signal time would be. Before morning I had these despatches: —

14. "Write to all hands that we are doing well. Langdon's baby is named Io, and Leonard's is named Phœbe."

How queer that was! What a coincidence! And they had some humor there.

15 was: "Our atmosphere stuck to us. It weighs three tenths of an inch — our weight."

16. "Our rain-fall is regular as the clock. We have made a cistern of Kilpatrick."

This meant the spherical chamber of that name.

17. "Write to Darwin that he is all right. We began with lichens and have come as far as palms and hemlocks."

These were the first night's messages. I had scarcely covered the eye-glasses and adjusted the equatorial for the day, when the bell announced the carriage in which Polly and the children came from the station to relieve me in my solitary service as janitor. I had the joy of showing her the good news. This night's work seemed to fill our cup. For all the day before, when I was awake, I had been haunted by the fear of famine for them. True, I knew that they had stored away in chambers H, I, and J the pork and flour which we had sent up for the workmen through the summer, and the corn and oats for the horses. But this could not last forever.

Now, however, that it proved that in a tropical climate they were forming their own soil, developing their own palms, and eventually even their bread-fruit and bananas, planting their own oats and maize, and developing rice, wheat, and all other cereals, harvesting these six, eight, or ten times — for aught I could see — in one of our years, — why, then, there was no danger of famine for them. If, as I thought, they carried up with them heavy drifts of ice and snow in the two chambers which were not covered in when they started, why, they had waters in their firmament quite sufficient for all purposes of thirst and of ablution. And what I had seen of their exercise showed that they were in strength sufficient for the proper development of their little world.

Polly had the messages by heart before an hour was over, and the little girls, of course, knew them sooner than she.

Haliburton, meanwhile, had brought out the Shubael refractor (Alvan Clark), and by night of Friday was in readiness to see what he could see. Shubael of course gave him no such luxury of detail as did my fifteen-inch equatorial. But still he had no difficulty in making out groves of hemlock, and the circular openings. And although he could not make out my thirty-seven flies, still when 10.15 came he saw distinctly the black square crossing from hole Mary to the edge, and beginning its Dervish dances. They were on his edge more precisely than on mine. For Orcutt knew nothing of Tamworth, and had thought his best chance was to display for No. 9. So was it that, at the same moment with me, Haliburton also was spelling out Orcutt & Co.'s joyous "Hurrah!"

"Thtephen," lisps Celia, "promith that you will look at yon moon [old Thornbush] at the inthtant I do." So was it with me and Haliburton.

He was of course informed long before the Moores' messenger came, that, in Orcutt's judgment, twenty feet of length were sufficient for his signals. Orcutt's atmosphere, of course, must be exquisitely clear.

So, on Saturday, Rob. and Haliburton pulled up all their cambric and arranged it on the Flat again, in letters of twenty feet, in this legend:—

RAH. AL WEL.

Haliburton said he could not waste flat or cambric on spelling.

He had had all night since half-past ten to consider what next was most important for them to know; and a very difficult question it was, you will observe. They had been gone nearly two years, and much had happened. Which thing was, on the whole, the most interesting and important? He had said we were all well. What then?

Did you never find yourself in the same difficulty? When your husband had come home from sea, and kissed you and the children, and wondered at their size, did you never sit silent and have to think what you should say? Were you never fairly relieved when little Phil said, blustering, "I got three eggs to-day." The truth is, that silence is very satisfactory intercourse, if we only know all is well. When De Sauty got his original cable going, he had not much to tell after all; only that consols were a quarter per cent higher than they were the day before. "Send me news," lisped he — poor lonely myth! — from Bull's Bay to Valentia, — "send me news; they are mad for news." But how if there be no news worth sending? What do I read in my cable despatch to-day? Only that the Harvard crew pulled at Putney yesterday, which I knew before I opened the paper, and that there had been a riot in Spain, which I also knew. Here is a letter just brought me by the mail from Moreau, Tazewell County, Iowa. It is written by Follansbee, in a good cheerful hand. How glad I am to hear from Follansbee! Yes; but do I care one straw whether Follansbee planted spring wheat or winter wheat? Not I. All I care for is Follansbee's way of telling it. All these are the remarks by which Haliburton explains the character of the messages he sent in reply to George Orcutt's autographs, which were so thoroughly satisfactory.

Should he say Mr. Borie had left the Navy Department and Mr. Robeson come in? Should he say the Lords had backed down on the Disendowment Bill? Should he say the telegraph had been landed at Duxbury? Should he say Ingham had removed to Tamworth? What did they care for this? What does anybody ever care for facts? Should he say that the State Constable was enforcing the liquor law on whiskey, but was winking at lager? All this would take him a week, in the most severe condensation, — and for what good? as Haliburton asked. Yet these were the things that the newspapers told, and they told nothing else. There was a nice little poem of Jean Ingelow's in a Transcript Haliburton had with him. He said he was really tempted to spell that out. It was better worth it than all the rest of the newspaper stuff, and would be remembered a thousand years after that was forgotten. "What they wanted," says Haliburton, "was sentiment. That is all that survives and is eternal." So he and Rob. laid out their cambric thus: —

RAH. AL WEL. SO GLAD.

Haliburton hesitated whether he would not add, "Power 5000," to indicate the full power I was using at Tamworth. But he determined not to, and, I think, wisely. The convenience was so great, of receiving the signal at the spot where it could be answered, that for the present he thought it best that they should go on as they did. That night, however, to his dismay, clouds gathered and a grim snow-storm began. He got no observations; and the next day it stormed so heavily that he could not lay his signals out. For me at Tamworth, I had a heavy storm all day, but at midnight it was clear; and as soon as the regular eclipse was past, George began with what we saw was an account of the great anaclysm which sent them there. You observe that Orcutt had far greater power of communicating with us than we had with him. He knew this. And it was fortunate he had. For he had, on his little world, much more of interest to tell than we had on our large one.

18. "It stormed hard. We were all asleep, and knew nothing till morning; the hammocks turned so slowly."

Here was another revelation and relief. I had always supposed that if they knew anything before they were roasted to death, they had had one wild moment of horror. Instead of this, the gentle slide of the MOON had not wakened them, the flight upward had been as easy as it was rapid, the change from one centre of gravity to another had of course been slow, — and they had actually slept through the whole. After the dancers had rested once, Orcutt continued: —

19. "We cleared E. A. in two seconds, I think. Our outer surface fused and cracked somewhat. So much the better for us."

They moved so fast that the heat of their friction through the air could not propagate itself through the whole brick surface. Indeed, there could have been but little friction after the first five or ten miles. By E. A. he means earth's atmosphere.

His 20th despatch is: "I have no observations of ascent. But by theory our positive ascent ceased in two minutes five seconds, when we fell into our proper orbit, which, as I calculate, is 5,109 miles from your mean surface."

In all this, observe, George dropped no word of regret through these five thousand miles.

His 21st despatch is: "Our rotation on our axis is made once in seven hours, our axis being exactly vertical to the plane of our own orbit. But in each of your daily rotations we get sunned all round."

Of course, they never had lost their identity with us, so far as our rotation and revolution went: our inertia was theirs; all the fatal Fly-Wheels had given them was an additional motion in space of their own.

This was the last despatch before daylight of Sunday morning; and the terrible snow-storm of March, sweeping our hemisphere, cut off our communication with them, both at Tamworth and No. 9, for several days.

But here was ample food for reflection. Our friends were in a world of their own, all thirty-seven of them well, and it seemed they had two more little girls added to their number since they started. They had plenty of vegetables to eat, with prospect of new tropical varieties according to Dr. Darwin. Rob. Shea was sure that they carried up hens; he said he knew Mrs. Whitman had several Middlesexes and Mrs. Leonard two or three Black Spanish fowls, which had been given her by some friends in Foxcroft. Even if they had not yet had time enough for these to develop into Alderneys and venison, they would not be without animal food.

When at last it cleared off, Haliburton had to telegraph: "Repeat from 21"; and this took all his cambric, though he had doubled his stock. Orcutt replied the next night: —

22. "I can see your storms. We have none. When we want to change climate we can walk in less than a minute from midsummer to the depth of winter. But in the inside we have eleven different temperatures, which do not change."

On the whole there is a certain convenience in such an arrangement. With No. 23 he went back to his story: —

It took us many days, one or two of our months, to adjust ourselves to our new condition. Our greatest grief is that we are not on the meridian. Do you know why?"

Loyal George! He was willing to exile himself and his race from the most of mankind, if only the great purpose of his life could be fulfilled. But his great regret was that it was not fulfilled. He was not on the meridian. I did not know why. But Haliburton, with infinite labor, spelt out on the Flat,

CYC. PROJECT. AD FIN.,

by which he meant, "See article Projectiles in the Cyclopædia at the end"; and there indeed is the only explanation to be given. When you fire a shot, why does it ever go to the right or left of the plane in which it is projected? Dr. Hutton ascribes it to a whirling motion acquired by the bullet by friction with the gun. Euler thinks it due chiefly to the irregularity of the shape of the ball. In our case the B. M. was regular enough. But on one side, being wholly unprepared for flight, she was heavily stored with pork and corn, while her other chambers had in some of them heavy drifts of snow, and some only a few men and women and hens.

Before Orcutt saw Haliburton's advice, he had sent us 24 and 25.

24. "We have established a Sandemanian church, and Brannan preaches. My son Edward and Alice Whitman are to be married this evening."

This despatch unfortunately did not reach Haliburton, though I got it. So, all the happy pair received for our wedding-present was the advice to look in the Cyclopædia at article Projectiles near the end.

25 was: —

"We shall act 'As You Like It' after the wedding. Dead-head tickets for all of the old set who will come."

Actually, in one week's reunion we had come to joking.

The next night we got 26: —

"Alice says she will not read the Cyclopædia in the honeymoon, but is much obliged to Mr. Haliburton for his advice."

"How did she ever know it was I?" wrote the matter-of-fact Haliburton to me.

27. "Alice wants to know if Mr. Haliburton will not send here for some rags; says we have plenty, with little need for clothes."

And then despatches began to be more serious again. Brannan and Orcutt had failed in the great scheme for the longitude, to which they had sacrificed their lives, — if, indeed, it were a sacrifice to retire with those they love best to a world of their own. But none the less did they devote themselves, with the rare power of observation they had, to the benefit of our world. Thus, in 28: —

"Your North Pole is an open ocean. It was black, which we think means water, from August 1st to September 29th. Your South Pole is on an island bigger than New Holland. Your Antarctic Continent is a great cluster of islands."

29. "Your Nyanzas are only two of a large group of African lakes. The green of Africa, where there is no water, is wonderful at our distance."

30. "We have not the last numbers of 'Foul Play.' Tell us, in a word or two, how they got home. We can see what we suppose their island was."

31. "We should like to know who proved Right in 'He Knew He was Right.'"

This was a good night's work, as they were then telegraphing. As soon as it cleared, Haliburton displayed, —

BEST HOPES. CARRIER DUCKS.

This was Haliburton's masterpiece. He had no room for more, however, and was obliged to reserve for the next day his answer to No. 31, which was simply,

SHE.

A real equinoctial now parted us for nearly a week, and at the end of that time they were so low in our northern horizon that we could not make out their signals; we and they were obliged to wait till they had passed through two-thirds of their month before we could communicate again. I used the time in speeding to No. 9. We got a few carpenters together, and arranged on the Flat two long movable black platforms, which ran in and out on railroad-wheels on tracks, from under green platforms; so that we could display one or both as we chose, and then withdraw them. With this apparatus we could give forty-five signals in a minute, corresponding to the line and dot of the telegraph; and thus could compass some twenty letters in that time, and make out perhaps two hundred and fifty words in an hour. Haliburton thought that, with some improvements, he could send one of Mr. Buchanan's messages up in thirty-seven working-nights.

IV

INDEPENDENCE

I OWN to a certain mortification in confessing that after this interregnum, forced upon us by so long a period of non-intercourse, we never resumed precisely the same constancy of communication as that which I have tried to describe at the beginning. The apology for this benumbment, if I may so call it, will suggest itself to the thoughtful reader.

It is indeed astonishing to think that we so readily accept a position when we once understand it. You buy a new house. You are fool enough to take out a staircase that you may put in a bathing-room. This will be done in a fortnight, everybody tells you, and then everybody begins. Plumbers, masons, carpenters, plasterers, skimmers, bell-hangers, speaking-tube men, men who make furnace-pipe, paper-hangers, men who scrape off the old paper, and other men who take off the old paint with alkali, gas men, city-water men, and painters begin. To them are joined a considerable number of furnace-men's assistants, stovepipe-men's assistants, mason's assistants, and hodmen who assist the assistants of the masons, the furnace-men, and the pipe-men. For a day or two these all take possession of the house and reduce it to chaos. In the language of Scripture, they enter in and dwell there. Compare, for the details, Matt. xii. 45. Then you revisit it at the end of the fortnight, and find it in chaos, with the woman whom you employed to wash the attics the only person on the scene. You ask her where the paper-hanger is; and she says he can do nothing because the plaster is not dry. You ask why the plaster is not dry, and are told it is because the furnace-man has not come. You send for him, and he says he did come, but the stove-pipe man was away. You send for him, and he says he lost a day in coming, but that the mason had not cut the right hole in the chimney. You go and find the mason, and he says they are all fools, and that there is nothing in the house that need take two days to finish.

Then you curse, not the day in which you were born, but the day in which bath-rooms were invented. You say, truly, that your father and mother, from whom you inherit every moral and physical faculty you prize, never had a bath-room till they were past sixty, yet they thrived, and their children. You sneak through back streets, fearful lest your friends shall ask you when your house will be finished. You are sunk in wretchedness, unable even to read your proofs accurately, far less able to attend the primary meetings of the party with which you vote, or to discharge any of the duties of a good citizen. Life is wholly embittered to you.

Yet, six weeks after, you sit before a soft-coal

fire in your new house, with the feeling that you have always lived there. You are not even grateful that you are there. You have forgotten the plumber's name; and if you met in the street that nice carpenter that drove things through, you would just nod to him, and would not think of kissing him or embracing him.

Thus completely have you accepted the situation.

Let me confess that the same experience is that with which, at this writing, I regard the BRICK MOON. It is there in ether. I cannot keep it. I cannot get it down. I cannot well go to it, — though possibly that might be done, as you will see. They are all very happy there, — much happier, as far as I can see, than if they lived in sixth floors in Paris, in lodgings in London, or even in tenement-houses in Phœnix Place, Boston. There are disadvantages attached to their position; but there are also advantages. And what most of all tends to our accepting the situation is, that there is "nothing that we can do about it," as Q. says, but to keep up our correspondence with them, and to express our sympathies.

For them, their responsibilities are reduced in somewhat the same proportion as the gravitation which binds them down, — I had almost said to earth, — which binds them down to brick, I mean. This decrease of responsibility must make them as light-hearted as the loss of gravitation makes them light-bodied.

On which point I ask for a moment's attention. And as these sheets leave my hand, an illustration turns up which well serves me. It is the 23d of October. Yesterday morning all wakeful women in New England were sure there was some one under the bed. This is a certain sign of an earthquake. And when we read the evening newspapers, we were made sure there had been an earthquake. What blessings the newspapers are, — and how much information they give us! Well, they said it was not very severe, here, but perhaps it was more severe elsewhere; hopes really arising in the editorial mind that in some Caraccas or Lisbon all churches and the cathedral might have fallen. I did not hope for that. But I did have just the faintest feeling that *if* — if — if — it should prove that the world had blown up into six or eight pieces, and they had gone off into separate orbits, life would be vastly easier for all of us, on whichever bit we happened to be.

That thing has happened, they say, once. Whenever the big planet between Mars and Jupiter blew up, and divided himself into one hundred and two or more asteroids, the people on each one only knew there had been an earthquake when and after they read their morning journals. And then, all that they knew at first was that telegraphic communication had ceased beyond — say two hundred miles. Gradually people and despatches came in, who said that they had parted company with some of the other islands and continents. But, as I say, on each piece the people not only weighed much less, but were much lighter-hearted, had less responsibility.

Now will you imagine the enthusiasm here, at Miss Hale's school, when it should be announced that geography, in future, would be confined to the study of the region east of the Mississippi and west of the Atlantic, — the earth having parted at the seams so named. No more study of Italian, German, French, or Sclavonic, — the people speaking those languages being now in different orbits or other worlds. Imagine also the superior ease of the office-work of the A. B. C. F. M. and kindred societies, the duties of instruction and civilizing, of evangelizing in general, being reduced within so much narrower bounds. For you and me also, who cannot decide what Mr. Gladstone ought to do with the land tenure in Ireland, and who distress ourselves so much about it in conversation, what a satisfaction to know that Great Britain is flung off with one rate of movement, Ireland with another, and the Isle of Man with another, into space, with no more chance of meeting again than there is that you shall have the same hand at whist to-night that you had last night! Even Victoria would sleep easier, and I am sure Mr. Gladstone would.

Thus, I say, were Orcutt's and Brannan's responsibilities so diminished, that after the first I began to see that their contracted position had its decided compensating ameliorations.

In these views, I need not say, the women of our little circle never shared. After we got the new telegraph arrangement in good running-order, I observed that Polly and Annie Haliburton had many private conversations, and the secret came out one morning, when, rising early in the cabins, we men found they had deserted us; and then, going in search of them, found them running the signal boards in and out as rapidly as they could, to tell Mrs. Brannan and the bride, Alice Orcutt, that flounces were worn an inch and a half deeper, and that people trimmed now with harmonizing colors and not with contrasts. I did not say that I believed they wore fig-leaves in B. M., but that was my private impression.

After all, it was hard to laugh at the girls, as these ladies will be called, should they live to be as old as Helen was when she charmed the Trojan senate (that was ninety-three, if Heyne be right in his calculations). It was hard to laugh at them because this was simple benevolence, and the same benevolence led to a much more practical suggestion when Polly came to me and told me she had been putting up some baby things for little Io and Phœbe, and some playthings for the older children, and she thought we might "send up a bundle."

Of course we could. There were the Flies still moving! or we might go ourselves!

[And here the reader must indulge me in a long parenthesis. I beg him to bear me witness that I never made one before. This parenthesis is on the tense that

I am obliged to use in sending to the press these minutes. The reader observes that the last transactions mentioned happen in April and May, 1871. Those to be narrated are the sequence of those already told. Speaking of them in 1870 with the coarse tenses of the English language is very difficult. One needs, for accuracy, a sure future, a second future, a paulo-post future, and a paulum-ante future, none of which does this language have. Failing this, one would be glad of an a-orist, — tense without time, — if the grammarians will not swoon at hearing such language. But the English tongue hath not that, either. Doth the learned reader remember that the Hebrew — language of history and prophecy — hath only a past and a future tense, but hath no present? Yet that language succeeded tolerably in expressing the present griefs or joys of David and of Solomon. Bear with me, then, O critic! if even in 1870 I use the so-called past tenses in narrating what remaineth of this history up to the summer of 1872. End of the parenthesis.]

On careful consideration, however, no one volunteers to go. To go, if you observe, would require that a man envelop himself thickly in asbestos or some similar non-conducting substance, leap boldly on the rapid Flies, and so be shot through the earth's atmosphere in two seconds and a fraction, carrying with him all the time in a non-conducting receiver the condensed air he needed, and landing quietly on B. M. by a precalculated orbit. At the bottom of our hearts I think we were all afraid. Some of us confessed to fear; others said, and said truly, that the population of the Moon was already dense, and that it did not seem reasonable or worth while, on any account, to make it denser. Nor has any movement been renewed for going. But the plan of the bundle of "things" seemed more feasible, as the things would not require oxygen. The only precaution seemed to be that which was necessary for protecting the parcel against combustion as it shot through the earth's atmosphere. We had not asbestos enough. It was at first proposed to pack them all in one of Professor Horsford's safes. But when I telegraphed this plan to Orcutt, he demurred. Their atmosphere was but shallow, and with a little too much force the corner of the safe might knock a very bad hole in the surface of his world. He said if we would send up first a collection of things of no great weight, but of considerable bulk, he would risk that, but he would rather have no compact metals.

I satisfied myself, therefore, with a plan which I still think good. Making the parcel up in heavy old woollen carpets, and cording it with worsted cords, we would case it in a carpet-bag larger than itself and fill in the interstice with dry sand, as our best non-conductor; cording this tightly again, we would renew the same casing with more sand; and so continually offer surfaces of sand and woollen, till we had five separate layers between the parcel and the air. Our calculation was that a perceptible time would be necessary for the burning and disintegrating of each sand-bag. If each one, on the average, would stand two-fifths of a second, the inner parcel would get through the earth's atmosphere unconsumed. If, on the other hand, they lasted a little longer, the bag, as it fell on B. M., would not be unduly heavy. Of course we could take their night for the experiment, so that we might be sure they should all be in bed and out of the way.

We had very funny and very merry times in selecting things important enough and at the same time bulky and light enough to be safe. Alice and Bertha at once insisted that there must be room for the children's playthings. They wanted to send the most approved of the old ones, and to add some new presents. There was a woolly sheep in particular, and a watering-pot that Rose had given Fanny, about which there was some sentiment; boxes of dominos, packs of cards, magnetic fishes, bows and arrows, checker-boards and croquet sets. Polly and Annie were more considerate. Down to Coleman and Company they sent an order for pins, needles, hooks and eyes, buttons, tapes, and I know not what essentials. India-rubber shoes for the children Mrs. Haliburton insisted on sending. Haliburton himself bought open-eye-shut-eye dolls, though I felt that wax had been, since Icarus's days, the worst article in such an adventure. For the babies he had india-rubber rings: he had tin cows and carved wooden lions for the bigger children, drawing-tools for those older yet, and a box of crochet tools for the ladies. For my part I piled in literature, — a set of my own works, the Legislative Reports of the State of Maine, Jean Ingelow, as I said or intimated, and both volumes of the "Earthly Paradise." All these were packed in sand, bagged and corded, — bagged, sanded and corded again, — yet again and again, — five times. Then the whole awaited Orcutt's orders and our calculations.

At last the moment came. We had, at Orcutt's order, reduced the revolutions of the Flies to 7230, which was, as nearly as he knew, the speed on the fatal night. We had soaked the bag for near twelve hours, and, at the moment agreed upon, rolled it on the Flies and saw it shot into the air. It was so small that it went out of sight too soon for us to see it take fire.

Of course we watched eagerly for signal time. They were all in bed on B. M. when we let fly. But the despatch was a sad disappointment.

107. "Nothing has come through but two croquet balls and a china horse. But we shall send the boys hunting in the bushes, and we may find more."

108. "Two Harpers and an Atlantic, badly singed. But we can read all but the parts which were most dry."

109. "We see many small articles revolving round us which may perhaps fall in."

They never did fall in, however. The truth was that all the bags had burned through. The sand, I suppose, went to its place, wherever that was. And all the other things in our bundle became little asteroids or aerolites in orbits of their own, except a well-disposed score or two, which persevered far enough to get within the attraction of Brick Moon and to take to revolving there, not having hit quite square, as the croquet balls did. They had five volumes of the "Congressional Globe" whirling round like bats within a hundred feet of their heads. Another body, which I am afraid was "The Ingham Papers," flew a little higher, not quite so heavy. Then there was an absurd procession of the woolly sheep, a china cow, a pair of india-rubbers, a lobster Haliburton had chosen to send, a wooden lion, the wax doll, a Salter's balance, the "New York Observer," the bow and arrows, a Nuremberg nanny-goat, Rose's watering-pot, and the magnetic fishes, which gravely circled round and round them slowly and made the petty zodiac of their petty world.

We have never sent another parcel since, but we probably shall at Christmas, gauging the Flies perhaps to one revolution more. The truth is, that although we have never stated to each other in words our difference of opinion or feeling, there is a difference of habit of thought in our little circle as to the position which the B. M. holds. Somewhat similar is the difference of habit of thought in which different statesmen of England regard their colonies.

Is B. M. a part of our world, or is it not? Should its inhabitants be encouraged to maintain their connections with us, or is it better for them to "accept the situation" and gradually wean themselves from us and from our affairs? It would be idle to determine this question in the abstract: it is perhaps idle to decide any question of casuistry in the abstract. But, in practice, there are constantly arising questions which really require some decision of this abstract problem for their solution.

For instance, when that terrible breach occurred in the Sandemanian church, which parted it into the Old School and New School parties, Haliburton thought it very important that Brannan and Orcutt and the church in B. M. under Brannan's ministry should give in their adhesion to our side. Their church would count one more in our registry, and the weight of its influence would not be lost. He therefore spent eight or nine days in telegraphing, from the early proofs, a copy of the address of the Chautauqua Synod to Brannan, and asked Brannan if he were not willing to have his name signed to it when it was printed. And the only thing which Haliburton takes sorely in the whole experience of the Brick Moon, from the beginning, is that neither Orcutt nor Brannan has ever sent one word of acknowledgment of the despatch. Once, when Haliburton was very low-spirited, I heard him even say that he believed they had never read a word of it, and that he thought he and Rob. Shea had had their labor for their pains in running the signals out and in.

Then he felt quite sure that they would have to establish civil government there. So he made up an excellent collection of books, — De Lolme on the British Constitution; Montesquieu on Laws; Story, Kent, John Adams, and all the authorities here; with ten copies of his own address delivered before the Young Men's Mutual Improvement Society of Podunk, on the "Abnormal Truths of Social Order." He telegraphed to know what night he should send them, and Orcutt replied: —

129. "Go to thunder with your old law-books. We have not had a primary meeting nor a justice court since we have been here, and, D. V., we never will have."

Haliburton says this is as bad as the state of things in Kansas, when, because Frank Pierce would not give them any judges or laws to their mind, they lived a year or so without any. Orcutt added in his next despatch: —

130. "Have not you any new novels? Send up Scribe and the 'Arabian Nights' and 'Robinson Crusoe' and the 'Three Guardsmen,' and Mrs. Whitney's books. We have Thackeray and Miss Austen."

When he read this, Haliburton felt as if they

were not only light-footed but light-headed. And he consulted me quite seriously as to telegraphing to them "Pycroft's Course of Reading." I coaxed him out of that, and he satisfied himself with a serious expostulation with George as to the way in which their young folks would grow up. George replied by telegraphing Brannan's last sermon, 1 Thessalonians iv. 11. The sermon had four heads, must have occupied an hour and a half in delivery, and took five nights to telegraph. I had another engagement, so that Haliburton had to sit it all out with his eye to Shubael, and he has never entered on that line of discussion again. It was as well, perhaps, that he got enough of it.

The women have never had any misunderstandings. When we had received two or three hundred despatches from B. M., Annie Haliburton came to me and said, in that pretty way of hers, that she thought they had a right to their turn again. She said this lore about the Albert Nyanza and the North Pole was all very well, but, for her part, she wanted to know how they lived, what they did, and what they talked about, whether they took summer journeys, and how and what was the form of society where thirty-seven people lived in such close quarters. This about "the form of society" was merely wool pulled over my eyes. So she said she thought her husband and I had better go off to the Biennial Convention at Assampink, as she knew we wanted to do, and she and Bridget and Polly and Cordelia would watch for the signals, and would make the replies. She thought they would get on better if we were out of the way.

So we went to the convention, as she called it, which was really not properly a convention, but the Forty-fifth Biennial General Synod, and we left the girls to their own sweet way.

Shall I confess that they kept no record of their own signals, and did not remember very accurately what they were? "I was not going to keep a string of 'says I's' and 'says she's,'" said Polly, boldly. "It shall not be written on my tomb that I have left more annals for people to file or study or bind or dust or catalogue." But they told us that they had begun by asking the "bricks" if they remembered what Maria Theresa said to her ladies-in-waiting.[1] Quicker than any signal had ever been answered, George Orcutt's party replied from the Moon, "We hear, and we obey." Then the women-kind had it all to themselves. The brick-women explained at once to our girls that they had sent their men round to the other side to cut ice, and that they were manning the telescope, and running the signals for themselves, and that they could have a nice talk without any bother about the law-books or

[1] Maria Theresa's husband, Francis, Duke of Tuscany, was hanging about loose one day, and the Empress, who had got a little tired, said to the maids of honor, "Girls, whenever you marry, take care and choose a husband who has something to do outside of the house."

the magnetic pole. As I say, I do not know what questions Polly and Annie put; but — to give them their due — they had put on paper a coherent record of the results arrived at in the answers; though, what were the numbers of the despatches, or in what order they came, I do not know; for the session of the synod kept us at Assampink for two or three weeks.

Mrs. Brannan was the spokesman. "We tried a good many experiments about day and night. It was very funny at first not to know when it would be light and when dark, for really the names day and night do not express a great deal for us. Of course the pendulum clocks all went wrong till the men got them overhauled, and I think watches and clocks both will soon go out of fashion. But we have settled down on much the old hours, getting up, without reference to daylight, by our great gong, at your eight o'clock. But when the eclipse season comes, we vary from that for signalling.

"We still make separate families, and Alice's is the seventh. We tried hotel life and we liked it, for there has never been the first quarrel here. You can't quarrel here, where you are never sick, never tired, and need not be ever hungry. But we were satisfied that it was nicer for the children and for all round to live separately and come together at parties, to church, at signal time, and so on. We had something to say then, something to teach, and something to learn.

"Since the carices developed so nicely into flax, we have had one great comfort, which we had lost before, in being able to make and use paper. We have had great fun, and we think the children have made great improvement in writing novels for the Union. The Union is the old Union for Christian work that we had in dear old No. 9. We have two serial novels going on, one called 'Diana of Carrotook,' and the other called 'Ups and Downs'; the first by Levi Ross, and the other by my Blanche. They are really very good, and I wish we could send them to you. But they would not be worth despatching.

"We get up at eight; dress, and fix up at home; a sniff of air, as people choose; breakfast; and then we meet for prayers outside. Where we meet depends on the temperature; for we can choose any temperature we want, from boiling water down, which is convenient. After prayers an hour's talk, lounging, walking, and so on; no flirting, but a favorite time with the young folks.

"Then comes work. Three hours' head-work is the maximum in that line. Of women's work, as in all worlds, there are twenty-four in one of your days, but for my part I like it. Farmers and carpenters have their own laws, as the light serves and the seasons. Dinner is seven hours after breakfast began; always an hour long, as breakfast was. Then every human being sleeps for an hour. Big gong again, and we ride, walk, swim, telegraph, or what not, as the case may be.

We have no horses yet, but the Shanghaes are coming up into very good dodos and ostriches, quite big enough for a trot for the children.

"Only two persons of a family take tea at home. The rest always go out to tea without invitation. At 8 P. M. big gong again, and we meet in 'Grace,' which is the prettiest hall, church, concert-room, that you ever saw. We have singing, lectures, theatre, dancing, talk, or what the mistress of the night determines, till the curfew sounds at ten, and then we all go home. Evening prayers are in the separate households, and every one is in bed by midnight. The only law on the statute-book is that every one shall sleep nine hours out of every twenty-four.

"Only one thing interrupts this general order. Three taps on the gong means 'telegraph,' and then, I tell you, we are all on hand.

"You cannot think how quickly the days and years go by!"

Of course, however, as I said, this could not last. We could not subdue our world and be spending all our time in telegraphing our dear B. M. Could it be possible—perhaps it was possible—that they there had something else to think of and to do besides attending to our affairs? Certainly their indifference to Grant's fourth Proclamation, and to Mr. Fish's celebrated protocol in the Tahiti business, looked that way. Could it be that that little witch of a Belle Brannan really cared more for their performance of "Midsummer Night's Dream," or her father's birthday, than she cared for that pleasant little account I telegraphed up to all the children, of the way we went to muster when we were boys together? Ah well! I ought not to have supposed that all worlds were like this old world. Indeed, I often say this is the queerest world I ever knew. Perhaps theirs is not so queer, and it is I who am the oddity.

Of course it could not last. We just arranged correspondence days, when we would send to them, and they to us. I was meanwhile turned out from my place at Tamworth Observatory. Not but I did my work well, and Polly hers. The observer's room was a miracle of neatness. The children were kept in the basement. Visitors were received with great courtesy; and all the fees were sent to the treasurer; he got three dollars and eleven cents one summer, — that was the year General Grant came there; and that was the largest amount that they ever received from any source but begging. I was not unfaithful to my trust. Nor was it for such infidelity that I was removed. No! But it was discovered that I was a Sandemanian; a Glassite, as in derision I was called. The annual meeting of the trustees came round. There was a large Mechanics' Fair in Tamworth at the time, and an Agricultural Convention. There was no horse-race at the convention, but there were two competitive examinations in which running horses competed with each other, and trotting horses competed with each other, and five thousand dollars was given to the best runner and the best trotter. These causes drew all the trustees together. The Rev. Cephas Philpotts presided. His doctrines with regard to free agency were considered much more sound than mine. He took the chair, — in that pretty observatory parlor, which Polly had made so bright with smilax and ivy. Of course I took no chair; I waited, as a janitor should, at the door. Then a brief address. Dr. Philpotts trusted that the observatory might always be administered in the interests of science, of true science; of that science which rightly distinguishes between unlicensed liberty and true freedom; between the unrestrained volition and the freedom of the will. He became eloquent, he became noisy. He sat down. Then three other men spoke, on similar subjects. Then the executive committee which had appointed me was dismissed with thanks. Then a new executive committee was chosen, with Dr. Philpotts at the head. The next day I was discharged. And the next week the Philpotts family moved into the observatory, and their second girl now takes care of the instruments.

I returned to the cure of souls and to healing the hurt of my people. On observation days somebody runs down to No. 9, and by means of Shubael communicates with B. M. We love them, and they love us all the same.

Nor do we grieve for them as we did. Coming home from Pigeon Cove in October with those nice Wadsworth people, we fell to talking as to the why and wherefore of the summer life we had led. How was it that it was so charming? And why were we a little loath to come back to more comfortable surroundings? "I hate the school," said George Wadsworth. "I hate the making calls," said his mother. "I hate the office hour," said her poor husband; "if there were only a dozen I would not mind, but seventeen hundred thousand in sixty minutes is too many." So that led to asking how many of us there had been at Pigeon Cove. The children counted up all the six families, — the Haliburtons, the Wadsworths, the Pontefracts, the Midges, the Hayeses, and the Inghams, and the two good-natured girls, — thirty-seven in all, — and the two babies born this summer. "Really," said Mrs. Wadsworth, "I have not spoken to a human being besides these since June; and what is more, Mrs. Ingham, I have not wanted to. We have really lived in a little world of our own."

"World of our own!" Polly fairly jumped from her seat, to Mrs. Wadsworth's wonder. So we had — lived in a world of our own. Polly reads no newspaper since the "Sandemanian" was merged. She has a letter or two tumble in sometimes, but not many; and the truth was that she had been more secluded from General Grant and Mr. Gladstone and the Khedive, and the rest of the important people, than had Brannan or Ross or any of them!

And it had been the happiest summer she had ever known.

Can it be possible that all human sympathies can thrive, and all human powers be exercised, and all human joys increase, if we live with all our might with the thirty or forty people next to us, telegraphing kindly to all other people, to be sure? Can it be possible that our passion for large cities, and large parties, and large theatres, and large churches, develops no faith nor hope nor love which would not find aliment and exercise in a little "world of our own"?

CRUSOE IN NEW YORK

CRUSOE IN NEW YORK

PART I

I WAS born in the year 1842, in the city of New York, of a good family, though not of that country, my father being a foreigner of Bremen, who settled first in England. He got a good estate by merchandise, and afterward lived at New York. But first he had married my mother, whose relations were named Robinson — a very good family in her country — and from them I was named.

My father died before I can remember — at least, I believe so. For, although I sometimes figure to myself a grave, elderly man, thickset and wearing a broad-brimmed hat, holding me between his knees and advising me seriously, I cannot say really whether this were my father or no; or, rather, whether this is really some one I remember or no. For my mother, with whom I have lived alone much of my life, as the reader will see, has talked to me of my father so much, and has described him to me so faithfully, that I cannot tell but it is her description of him that

I recollect so easily. And so, as I say, I cannot tell whether I remember him or no.

He never lost his German notions, and perhaps they gained in England some new force as to the way in which boys should be bred. At least, for myself, I know that he left to my mother strict charge that I should be bound 'prentice to a carpenter as soon as I was turned of fourteen. I have often heard her say that this was the last thing he spoke to her of when he was dying; and with the tears in her eyes, she promised him it should be so. And though it cost her a world of trouble — so changed were times and customs — to find an old-fashioned master who would take me for an apprentice, she was as good as her word.

I should like to tell the story of my apprenticeship, if I supposed the reader cared as much about it as I do; but I must rather come to that part of my life which is remarkable, than hold to that which is more like the life of many other boys. My father's property was lost or was wasted, I know not how, so that my poor mother had but a hard time of it; and when I was just turned of twenty-one and was free of my apprenticeship, she had but little to live upon but what I could bring home, and what she could earn by her needle. This was no grief to me, for I was fond of my trade, and I had learned it well. My old master was fond of me, and would trust me with work of a good deal of responsibility. I neither drank nor smoked, nor was I over-fond of the amusements which took up a good deal of the time of my fellow-workmen. I was most pleased when, on pay-day, I could carry home to my mother ten, fifteen, or even twenty dollars — could throw it into her lap, and kiss her and make her kiss me.

"Here is the oil for the lamp, my darling," I would say; or, "Here is the grease for the wheels"; or, "Now you must give me white sugar twice a day." She was a good manager, and she made both ends meet very well.

I had no thought of leaving my master when my apprenticeship was over, nor had he any thought of letting me go. We understood each other well, he liked me and I liked him. He knew that he had in me one man who was not afraid of work, as he would say, and who would not shirk it. And so, indeed, he would often put me in charge of parties of workmen who were much older than I was.

So it was that it happened, perhaps some months after I had become a journeyman, that he told me to take a gang of men, whom he named, and to go quite up-town in the city, to put a close wooden fence around a vacant lot of land there. One of his regular employers had come to him, to say that this lot of land was to be enclosed, and the work was to be done by him. He had sent round the lumber, and he told me that I would find it on the ground. He gave me, in writing, the general directions by which the fence was ordered, and told me to use my best judgment in carrying them out. "Only take care," said he, "that you do it as well as if I was there myself. Do not be in a hurry, and be sure your work stands."

I was well pleased to be left thus to my own judgment. I had no fear of failing to do the job well, or of displeasing my old master or his employer. If I had any doubts, they were about the men who were to work under my lead, whom I did not rate at all equally; and, if I could have had my pick, I should have thrown out some of the more sulky and lazy of them, and should have chosen from the other hands. But youngsters must not be choosers when they are on their first commissions.

I had my party well at work, with some laborers whom we had hired to dig our post-holes, when a white-haired old man, with gold spectacles and a broad-brimmed hat, alighted from a cab upon the sidewalk, watched the men for a minute at their work, and then accosted me. I knew him perfectly, though of course he did not remember me. He was, in fact, my employer in this very job, for he was old Mark Henry, a Quaker gentleman of Philadelphia, who was guardian of the infant heirs who owned this block of land which we were enclosing. My master did all the carpenter's work in the New York houses which Mark Henry or any of his wards owned, and I had often seen him at the shop in consultation. I turned to him and explained to him the plans for the work. We had already some of the joists cut, which were to make the posts to our fence. The old man measured them with his cane, and said he thought they would not be long enough.

I explained to him that the fence was to be eight feet high, and that these were quite long enough for that.

"I know," he said, "I know, my young friend, that my order was for a fence eight feet high, but I do not think that will do."

With some surprise I showed him, by a "ten-foot pole," how high the fence would come.

"Yes, my young friend, I see, I see. But I tell thee, every beggar's brat in the ward will be over thy fence before it has been built a week, and there will be I know not what devices of Satan carried on in the inside. All the junk from the North River will be hidden there, and I shall be in luck if some stolen trunk, nay, some dead man's body, is not stowed away there. Ah, my young friend, if thee is ever unhappy enough to own a vacant lot in the city, thee will know much that thee does not know now of the exceeding sinfulness of sin. Thee will know of trials of the spirit and of the temper that thee has never yet experienced."

I said I thought this was probable, but I thought inwardly that I would gladly be tried that way. The old man went on:—

"I said eight feet to friend Silas, but thee may say to him that I have thought better of it, and that I have ordered thee to make the fence ten feet high. Thee may say that I am now going to Philadelphia, but that I will write to him my order when I arrive. Meanwhile thee will go on with the fence as I bid thee."

And so the old man entered his cab again and rode away.

I amused myself at his notion, for I knew very well that the street-boys and other loafers would storm his ten-foot wall as readily as they would have stormed the Malakoff or the Redan, had they supposed there was anything to gain by doing it. I had, of course, to condemn some of my posts, which were already cut, or to work them in to other parts of the fence. My order for spruce boards was to be enlarged by twenty per cent by the old man's direction, and this, as it happened, led to a new arrangement of my piles of lumber on my vacant land.

And all this it was which set me to thinking that night, as I looked on the work, that I might attempt another enterprise, which, as it proved, lasted me for years, and which I am now going to describe.

I had worked diligently with the men to set up some fifty feet of the fence where it parted us from an alley-way, for I wanted a chance to dry some of the boards, which had just been hauled from a raft in the North River. The truckmen had delivered them helter-skelter, and they lay, still soaking, above each other on our vacant lot.

We turned all our force on this first piece of fence, and had so much of it done that, by calling off the men just before sundown, I was able to set up all the wet boards, each with one end resting on the fence and the other on the ground, so that they took the air on both sides, and would dry more quickly. Of course this left a long, dark tunnel underneath.

As the other hands gathered up their tools and made ready to go, a fellow named McLoughlin, who had gone out with one of the three months' regiments not long before, said:—

"I would not be sorry to sleep there. I have slept in many a worse place than that in Dixie"; and on that he went away, leaving me to make some measurements which I needed the next day. But what he said rested in my mind, and, as it happened, directed the next twelve years of my life.

Why should not I live here? How often my mother had said that if she had only a house of her own she should be perfectly happy! Why should not we have a house of our own here, just as comfortable as if we had gone a thousand miles out on the prairie to build it, and a great deal nearer to the book-stores, to the good music, to her old friends, and to my good wages? We had talked a thousand times of moving together to Kansas, where I was to build a little hut for her, and we were to be very happy together. But why not do as the minister had bidden us only the last Sunday — seize on to-day, and take what Providence offered now?

I must acknowledge that the thought of paying any ground rent to old Mr. Henry did not occur to me then — no, nor for years afterward. On the other hand, all that I thought of was this, — that here was as good a chance as there was in Kansas to live without rent, and that rent had been, was still, and was likely to be my bugbear, unless I hit on some such scheme as this for abating it.

The plan, to be short, filled my mind. There was nothing in the way of house-building which I shrank from now, for, in learning my trade, I had won my Aladdin's lamp, and I could build my mother a palace, if she had needed one. Pleased with my fancy, before it was dark I had explored my principality from every corner, and learned all its capabilities.

The lot was an oblong, nearly three times as long as it was wide. On the west side, which was one of the short sides, it faced what I will call the Ninety-ninth Avenue, and on the south side, what I will call Fernando Street, though really it was one of the cross-streets with numbers. Running to the east it came to a narrow passage-way which had been reserved for the accommodation of the rear of a church which fronted on the street just north of us. Our back line was also the back line of the yards of the houses on the same street, but on our northeast corner the church ran back as far as the back line of both houses and yards, and its high brick wall — nearly fifty feet high — took the place there of the ten-foot brick wall, surmounted by bottle-glass, which made their rear defence.

The moment my mind was turned to the matter, I saw that in the rear of the church there was a corner which lay warmly and pleasantly to the southern and western sun, which was still out of eye-shot from the street, pleasantly removed from the avenue passing, and only liable to inspection, indeed, from the dwelling-houses on the opposite side of our street, — houses which, at this moment, were not quite finished, though they would be occupied soon.

If, therefore, I could hit on some way of screening my mother's castle from them — for a castle I called it from the first moment, though it was to be much more like a cottage — I need fear no observation from other quarters; for the avenue was broad, and on the other side from us there was a range of low, rambling buildings — an engine-house and a long liquor-saloon were two — which had but one story. Most of them had been built, I suppose, only to earn something for the land while it was growing valuable. The church had no windows in the rear, and that protected my castle — which was, indeed, still in the air — from all observation on that side.

I told my mother nothing of all this when I went home. But I did tell her that I had some calculations to make for my work, and that was enough. She went on, sweet soul! without speaking a word, with her knitting and her sewing at her end of the table, only getting up to throw a cloth over her parrot's cage when he was noisy; and I sat at my end of the table, at work over my figures, as silent as if I had been on a desert island.

Before bedtime I had quite satisfied myself with the plan of a very pretty little house which would come quite within our space, our means, and our shelter. There was a little passage which ran quite across from east to west. On the church side of this there was my mother's kitchen, which was to be what I fondly marked the "common-room." This was quite long from east to west, and not more than half as long the other way. But on the east side, where I could have no windows, I cut off, on its whole width, a deep closet; and this proved a very fortunate thing afterward, as you shall see. On the west side I made one large square window, and there was, of course, a door into the passage.

On the south side of the passage I made three rooms, each narrow and long. The two outside rooms I meant to light from the top. Whether I would put any skylight into the room between them, I was not quite so certain; I did not expect visitors in my new house, so I did not mark it a "guest-room" in the plan. But I thought of it as a store-room, and as such, indeed, for many years we used it; though at last I found it more convenient to cut a sky-light in the roof there also. But I am getting before my story.

Before I had gone to bed that night I had made a careful estimate as to how much lumber I should need, of different kinds, for my little house; for I had, of course, no right to use my master's lumber nor Mr. Henry's; nor had I any thought of doing so. I made out an estimate that would be quite full, for shingles, for clapboards, white pine for my floors and finish, — for I meant to make a good job of it if I made any, — and for laths for the inside work. I made another list of the locks, hinges, window furniture and other hardware I should need; but for this I cared less, as I need not order them so soon. I could scarcely refrain from showing my plan to my mother, so snug and comfortable did it look already; but I had already determined that the "city house" should be a present to her on her next birthday, and that till then I would keep it a secret from her, as from all the world; so I refrained.

The next morning I told my master what the old Quaker had directed about the fence, and I took his order for the new lumber we should need to raise the height as was proposed. At the same time I told him that we were all annoyed at the need of carrying our tools back and forth, and because we could only take the nails for one day's use; and that, if he were willing, I had a mind to risk an old chest I had with the nails in it and a few tools, which I thought I could so hide that the wharf-rats and other loafers should not discover it. He told me to do as I pleased, that he would risk the nails if I would risk my tools; and so, by borrowing what we call a hand-cart for a few days, I was able to take up my own little things to the lot without his asking any other questions, or without exciting the curiosity of McLoughlin or any other of the men. Of course, he would have sent up in the shop-wagon anything we needed; but it was far out of the way, and nobody wanted to drive the team back at night if we could do without. And so, as night came on, I left the men at their work, and having loaded my hand-cart with a small chest I had, I took that into the alley-way of which I told you before, carried my box of tools into the corner between the church and our fence, under the boards which we had set up that day, and covered it heavily, with McLoughlin's help, with joists and boards, so that no light work would remove them, if, indeed, any wanderer of the night suspected that the box was there. I took the hand-cart out into the alley-way and chained it, first by the wheel and then by the handle, in two staples which I drove there. I had another purpose in this, as you shall see; but most of all, I wanted to test both the police and the knavishness of the neighborhood by seeing if the hand-cart were there in the morning.

To my great joy it was, and to my greater joy it remained there unmolested all the rest of the week in which we worked there. For my master, who never came near us himself, increased our force for us on the third day, so that at the end of the week, or Saturday night, the job was nearly done, and well done, too.

On the third day I had taken the precaution to throw out in the inside of our enclosure a sort of open fence, on which I could put the wet boards to dry, which at first I had placed on our side fence. I told McLoughlin, what was true enough, that the south sun was better for them than the sun from the west. So I ran out what I may call a screen thirty-five feet from the church, and parallel with it, on which I set up these boards to dry, and to my great joy I saw that they would wholly protect the roof of my little house from any observation from the houses the other side of the way while the workmen were at work, or even after they were inhabited.

There was not one of the workmen with me who had forethought enough or care for our master's interest to ask whose boards those were which we left there, or why we left them there. Indeed, they knew the next Monday that I went up with Fergus, the Swede, to bring back such lumber as we did not use, and none of them knew or cared how much we left there.

For me, I was only eager to get to work, and that day seemed very long to me. But that Monday afternoon I asked my master if I might have the team again for my own use for an hour or so, to move some stuff of mine and my mother's, and he gave it to me readily.

I had then only to drive up-town to a friendly lumberman's, where my own stuff was already lying waiting for me to load up, with the assistance of the workmen there, and to drive as quickly as I could into the church alley. Here I looked around, and seeing a German who looked as if he were only a day from Bremen, I made signs to him that if he would help me I would give him a piece of scrip which I showed him. The man had been long enough in the country to know that the scrip was good for lager. He took hold manfully with me, and carried my timbers and boards into the enclosure through a gap I made in the fence for the purpose. I gave him his money and he went away. As he went to Minnesota the next day, he never mentioned to anybody the business he had been engaged in.

Meanwhile, I had bought my hand-cart of the man who owned it. I left a little pile of heavy cedar logs on the outside, spiking them to each other indeed, that they should not be easily moved. And to them and to my posts I padlocked the hand-cart; nor was it ever disturbed during my reign in those regions. So I had easy method enough when I wanted a bundle or two of laths, or a bunch of shingles, or anything else for my castle, to bring them up in the cool of the evening, and to discharge my load without special observation. My pile of logs, indeed, grew eventually into a blind or screen, which quite protected that corner of the church alley from the view of any passer-by in Fernando Street.

Of that whole summer, happy and bright as it all was, I look back most often on the first morning when I got fairly to work on my new home. I told my mother that for some weeks I should have to start early, and that she must not think of getting up for my breakfast. I told her that there was extra work on a job up-town, and that I had promised to be there at five every day while the summer lasted. She left for me a pot of coffee, which I promised her I would warm when the time for breakfast and dinner came; and for the rest, she always had my dinner ready in my tin dinner-pail. Little did she know then, sweet saint! that I was often at Fernando Street by half-past three in the first sweet gray of those summer days.

On that particular day, it was really scarcely light enough for me to find the nail I drew from the plank which I left for my entrance. When I was fairly within and the plank was replaced, I felt that I was indeed "monarch of all I surveyed." What did I survey? The church wall on the north; on the south, my own screen of spruce boards, now well dry; on the east and west, the ten-foot fences which I had built myself; and over that on the west, God's deep, transparent sky, in which I could still see a planet whose name I did not know. It was a heaven, indeed, which He had said was as much mine as his!

The first thing, of course, was to get out my frame. This was a work of weeks. The next thing was to raise it. And here the first step was the only hard one, nor was this so hard as it would seem. The highest wall of my house was no higher than the ten-foot fence we had already built on the church alley. The western wall, if, indeed, a frame house has any walls, was only eight feet high. For foundations and sills, I dug deep post-holes, in which I set substantial cedar posts which I knew would outlast my day, and I framed my sills into these. I made the frame of the western wall lie out upon the ground in one piece; and I only needed a purchase high enough, and a block with repeating pulleys strong enough, to be able to haul up the whole frame by my own strength, unassisted. The high purchase I got readily enough by making what we called a "three-leg," near twenty feet high, just where my castle was to stand. I had no difficulty in hauling this into its place by a solid staple and ring, which for this purpose I drove high in the church wall. My multiplying pulley did the rest; and after it was done, I took out the staple and mended the hole it had made, so the wall was as good as ever.

You see it was nobody's business what shanty or what tower old Mark Henry or the Fordyce heirs might or might not put on the vacant corner lot. The Fordyce heirs were all in nurseries and kindergartens in Geneva, and indeed would have known nothing of corner lots had they been living in their palace in Fourteenth Street. As for Mark Henry, that one great achievement by which he rode up to Fernando Street was one of the rare victories of his life, of which ninety-nine hundredths were spent in counting-houses. Indeed, if he had gone there, all he would have seen was his ten-foot fence, and he would have taken pride to himself that he had it built so high.

When the day of the first raising came, and the frame slipped into the mortises so nicely, as I had foreordained that it should do, I was so happy that I could scarcely keep my secret from my mother. Indeed, that day I did run back to dinner. And when she asked me what pleased me so, I longed to let her know; but I only smoothed her cheeks with my hands and kissed her on both of them, and told her it was because she was so handsome that I was so pleased. She said she knew I had a secret from her, and I owned that I had, but she said she would not try to guess, but would wait for the time for me to tell her.

And so the summer sped by. Of course I saw my sweetheart, as I then called my mother, less and less. For I worked till it was pitch-dark at the castle; and after it was closed in, so I could work inside, I often worked till ten o'clock by candlelight. I do not know how I lived with so little sleep; I am afraid I slept pretty late on Sundays. But the castle grew and grew, and the common-room, which I was most eager to finish wholly before cold weather, was in complete order three full weeks before my mother's birthday came.

Then camc thc joy of furnishing it. To this I had looked forward all the summer, and I had measured with my eye many a bit of furniture, and priced, in an unaffected way, many an impossible second-hand finery, so that I knew just what I could do and what I could not do.

My mother had always wanted a Banner stove. I knew this, and it was a great grief to me that she had none, though she would never say anything about it.

To my great joy, I found a second-hand Banner stove, No. 2, at a sort of old junk-shop, which was, in fact, an old curiosity shop not three blocks away from Ninety-ninth Avenue. Some one had sold this to them while it was really as good as new, and yet the keeper offered it to me at half-price.

I hung round the place a good deal, and when the man found I really had money and meant something, he took me into all sorts of alleys and hiding-places, where he stored his old things away. I made fabulous bargains there, for either the old Jew liked me particularly, or I liked things that nobody else wanted. In the days when his principal customers were wharf-rats, and his principal business the traffic in old cordage and copper, he had hung out as a sign an old tavern-sign of a ship that had come to him. His place still went by the name of "The Ship," though it was really, as I say, a mere wreck, a rambling, third-rate old furniture shop of the old-curiosity kind.

But after I had safely carried the Banner to my new house, and was sure the funnel drew well, and that the escape of smoke and sparks was carefully guarded, many a visit did I make to The Ship at early morning or late in the evening, to bring away one or another treasure which I had discovered there.

Under the pretence of new-varnishing some of my mother's most precious tables and her bureau, I got them away from her also. I knocked up, with my own hatchet and saw, a sitting-table which I meant to have permanent in the middle of the room, which was much more convenient than anything I could buy or carry.

And so, on the 12th of October, the eve of my mother's birthday, the common-room was all ready for her. In her own room I had a new carpet and a new set of painted chamber furniture, which I had bought at the maker's, and brought up piece by piece. It cost me nineteen dollars and a half, for which I paid him in cash, which indeed he wanted sadly.

So, on the morning of the 13th of October, I kissed my mother forty times, because that day she was forty years old. I told her that before midnight she should know what the great surprise was, and I asked her if she could hold out till then.

She let me poke as much fun at her as I chose, because she said she was so glad to have me at breakfast; and I stayed long after breakfast, for I had told my mother that it was her birthday, and that I should be late. And such a thing as my asking for an hour or two was so rare that I took it quite of course when I did ask. I came home early at night, too. Then I said, —

"Now, sweetheart, the surprise requires that you spend the night away from home with me. Perhaps, if you like the place, we will spend to-morrow there. So I will take Poll in her cage, and you must put up your night-things and take them in your hand."

She was surprised now, for such a thing as an outing over night had never been spoken of before by either of us.

"Why, Rob," she said, "you are taking too much pains for your old sweetheart, and spending too much money for her birthday. Now, don't you think that you should really have as good a time, say, if we went visiting together, and then came back here?"

For, you see, she never thought of herself at all; it was only what I should like most.

"No, sweetheart dear," said I. "It is not for me, this 13th of October, it is all for you. And to-night's outing is not for me, it is for you; and I think you will like it and I think Poll will like it, and I have leave for to-morrow, and we will stay away all to-morrow."

As for Tom-puss, I said, we would leave some milk where he could find it, and I would leave a bone or two for him. But I whistled Rip, my dog, after me. I took Poll's cage, my mother took her bag, and locked and left her door, unconscious that she was never to enter it again.

A Ninety-ninth Avenue car took us up to Fernando Street. It was just the close of twilight when we came there. I took my mother to Church Alley, muttered something about some friends, which she did not understand more than I did, and led her up the alley in her confused surprise. Then I pushed aside my movable board, and, while she was still surprised, led her in after me and slid it back again.

"What is it, dear Rob? Tell me — tell me!"

"This way, sweetheart, this way!" This was all I would say.

I drew her after me through the long passage, led her into the common-room, which was just lighted up by the late evening twilight coming in between the curtains of the great square window. Then I fairly pushed her to the great, roomy easy-chair which I had brought from The Ship, and placed it where she could look out on the evening glow, and I said, —

"Mother, dear, this is the surprise; this is your new home; and, mother dear, your own boy has made it with his own hands, all for you."

"But, Rob, I do not understand — I do not understand at all. I am so stupid. I know I am awake. But it is as sudden as a dream!"

So I had to begin and to explain it all, — how here was a vacant lot that Mark Henry had the care of, and how I had built this house for her upon it. And long before I had explained it all, it was quite dark. And I lighted up the pretty student's-lamp, and I made the fire in the new Banner with my own hands.

And that night I would not let her lift a kettle, nor so much as cut a loaf of bread. It was my feast, I said, and I had everything ready, round to a loaf of birthday-cake, which I had ordered at Taylor's, which I had myself frosted and dressed, and decorated with the initials of my mother's name.

And when the feast was over, I had the best surprise of all. Unknown to my mother, I had begged from my Aunt Betsy my own father's portrait, and I had hung that opposite the window, and now I drew the curtain that hid it, and told my sweetheart that this and the house were her birthday presents for this year!

. . . .

And this was the beginning of a happy life, which lasted nearly twelve years. I could make a long story of it, for there was an adventure in everything, — in the way we bought our milk, and the way we took in our coals. But there is no room for me to tell all that, and it might not interest other people as it does me. I am sure my mother was never sorry for the bold step she took when we moved there from our tenement. True, she saw little or no society, but she had not seen much before. The conditions of our life were such that she did not like to be seen coming out of Church Alley, lest people should ask how she got in, and excepting in the evening, I did not care to have her go. In the evening I could go with her. She did not make many calls, because she could not ask people to return them. But she would go with me to concerts, and to the church parlor meetings, and sometimes to exhibitions; and at such places, and on Sundays, she would meet, perhaps, one or another of the few friends she had in New York. But we cared for them less and less, I will own, and we cared more and more for each other.

As soon as the first spring came, I made an immense effort, and spaded over nearly half of the lot. It was ninety feet wide and over two hundred and sixty long — more than half an acre. So I knew we could have our own fresh vegetables, even if we never went to market. My mother was a good gardener, and she was not afraid even to hoe the corn when I was out of the way. I dare say that the people whom the summer left in the street above us often saw her from their back windows, but they did not know — as how should they? — who had the charge of this lot, and there was no reason why they should be surprised to see a cornfield there. We only raised green corn. I am fond of Indian cake, but I did not care to grind my own corn, and I could buy sweet meal without trouble. I settled the milk question, after the first winter, by keeping our own goats. I fenced in, with a wirc fence, the northwest corner of our little empire, and put there a milch goat and her two kids. The kids were pretty little things, and would come and feed from my mother's hand. We soon weaned them, so that we could milk their mother; and after that our flock grew and multiplied, and we were never again troubled for such little milk as we used.

Some old proprietor, in the old Dutch days, must have had an orchard in these parts. There were still left two venerable wrecks of ancient pear-trees; and although they bore little fruit, and what they bore was good for nothing, they still gave a compact and grateful shade. I sodded the ground around them and made a seat beneath, where my mother would sit with her knitting all the afternoon. Indeed, after the sods grew firm, I planted hoops there, and many a good game of croquet have she and I had together there, playing so late that we longed for the chance they have in Sybaris, where, in the evening, they use balls of colored glass, with fireflies shut up inside.

On thc 11th of February, in the year 1867, my old master died, to my great regret, and I truly believe to that of his widow and her children. His death broke up the establishment, and I, who was always more of a cabinet-maker or joiner than carpenter or builder, opened a little shop of my own, where I took orders for cupboards, drawers, stairs, and other finishing work, and where I employed two or three German journeymen, and was thus much more master of my own time. In particular, I had two faithful fellows, natives of my own father's town of Bremen. While they were with me I could leave them a whole afternoon at a time, while I took any little job there might be, and worked at it at my own house at home. Where my house was, except that it was far uptown, they never asked, nor ever, so far as I know, cared. This gave me the chance for many a pleasant afternoon with my mother, such as we had dreamed of in the old days when we talked of Kansas. I would work at the lathe or the bench and she would read to me. Or we would put off the bench till the evening, and we would both go out into the cornfield together.

And so we lived year after year. I am afraid that we worshipped each other too much. We were in the heart of a crowded city, but there was that in our lives which tended a little to habits of loneliness, and I suppose a moralist would say that our dangers lay in that direction.

On the other hand, I am almost ashamed to say that, as I sat in a seat I had made for myself in old Van der Tromp's pear-tree, I would look upon my corn and peas and squashes and tomatoes with a satisfaction which I believe many a nobleman in England does not enjoy.

Till the youngest of the Fordyce heirs was of age, and that would not be till 1880, this was all my own. I was, by right of possession and my own labors, lord of all this region. How else did the writers on political economy teach me that any property existed!

I surveyed it with a secret kind of pleasure. I had not abundance of pears; what I had were poor and few. But I had abundance of sweet corn, of tomatoes, of peas, and of beans. The tomatoes were as wholesome as they were plentiful, and as I sat I could see the long shelves of them which my mother had spread in the sun to ripen, that we might have enough of them canned when winter should close in upon us. I knew I should have potatoes enough of my own raising also to begin the winter with. I should have been glad of more. But as by any good day's work I could buy two barrels of potatoes, I did not fret myself that my stock was but small.

Meanwhile my stock in bank grew fast. Neither my mother nor I had much occasion to buy new clothes. We were at no charge for house-rent, insurance, or taxes. I remember that a Spanish gentleman, who was fond of me, for whom I had made a cabinet with secret drawers, paid me in moidores and pieces-of-eight, which in those times of paper were a sight to behold.

I carried home the little bag and told my mother that this was a birthday present for her; indeed, that she was to put it all in her bed that night, that she might say she had rolled in gold and silver. She played with the pieces, and we used them to count with as we played our game of cribbage.

"But really, Robin, boy," said she, "it is as the dirt under our feet. I would give it all for three or four pairs of shoes and stockings, such as we used to buy in York, but such as these Lynn-built shoes and steam-knit stockings have driven out of the market."

Indeed, we wanted very little in our desert home.

And so for many years we led a happy life, and we found more in life than would have been possible had we been all tangled up with the cords of artificial society. I say "we," for I am sure I did, and I think my dear mother did.

But it was in the seventh year of our residence in the hut that of a sudden I had a terrible shock or fright, and this I must now describe to you.

It comes in about the middle of this history, and it may end this chapter.

It was one Sunday afternoon, when I had taken the fancy, as I often did of Sundays, to inspect my empire. Of course, in a certain way, I did this every time I climbed old Van der Tromp's pear-tree, and sat in my hawk's-nest there. But a tour of inspection was a different thing. I walked close round the path which I had made next the fence of the enclosure. I went in among my goats, — even entered the goat-house and played with my kids. I tried the boards of the fence and the timber-stays, to be sure they all were sound. I had paths enough between the rows of corn and potatoes to make a journey of three miles and half a furlong, with two rods more, if I went through the whole of them. So at half-past four on this fatal afternoon I bade my mother good-by, and kissed her. I told her I should not be back for two hours, because I was going to inspect my empire, and I set out happily.

But in less than an hour — I can see the face of the clock now: it was twenty-two minutes after five — I flung myself in my chair, panting for breath, and, as my mother said, as pale as if I had seen a ghost. But I told her it was worse than that.

I had come out from between two high rows of corn, which wholly covered me, upon a little patch which lay warm to the south and west, where I had some melons a-ripening, and was just lifting one of the melons, to be sure that the under surface did not rot, when close behind it I saw the print of a man's foot, which was very plain to be seen in the soft soil.

I stood like one thunderstruck, or as if I had seen an apparition. I listened; I looked round me. I could hear nothing but the roar of the omnibuses, nor could I see anything. I went up and down the path, but it was all one. I could see no other impression but that one. I went to it again, to see if there were any more, and to observe if it might not be my fancy. But there was no room for that, for there was exactly the print of an Englishman's hobnailed shoe, — the heavy heel, the prints of the heads of the nails. There was even a piece of patch which had been put on it, though it had never been half-soled.

How it came there I knew not; neither could I in the least imagine. But, as I say, like a man perfectly confused and out of myself, I rushed home into my hut, not feeling the ground I went upon. I fled into it like one pursued, and, as my mother said, when I fell into my chair, panting, I looked as if I had seen a ghost.

It was worse than that, as I said to her.

PART II

I CANNOT well tell you how much dismay this sight of a footprint in the ground gave me, nor how many sleepless nights it cost me. All the time I was trying to make my mother think that there was no ground for anxiety, and yet all the time I was showing her that I was very anxious. The more I pretended that I was not troubled, the more absent-minded, and so the more troubled, I appeared to her. And yet, if I made no pretence, and told her what I really feared, I should have driven her almost wild by the story of my terrors. To have our pretty home broken up, perhaps to be put in the newspapers — which was a lot that, so far, we had always escaped in our quiet and modest life — all this was more than she or I could bear to think of.

In the midst of these cogitations, apprehensions, and reflections, it came into my thoughts one day, as I was working at my shop down-town with my men, that all this might be a chimera of my own, and that the foot might be the print of my own boot as I had left it in the soil some days before when I was looking at my melons. This cheered me up a little, too. I considered that I could by no means tell for certain where I had trod and where I had not, and that if at last this was the print of my own boot, I had played the part of those fools who strive to make stories of spectres, and then are themselves frightened at them more than anybody else.

So I returned home that day in very good spirits. I carried to my mother a copy of Frank Leslie's Illustrated Newspaper, which had in it some pictures that I knew would please her, and I talked with her in as light-hearted a way as I could, to try to make her think that I had forgotten my alarm. And afterward we played two or three games of Egyptian solitaire at the table, and I went to bed unusually early. But, at the first break of day, when I fancied or hoped that she was still asleep, I rose quickly, and half-dressing myself, crept out to the melon-patch to examine again the imprint of the foot and to make sure that it was mine.

Alas! it was no more mine than it was Queen Victoria's. If it had only been cloven, I could easily have persuaded myself whose it was, so much grief and trouble had it cost me. When I came to measure the mark with my own boot, I found, just as I had seen before, that mine was not nearly so large as this mark was. Also, this was, as I have said, the mark of a heavy brogan — such as I never wore — and there was the mark of a strange patch near the toe, such as I had never seen, nor, indeed, have seen since, from that hour to this hour. All these things renewed my terrors. I went home like a whipped dog, wholly certain now that some one had found the secret of our home: we might be surprised in it before I was aware; and what course to take for my security I knew not.

As we breakfasted, I opened my whole heart to my mother. If she said so, I would carry all our little property, piece by piece, back to old Thunberg, the junk-dealer, and with her parrot and my umbrella we would go out to Kansas, as we used to propose. We would give up the game. Or, if she thought best, we would stand on the defensive. I would put bottle-glass on the upper edges of the fences all the way round.

There were four or five odd revolvers at The Ship, and I would buy them all, with powder and buck-shot enough for a long siege. I would teach her how to load, and while she loaded I would fire, till they had quite enough of attacking us in our home. Now it has all gone by, I should be ashamed to set down in writing the frightful contrivances I hatched for destroying these "creatures," as I called them, or, at least, frightening them, so as to prevent their coming thither any more.

"Robin, my boy," said my mother to me, when I gave her a chance at last, "if they came in here to-night — whoever 'they' may be — very little is the harm that they could do us. But if Mr. Kennedy and twenty of his police should come in here over the bodies of — five times five are twenty-five, twenty-five times eleven are — two hundred and seventy-five people whom you will have killed by that time, if I load as fast as thee tells me I can, why, Robin, my boy, it will go hard for thee and me when the day of the assizes comes. They will put handcuffs on thy poor old mother and on thee, and if they do not send thee to Jack Ketch, they will send thee to Bloomingdale."

I could not but see that there was sense in what she said. Anyway, it cooled me down for the time, and I kissed her and went to my work less eager, and, indeed, less anxious, than I had been the night before. As I went down-town in the car, I had a chance to ask myself what right I had to take away the lives of these poor savages of the neighborhood merely because they entered on my possessions. Was it their fault that they had not been apprenticed to carpenters? Could they help themselves in the arrangements which had left them savages? Had any one ever given them a chance to fence in an up-town lot? Was it, in a word, I said to myself — was it my merit or my good luck which made me as good as a landed proprietor, while the Fordyce heirs had their education? Such thoughts, before I came to my shop, had quite tamed me down, and when I arrived there I was quite off my design, and I concluded that I had taken a wrong measure in my resolution to attack the savages, as I had begun to call men who might be merely harmless loafers.

It was clearly not my business to meddle with them unless they first attacked me. This it was my business to prevent; if I were discovered and attacked, then I knew my duty.

With these thoughts I went into my shop that day, and with such thoughts as these, and with my mother's good sense in keeping me employed in pleasanter things than hunting for traces of savages, I got into a healthier way of thinking.

The crop of melons came in well, and many a good feast we had from them. Once and again I was able to carry a nice fresh melon to an old lady my mother was fond of, who now lay sick with a tertian ague.

Then we had the best sweet corn for dinner every day that any man had in New York. For at Delmonico's itself, the corn the grandees had had been picked the night before, and had started at two o'clock in the morning on its long journey to town. But my mother picked my corn just at the minute when she knew I was leaving my shop. She husked it and put it in the pot, and by the time I had come home, had slipped up the board in the fence that served me for a door, and had washed my face and hands in my own room, she would have dished her dinner, would have put her fresh corn upon the table, covered with a pretty napkin; and so, as I say, I had a feast which no nabob in New York had. No indeed, nor any king that I know of, unless it were the King of the Sandwich Islands, and I doubt if he were as well served as I.

So I became more calm and less careworn,

though I will not say but sometimes I did look carefully to see if I could find the traces of a man's foot; but I never saw another.

Unless we went out somewhere during the evening, we went to bed early. We rose early as well, for I never lost the habits of my apprenticeship. And so we were both sound asleep in bed one night when a strange thing happened, and a sudden fright came to us, of which I must tell quite at length, for it made, indeed, a very sudden change in the current of our lives.

I was sound asleep, as I said, and so, I found, was my mother also. But I must have been partly waked by some sudden noise in the street, for I knew I was sitting up in my bed in the darkness when I heard a woman scream, — a terrible cry, — and while I was yet startled, I heard her scream again, as if she were in deadly fear. My window was shaded by a heavy green curtain, but in an instant I had pulled it up, and by the light of the moon I seized my trousers and put them on.

I was well awake by this time, and when I flung open the door of my house, so as to run into my garden, I could hear many wild voices, some in English, some in German, some in Irish, and some with terrible cries, which I will not pretend I could understand.

There was no cry of a woman now, but only the howling of angry or drunken men, when they are in a rage with some one or with each other.

What startled me was that, whereas the woman's cry came from the street south of me, which I have called Fernando Street, the whole crowd of men, as they howled and swore, were passing along that street rapidly, and then stopped for an instant, as if they were coming up what I called Church Alley. There must have been seven or eight of them.

Now, it was by Church Alley that my mother and I always came into our house, and so into our garden. In the eight years, or nearly so, that I had lived there, I had by degrees accumulated more and more rubbish near the furthest end of the alley as a screen, so to speak, that when my mother or I came in or out, no one in the street might notice us. I had even made a little wing-fence out from my own, to which my hand-cart was chained. Next this I had piled broken brick-bats and paving-stones, and other heavy things, that would not be stolen. There was the stump and the root of an old pear-tree there, too heavy to steal, and too crooked and hard to clean or saw. There was a bit of curbstone from the street, and other such trash, which quite masked the fence and the hand-cart.

On the other side — that is, the church side, or the side furthest from the street — was the sliding-board in the fence, where my mother and I came in. So soon as it was slid back, no man could see that the fence was not solid.

At this moment in the night, however, when I

found that this riotous, drunken crew were pausing at the entrance of Church Alley, as doubting if they would not come down, I ran back through the passage, knocking loudly for my mother as I passed, and coming to my coal-bin, put my eye at the little hole through which I always reconnoitred before I slid the door. I could see nothing, nor at night ought I to have expected to do so.

But I could hear, and I heard what I did not expect. I could hear the heavy panting of one who had been running, and as I listened I heard a gentle, low voice sob out, "Ach, ach, mein Gott! Ach, mein Gott!" or words that I thought were these, and I was conscious, when I tried to move the door, that some one was resting close upon it.

All the same, I put my shoulder stoutly to the cross-bar, to which the boards of the door were nailed; I slid it quickly in its grooves, and as it slid, a woman fell into the passage.

She was wholly surprised by the motion, so that she could not but fall. I seized her and dragged her in, saying, "Hush, hush, hush!" as I did so. But not so quick was I but that she screamed once more as I drew to the sliding-door and thrust in the heavy bolt which held it.

In an instant my mother was in the passage with a light in her hand. In another instant I had seized the light and put it out. But that instant was enough for her and me to see that here was a lovely girl, with no hat or bonnet on, with her hair floating wildly, both her arms bleeding, and her clothes all stained with blood. She could see my mother's face of amazement, and she could see my finger on my mouth, as with the other I dashed out the candle. We all thought quickly, and we all knew that we must keep still.

But that unfortunate scream of hers was enough. Though no one of us all uttered another sound, this was like a "view-halloo," to bring all those dogs down upon us. The passage was dark, and, to my delight, I heard some of them breaking their shins over the curbstone and old pear-tree of my defences. But they were not such hounds as were easily thrown off the scent, and there were enough to persevere while the leaders picked themselves up again.

Then how they swore and cursed and asked questions! And we three stood as still as so many frightened rabbits. In an instant more one of them, who spoke in English, said he would be hanged if he thought she had gone into the church, that he believed she had got through the fence; and then, with his fist, or something harder, he began trying the boards on our side, and others of them we could hear striking those on the other side of the alley-way.

When it came to this, I whispered to my mother that she must never fear, only keep perfectly still. She dragged the frightened girl into our kitchen, which was our sitting-room, and they both fell, I know not how, into the great easy-chair.

For my part, I seized the light ladder, which always hung ready at the door, and ran with it at my full speed to the corner of Fernando Street and the alley. I planted the ladder, and was on the top of the fence in an instant

Then I sprang my watchman's rattle, which had hung by the ladder, and I whirled it round well. It wholly silenced the sound of the swearing fellows up the passage, and their pounding. When I found they were still, I cried out: —

"This way, 24! this way, 47! I have them all penned up here! Signal the office, 42, and bid them send us a sergeant. This way, fellows — up Church Alley!"

With this I was down my ladder again. But my gang of savages needed no more. I could hear them rushing out of the alley as fast as they might, not one of them waiting for 24 or 47. This was lucky for me, for as it happened I was ten minutes older before I heard two patrolmen on the outside, wondering what frightened old cove had been at the pains to spring a rattle.

The moonlight shone in at the western window of the kitchen, so that as I came in I could just make out the figure of my mother and of the girl, lying, rather than sitting, in her lap and her arms. I was not afraid to speak now, and I told my mother we were quite safe again, and she told the poor girl so. I struck a match and lighted the lamp as soon as I could. The poor, frightened creature started as I did so, and then fell on her knees at my mother's feet, took both her hands in her own, and seemed like one who begs for mercy, or, indeed, for life.

My poor, dear mother was all amazed, and her eyes were running with tears at the sight of the poor thing's terror. She kissed her again and again; she stroked her beautiful golden hair with her soft hands; she said in every word that she could think of that she was quite safe now, and must not think of being frightened any more.

But it was clear in a moment that the girl could not understand any language that we could speak. My mother tried her with a few words of German, and she smiled then; but she shook her head prettily, as if to say that she thanked her, but could not speak to her in that way either. Then she spoke eagerly in some language that we could not understand. But had it been the language of Hottentots, we should have known that she was begging my mother not to forsake her, so full of entreaty was every word and every gesture.

My dear, sweet mother lifted her at last into the easy-chair and made her lie there while she dipped some hot water from her boiler and filled a large basin in her sink. Then she led the pretty creature to it, and washed from her arms, hands, and face the blood that had hardened upon them, and looked carefully to find what her wounds were. None of them were deep, though there were ugly scratches on her beautiful arms; they were cut by glass, as I guessed then, and as we learned from her afterward. My mother was wholly prepared for all such surgery as was needed here; she put on two bandages where she thought they were needed, she plastered up the other scratches with court-plaster, and then, as if the girl understood her, she said to her, "And now, my dear child, you must come to bed; there is no danger for you more."

The poor girl had grown somewhat reassured in the comfortable little kitchen, but her terror seemed to come back at any sign of removal; she started to her feet, almost as if she were a wild creature. But I would defy any one to be afraid of my dear mother, or indeed to refuse to do what she bade, when she smiled so in her inviting way and put out her hand; and so the girl went with her, bowing to me, or dropping a sort of courtesy in her foreign fashion, as she went out of the door, and I was left to see what damage had been done to my castle by the savages, as I called them.

I had sprung the rattle none too soon; for one of these rascals, as it proved — I suppose it was the same who swore that she had not gone into the church — with some tool or other he had in his hand, had split out a bit of the fence and had pried out a part of a plank. I had done my work too well for any large piece to give way. But the moment I looked into my coal-bin I saw that something was amiss. I did not like very well to go to the outside, but I must risk something; so I took out a dark lantern which I always kept ready. Sure enough, as I say, the fellow had struck so hard and so well that he had split out a piece of board, and a little coal even had fallen upon the passage-way. I was not much displeased at this, for if he thought no nearer the truth than that he had broken into a coal-bin of the church, why, he was far enough from his mark for me. After finding this, however, I was anxious enough, lest any of them should return, not to go to bed again that night; but all was still as death, and, to tell the truth, I fell asleep in my chair. I doubt whether my mother slept, or her frightened charge.

I was at work in the passage early the next morning with some weather-stained boards I had, and before nine o'clock I had doubled all that piece of fence, from my wing where my hand-cart was to the church, and I had spiked the new boards on, which looked like old boards, as I said, with tenpenny nails; so that he would be a stout burglar who would cut through them unless he had tools for his purpose and daylight to work by. As I was gathering up my tools to go in, a coarse, brutal-looking Irishman came walking up the alley and looked round. My work was so well done, and I had been so careful to leave no chips, that even then he could not have guessed that I had been building the fence anew, though

I fancied he looked at it. He seemed to want to excuse himself for being there at all, and asked me, with an oath and in a broad Irish brogue, if there were no other passage through. I had the presence of mind to say in German, "*Wollen sie sprechen Deutsch?*" and so made as if I could not understand him; and then, kneeling on the cellar-door of the church, pretended to put a key into the lock, as if I were making sure that I had made it firm.

And with that, he turned round with another oath, as if he had come out of his way, and went out of the alley, closely followed by me. I watched him as long as I dared, but as he showed no sign of going back to the alley, I at last walked round a square with my tools, and so came back to my mother and the pretty stranger.

My mother had been trying to get at her story. She made her understand a few words of German, but they talked by signs and smiles and tears and kisses much more than by words; and by this time they understood each other so well that my mother had persuaded her not to go away that day.

Nor did she go out for many days after; I will go before my story far enough to say that. She had, indeed, been horribly frightened that night, and she was as loath to go out again into the streets of New York as I should be to plunge from a safe shore into some terrible, howling ocean; or, indeed, as one who found himself safe at home would be to trust himself to the tender mercies of a tribe of cannibals.

Two such loving women as they were were not long in building up a language, especially as my mother had learned from my father and his friends, in her early life, some of the common words of German — what she called a bread-and-butter German. For our new inmate was a Swedish girl. Her story, in short, was this: —

She had been in New York but two days. On the voyage over, they had had some terrible sickness on the vessel, and the poor child's mother had died very suddenly and had been buried in the sea. Her father had died long before.

This was, as you may think, a terrible shock to her. But she had hoped and hoped for the voyage to come to an end, because there was a certain brother of hers in America whom they were to meet at their landing, and though she was very lonely on the packet-ship, in which she and her mother and a certain family of the name of Hantsen — of whom she had much to say — were the only Swedes, still she expected to find the brother almost as soon, as I may say, as they saw the land.

She felt badly enough that he did not come on board with the quarantine officer. When the passengers were brought to Castle Garden, and no brother came, she felt worse. However, with the help of the clerks there, she got off a letter to him, somewhere in Jersey, and proposed to wait as long as they would let her, till he should come.

The second day there came a man to the Garden, who said he was a Dane, but he spoke Swedish well enough. He said her brother was sick, and had sent him to find her. She was to come with her trunks, and her mother's, and all their affairs, to his house, and the same afternoon they should go to where the brother was.

Without doubt or fear she went with this man, and spent the day at a forlorn sort of hotel which she described, but which I never could find again. Toward night the man came again and bade her take a bag, with her one change of dress, and come with him to her brother.

After a long ride through the city, they got out at a house which, thank God! was only one block from Fernando Street. And there this simple, innocent creature, as she went in, asked where her brother was, to meet only a burst of laughter from one or two coarse-looking men, and from half-a-dozen brazen-faced girls whom she hated, she said, the minute she saw them.

Except that an old woman took off her shawl and cloak and bonnet, and took away from her the travelling things she had in her hand, nobody took any care of her but to laugh at her, and mock her if she dared say anything.

She tried to go out to the door to find even the

Dane who had brought her there, but she was given to understand that he was coming again for her, and that she must wait till he came. As for her brother, there was no brother there, nor had been any. The poor girl had been trapped, and saw that she had been trapped; she had been spirited away from everybody who ever heard of her mother, and was in the clutches, as she said to my mother afterward, of a crew of devils who knew nothing of love or of mercy.

They did try to make her eat and drink, — tried to make her drink champagne, or any other wine; but they had no fool to deal with. The girl did not, I think, let her captors know how desperate were her resolutions. But her eyes were wide open, and she was not going to lose any chance. She was all on the alert for her escape when, at eleven o'clock, the Dane came at last whom she had been expecting so anxiously.

The girl asked him for her brother, only to be put off by one excuse or another, and then to hear from him the most loathsome talk of his admiration, not to say his passion, for her.

They were nearly alone by this time, and he led her unresisting, as he thought, into another smaller room, brilliantly lighted, and, as she saw in a glance, gaudily furnished, with wine and fruit and cake on a side-table, — a room where they would be quite alone.

She walked simply across and looked at herself in the great mirror. Then she made some foolish little speech about her hair, and how pale she looked. Then she crossed to the sofa, and sat upon it with as tired an air as he might have expected of one who had lived through such a day. Then she looked up at him and even smiled upon him, she said, and asked him if he would not ask them for some cold water.

The fellow turned into the passage-way, well pleased with her submission, and in the same instant the girl was at the window as if she had flown across the room.

Fool! The window was made fast, not by any moving bolt, either. It was nailed down, and it did not give a hair's-breadth to her hand.

Little cared she for that. She sat on the window-seat, which was broad enough to hold her; she braced her feet against the foot of the bedstead, which stood just near enough to her; she turned enough to bring her shoulder against the window-sash, and then with her whole force she heaved herself against the sash, and the entire window, of course, gave way.

The girl caught herself upon the blind, which swung open before her. She pulled herself free from the sill and window-seat, and dropped fearless into the street.

The fall was not long. She lighted on her feet and ran as only fear could teach her to run. Where to, she knew not; but she thought she turned a corner before she heard any voices from behind.

Still she ran. And it was when she came to the corner of the next street that she heard for the first time the screams of pursuers.

She turned again, like a poor hunted hare as she was. But what was her running to theirs? She was passing our long fence in Fernando Street, and then for the first time she screamed for help.

It was that scream which waked me.

She saw the steeple of the church. She had a dim feeling that a church would be an asylum. So was it that she ran up our alley, to find that she was in a trap there.

And then it was that she fell against my door, that she cried twice, "Oh, my God! Oh, my God!" and that the good God, who had heard her, sent me to draw her in.

We had to learn her language, in a fashion, and she to learn ours, before we understood her story in this way. But at the very first my mother made out that the girl had fled from savages who meant worse than death for her. So she understood why she was so frightened at every sound, and why at first she was afraid to stay with us, yet more afraid to go.

But this passed off in a day or two. She took to my mother with a sort of eager way which showed how she must have loved her own mother, and how much she lost when she lost her. And that was one of the parts of her sad story that we understood.

No one, I think, could help loving my mother; but here was a poor, storm-tossed creature who, I might say, had nothing else to love, seeing she had lost all trace of this brother, and here was my mother, soothing her, comforting her, dressing her wounds for her, trying to make her feel that God's world was not all wickedness; and the girl in return poured out her whole heart.

When my mother explained to her that she should not let her go away till her brother was found, then for the first time she seemed perfectly happy. She was indeed the loveliest creature I ever put my eyes on.

She was then about nineteen years old, of a delicate complexion naturally, which was now a little browned by the sea-air. She was rather tall than otherwise, but her figure was so graceful that I think you never thought her tall. Her eyes were perhaps deep-set, and of that strange gray which I have heard it said the goddesses in the Greek poetry had. Still, when she was sad, one saw the less of all this. It was not till she forgot her grief for the instant in the certainty that she might rest with my mother, so that her whole face blazed with joy, that I first knew what the perfect beauty of a perfect woman was.

Her name, it seemed, was Frida, — a name made from the name of one of the old goddesses among the Northmen, the same from whom our day Friday is named. She is the half-sister of Thor, from whom Thursday is named, and the daughter of Wodin, from whom Wednesday is named.

I knew little of all this then, but I did not wonder when I read afterward that this northern goddess was the Goddess of Love, the friend of song, the most beautiful of all their divinities, — queen of spring and light and everything lovely.

But surely never any one took fewer of the airs of a goddess than our Frida did while she was with us. She would watch my mother, as if afraid that she should put her hand to a gridiron or a tin dipper. She gave her to understand, in a thousand pretty ways, that she should be her faithful, loving, and sincere servant. If she would only show her what to do, she would work for her as a child that loved her. And so indeed she did. My dear mother would laugh and say she was quite a fine lady now, for Frida would not let her touch broom nor mop, skimmer nor dusting-cloth.

The girl would do anything but go out upon an errand. She could not bear to see the other side of the fence. What she thought of it all I do not know. Whether she thought it was the custom in America for young men to live shut up with their mothers in enclosures of half an acre square, or whether she thought we two made some peculiar religious order, whose rules provided that one woman and one man should live together in a convent or monastery of their own, or whether she supposed half New York was made up, as

Marco Polo found Pekin, of cottages or of gardens, I did not know, nor did I much care. I could see that here was provided a companion for my mother, who was else so lonely, and I very soon found that she was as much a companion for me.

So soon as we could understand her at all, I took the name of her brother and his address. When he wrote last he was tending a saw-mill at a place about seven miles away from Tuckahoe, in Jersey. But he said he was going to leave there at once, so that they need not write there. He sent the money for their passage, and promised, as I said, to meet them at New York.

This was a poor clew at the best. But I put a good face on it, and promised her I would find him if he could be found. And I spared no pains. I wrote to the postmaster at Tuckahoe, and to a minister I heard of there. I inquired of the Swedish consuls in New York and Philadelphia. Indeed, in the end, I went to Tuckahoe myself, with her, to inquire. But this was long after. However, I may say here, once for all, to use an old phrase of my mother's, we never found "hide nor hair" of him. And although this grieved Frida, of course, yet it came on her gradually, and as she had never seen him to remember him, it was not the same loss as if they had grown up together.

Meanwhile that first winter was, I thought, the pleasantest I had ever known in my life. I did not have to work very hard now, for my business was rather the laying out work for my men, and sometimes a nice job which needed my hand on my lathe at home, or in some other delicate affair that I could bring home with me.

We were teaching Frida English, my mother and I, and she and I made a great frolic of her teaching me Swedish. I would bring home Swedish newspapers and stories for her, and we would puzzle them out together, — she as much troubled to find the English word as I to find out the Swedish. Then she sang like a bird when she was about her household work, or when she sat sewing for my mother, and she had not lived with us a fortnight before she began to join us on Sunday evenings in the choruses of the Methodist hymns which my mother and I sang together. So then we made her sing Swedish hymns to us. And before she knew it, the great tears would brim over her deep eyes and would run down in pearls upon her cheek. Nothing set her to thinking of her old home as those Sunday evenings did. Of a Sunday evening we could make her go out with us to church sometimes. Not but then she would half cover her face with a veil, so afraid was she that we might meet the Dane. But I told her that the last place we should find him at would be at church on Sunday evening.

I have come far in advance of my story, that I might make any one who reads this life of mine to understand how naturally and simply this poor lost bird nestled down into our quiet life, and how the house that was built for two proved big enough for three. For I made some new purchases now, and fitted up the little middle chamber for Frida's own use. We had called it the "spare chamber" before, in joke. But now my mother fitted pretty curtains to it, and other hangings, without Frida's knowledge. I had a square of carpet made up at the warehouse for the middle of the floor, and by making her do one errand and another in the corner of the garden one pleasant afternoon in November, we had it all prettily fitted up for her room before she knew it. And a great gala we made of it when she came in from gathering the seeds of the calystegia, which she had been sent for.

She looked like a northern Flora as she came in, with her arms all festooned by the vines she had been pulling down. And when my mother made her come out to the door she had never seen opened before, and led her in, and told her that this pretty chamber was all her own, the pretty creature flushed crimson red at first, and then her quick tears ran over, and she fell on my mother's neck and kissed her as if she would never be done. And then she timidly held her hand out to me, too, as I stood in the doorway, and said, in her slow, careful English, —

"And you, too — and you, too. I must tank you both, also, especially. You are so good — so good to de poor lost girl!" That was a very happy evening.

But, as I say, I have gone ahead of my story. For before we had these quiet evenings we were fated to have many anxious ones and one stormy one.

The very first day that Frida was with us, I felt sure that the savages would make another descent upon us. They had heard her scream, that was certain. They knew she had not passed them, that was certain. They knew there was a coal-bin on the other side of our fence, that was certain. They would have reason enough for being afraid to have her at large, if, indeed, there were no worse passion than fear driving some of them in pursuit of her. I could not keep out of my mind the beastly look of the Irishman who asked me, with such an ugly leer on his face, if there were no passage through. Not that I told either of the two women of my fears. But, all the same, I did not undress myself for a week, and sat in the great easy-chair in our kitchen through the whole of every night, waiting for the least sound of alarm.

Next to the savages, I had always lived in fear of being discovered in my retreat by the police, who would certainly think it strange to find a man and his mother living in a shed, without any practicable outside door, in what they called a vacant lot.

But I have read of weak nations in history which were fain to call upon one neighbor whom they did not like to protect them against another whom they liked less. I made up my mind, in like wise, to go round to the police-station nearest me.

And so, having dressed myself in my black coat, and put on a round hat and gloves, I bought me a Malacca walking-stick, such as was then in fashion, and called upon the captain in style. I told him I lived next the church, and that on such and such a night there was a regular row among roughs, and that several of them went storming up the alley in a crowd. I said, "Although your men were there as quick as they could come, these fellows had all gone before they came." But then I explained that I had seen a fellow hanging about the alley in the daytime, who seemed to be there for no good; that there was a hand-cart kept there by a workman, who seemed to be an honest fellow, and, perhaps, all they wanted was to steal that; that, if I could, I would warn him. But meanwhile, I said, I had come round to the station to give the warning of my suspicions, that if my rattle was heard again, the patrolmen might know what was in the wind.

The captain was a good deal impressed by my make-up and by the ease of my manner. He affected to be perfectly well acquainted with me, although we had never happened to meet at the Century Club or at the Union League. I confirmed the favorable impression I had made by leaving my card, which I had had handsomely engraved: "MR. ROBINSON CRUSOE." With my pencil I added my down-town address, where, I said, a note or telegram would find me.

I was not a day too soon with my visit to this gentleman. That very night, after my mother and Frida had gone to bed, as I sat in my easy-chair, there came over me one of those strange intimations which I have never found it safe to disregard. Sometimes it is of good, and sometimes of bad. This time it made me certain that all was not well. To relieve my fears I lifted my ladder over the wall and dropped it in the alley. I swung myself down and carried it to the very end of the alley, to the place where I had dragged poor Frida in. The moon fell on the fence opposite ours. My wing-fence and hand-cart were all in shade. But everything was safe there.

Again I chided myself for my fears, when, as I looked up the alley to the street, I saw a group of four men come in stealthily. They said not a word, but I could make out their forms distinctly against the houses opposite.

I was caught in my own trap!

Not quite! They had not seen me, for I was wholly in shadow. I stepped quickly in at my own slide. I pushed it back and bolted it securely, and with my heart in my mouth, I waited at my hole of observation. In a minute more they were close around me, though they did not suspect I was so near.

They also had a dark-lantern, and, I thought,

more than one. They spoke in low tones; but as they had no thought they had a hearer quite so near, I could hear all they said.

"I tell you it was this side, and this is the side I heard their deuced psalm-singing day before yesterday."

"What if he did hear psalm-singing? Are you going to break into a man's garden because he sings psalms? I came here to find out where the girl went to; and now you talk of psalm-singing and coal-bins." This from another, whose English was poor, and in whom I fancied I heard the Dane. It was clear enough that he spoke sense, and a sort of doubt fell on the whole crew; but speaker No. 1, with a heavy crowbar he had, smashed into my pine wall, as I have a right to call it now, with a force which made the splinters fly.

"I should think we were all at Niblo's," said a man of slighter build, "and that we were playing Humpty Dumpty. Because a girl flew out of a window, you think a fence opened to take her in. Why should she not go through a door?" and he kicked with his foot upon the heavy sloping cellar-door of the church, which just rose a little from the pavement. It was the doorway which they used there when they took in their supply of coal. The moon fell full on one side of it. To my surprise it was loose and gave way.

"Here is where the girl flew to, and here is

where Bully Bigg, the donkey, let her slip out of his fingers. I knew he was a fool, but I did not know he was such a fool," said the Dane (if he were the Dane).

I will not pretend to write down the oaths and foul words which came in between every two of the words I have repeated.

"Fool yourself!" replied the Bully; "and what sort of a fool is the man who comes up a blind alley looking after a girl that will not kiss him when he bids her?"

"Anyway," put in another of the crew, who had just now lifted the heavy cellar-door, "other people may find it handy to hop down here when the 'beaks' are too near them. It 's a handy place to know of in a dark night, if the dear deacons do choose to keep it open for a poor psalm-singing tramp, who has no chance at the station-house. Here, Lopp, you are the tallest, — jump in and tell us what is there;" and at this moment the Dane caught sight of my unfortunate ladder, lying full in the moonlight. I could see him seize it and run to the doorway with it with a deep laugh and some phrase of his own country talk, which I did not understand.

"The deacons are very good," said the savage who had lifted the cellar-door. "They make everything handy for us poor fellows."

And though he had not planted the ladder, he was the first to run down, and called for the rest to follow. The Dane was second, Lopp was third, and "The Bully," as the big rascal seemed to be called by distinction, was the fourth.

I saw him disappear from my view with a mixture of wonder and terror which I will not describe. I seized my light overcoat, which always hung in the passage. I flung open my sliding-door and shut it again behind me. I looked into the black of the cellar to see the reflections from their distant lanterns, and without a sound I drew up my ladder. Then I ran to the head of the alley and sounded my rattle as I would have sounded the trumpet for a charge in battle. The officers joined me in one moment.

"I am the man who spoke to the captain about these rowdies. Four of them are in the cellar of the church yonder now."

"Do you know who?"

"One they called Lopp, and one they called Bully Bigg," said I. "I do not know the others' names."

The officers were enraptured.

I led them, and two other patrolmen who joined us, to the shelter of my wing-wall. In a few minutes the head of the Dane appeared, as he was lifted from below. With an effort and three or four oaths, he struggled out upon the ground, to be seized and gagged the moment he stepped back. With varying fortunes, Bigg and Lopp emerged, and were seized and handcuffed in turn. The fourth surrendered on being summoned.

What followed comes into the line of daily life and the morning newspaper so regularly that I need not describe it. Against the Dane it proved that endless warrants could be brought immediately. His lair of stolen baggage and other property was unearthed, and countless sufferers claimed their own. I was able to recover Frida's and her mother's possessions — the locks on the trunks still unbroken. The Dane himself would have been sent to the Island on I know not how many charges, but that the Danish minister asked for him that he might be hanged in Denmark, and he was sent and hanged accordingly.

Lopp was sent to Sing-Sing for ten years, and has not yet been pardoned.

Bigg and Cordon were sent to Blackwell's Island for three years each. And so the land had peace for that time.

That winter, as there came on one and another idle alarm that Frida's brother might be heard from, my heart sank with the lowest terror lest she should go away. And in the spring I told her that if she went away I was sure I should die. And the dear girl looked down, and looked up, and said she thought — she thought she should, too. And we told my mother that we had determined that Frida should never go away while we stayed there. And she approved.

So I wrote a note to the minister of the church which had protected us so long, and one night we slid the board carefully, and all three walked round, fearless of the Dane, and Frida and I were married.

It was more than three years after, when I received by one post three letters, which gave us great ground for consultation. The first was from my old friend and patron, the Spaniard. He wrote to me from Chicago, where he, in his turn, had fallen in with a crew of savages, who had stripped him of all he had, under the pretext of a land-enterprise they engaged him in, and had left him without a real, as he said. He wanted to know if I could not find him some clerkship, or even some place as janitor, in New York.

The second letter was from old Mr. Henry in Philadelphia, who had always employed me after my old master's death. He said that the fence around the lot in Ninety-ninth Avenue might need some repairs, and he wished I would look at it. He was growing old, he said, and he did not care to come to New York. But the Fordyce heirs would spend ten years in Europe.

The third letter was from Tom Grinnell.

I wrote to Mr. Henry that I thought he had better let me knock up a little office, where a keeper might sleep, if necessary; that there was some stuff with which I could put up such an office, and that I had an old friend, a Spaniard, who was an honest fellow, and if he might have his bed in the office, would take gratefully whatever his services to the estate proved worth. He wrote me by the next day's mail that I might engage the Spaniard and finish the office. So I wrote to the Spaniard and got a letter from him, accepting the post provided for him. Then I wrote to Tom Grinnell.

The last day we spent at our dear old home, I occupied myself in finishing the office as Friend Henry bade me. I made a "practicable door," which opened from the passage on Church Alley. Then I loaded my hand-cart with my own chest and took it myself, in my working clothes, to the Vanderbilt Station, where I took a brass check for it.

I could not wait for the Spaniard, but I left a letter for him, giving him a description of the way I managed the goats, and directions to milk and fatten them, and to make both butter and cheese.

At half-past ten a "crystal," as those cabs were then called, came to the corner of Fernando Street and Church Alley, and so we drove to the station. I left the key of the office, directed to the Spaniard, in the hands of the baggage-master.

When I took leave of my castle, as I called it, I carried with me for relics the great straw hat I had made, my umbrella, and one of my parrots; also I forgot not to take the money I formerly mentioned, which had lain by me so long useless that it was grown rusty and tarnished, and could scarcely pass for money till it had been a little rubbed and handled. With these relics and with my wife's and mother's baggage and my own chest, we arrived at our new home.

BREAD ON THE WATERS

A WASHINGTON CHRISTMAS

BREAD ON THE WATERS

[No. This story also is "Invented Example." But it is founded on facts. It is a pleasure to me, writing fifty-four years after the commission intrusted to me by the late Mrs. Falcs, to say that that is a real name, and that her benevolence at a distance is precisely represented here.

Perhaps the large history of the world would be differently written but for that kindness of hers.

I was a very young clergyman, and the remittance she made to me was the first trust of the same kind which had ever been confided to me.]

CHAPTER I

MAKE READY

"ONLY think, Matty, papa passed right by me when I was sitting with my back to the fire and stitching away on his book-mark without my once seeing him! But he was so busy talking to mamma that he never saw what I was doing, and I huddled it under a newspaper before he came back again. Well, I have got papa's present done, but I cannot keep out of mamma's way. Matty, dear, if I will sit in the sun and keep a shawl on, may I not sit in your room and work? It is not one bit cold there.

Really, Matty, it is a great deal warmer than it was yesterday."

"Dear child," said Matty, to whom everybody came so readily for advice and help, "I can do better for you than that. You shall come into the study; papa will be away all the morning, and I will have the fire kept up there, — and mamma shall never come near you."

All this, and a thousand times more of plotting and counterplotting, was going on among four children and their elders in a comfortable, free-and-easy seeming household in Washington, as the boys and girls, young men and young women were in the last agonies of making ready for Christmas. Matty is fully entitled to be called a young woman, when we see her. She has just passed her twenty-first birthday. But she looks as fresh and pretty as when she was seventeen, and certainly she is a great deal pleasanter though she be wiser. She is the oldest of the troop. Tom, the next, is expected from Annapolis this afternoon, and Beverly from Charlotte. Then come four boys and girls whose ages and places the reader must guess at as we go on.

The youngest of the family were still young enough to write the names of the presents which they would be glad to receive, or to denote them by rude hieroglyphs, on large sheets of paper. They were wont to pin up these sheets on certain doors, which, by long usage in this free-and-easy family, had come to be regarded as the bulletin-boards of the establishment. Well-nigh every range of created things had some representation on these bulletins, — from an ambling pony round to a "boot-buttenner," thus spelled out by poor Laura, who was constantly in disgrace, because she always appeared latest at the door when the children started for church, to ride, or for school. The youngsters still held to the theory of announcing thus their wants in advance. Horace doubted whether he were not too old. But there was so much danger that nobody would know how much he needed a jig-saw, that he finally compromised with his dignity, wrote on a virgin sheet of paper, "gig-saw," signed his name, "Horace Molyneux, Dec. 21," and left his other presents to conjecture.

And of course at thc very end, as Santa Claus and his revels were close upon them, while the work done had been wonderful, that which we ought to have done but which we had left undone, was simply terrible. Here were pictures that must be brought home from the frame-man, who had never pretended he would send them; there were ferns and lycopodiums in pots which must be brought home from the greenhouse; here were presents for other homes, which must not only be finished, but must be put up in paper and sent before night, so as to appear on other trees. Every one of these must be shown to mamma, and approved by her and praised; and every one must be shown to dear Matty, and praised and approved by her. And yet by no accident must Matty see her own presents or dream that any child has remembered her, or mamma see *hers* or think herself remembered.

And Matty has all her own little list to see to, while she keeps a heart at leisure from itself to soothe and sympathize. She has to correct the mistakes, to repair the failures, to respect the wonder, to refresh the discouragement, of each and all the youngsters. Her own Sunday scholars are to be provided with their presents. The last orders are to be given for the Christmas dinners of half-a-dozen families of vassals, mostly black or of some shade of black, who never forgot their vassalage as Christmas came round. Turkey, cranberry, apples, tea, cheese, and butter must be sent to each household of these vassals, as if every member were paralyzed except in the muscles of the jaw. But, all the same, Matty or her mother must be in readiness all the morning and afternoon to receive the visits of all the vassals, — who, so far as this form of homage went, did not seem to be paralyzed at all.

For herself, Matty took possession of the dining-room, as soon as she could clear it of the breakfast equipage, of the children and of the servants, and here, with pen and ink, with wrapping-paper and twine, with telegraph blanks and with the directory, and with Venty as her Ariel messenger — not so airy and quick as Ariel, but quite as willing — Matty worked her wonders, and gave her audiences, whether to vassals from without or puzzled children from within.

Venty was short for Ventidius. But this name, given in baptism, was one which Venty seldom heard.

Matty corded up this parcel, and made Venty cord up that ; wrote this note of compliment, that of inquiry, that of congratulation, and sent Venty on this, that, and another errand with them; relieved Flossy's anxieties and poor Laura's in ways which have been described; made sure that the wagon should be at the station in ample time for Beverly's arrival; and at last, at nearly one o'clock, called Aunty Chloe (who was in waiting on everybody as a superserviceable person, on the pretence that she was needed), bade Aunty pick up the scraps, sweep the floor, and bring the room to rights. And so, having attended to everybody beside herself, to all their wishes and hopes and fears, poor Matty — or shall I say, dear Matty — ran off to her own room, to finish her own presents and make her own last preparations.

She had kept up her spirits as best she could all the morning, but, at any moment when she was alone, her spirits had fallen again. She knew it, and she knew why. And now she could not hold out any longer. She and her mother, thank God, never had any secrets. And as she ran by her mother's door she could not help tapping, to be sure if she had come home.

Yes, she had come home. "Come in!" and Matty ran in.

Her mother had not even taken off her hat or her gloves. She had flung herself on the sofa, as if her walk had been quite too much for her; her salts and her handkerchief were in her hands, and when she saw it was Matty, as she had hoped when she spoke, she would not even pretend she had not been in tears.

In a moment Matty was on her knees on the floor by the sofa, and somehow had her left arm round about her mother's neck.

"Dear, dear mamma! What is it, what is the matter?"

"My dear, dear Matty," replied her mother, just succeeding in speaking without sobs, and speaking the more easily because she stroked the girl's hair and caressed her as she spoke, "do not ask, do not try to know. You will know, if you do not guess, only too soon. And now the children will be better, and papa will get through Christmas better, if you do not know, my darling."

"No, dear mamma," said Matty, crossing her mother's purpose almost for the first time that she remembered, but wholly sure that she was right in doing so, — "No, dear mamma, it is not best so. Indeed, it is not, mamma! I feel in my bones that it is not!" This she said with a wretched attempt to smile, which was the more ghastly because the tears were running down from both their faces.

"You see I have tried, mamma. I knew all day yesterday that something was wrong, and at breakfast this morning I knew it. And I have had to hold up — with the children and all these people — with the feeling that any minute the hair might break and the sword fall. And I know I shall do better if you tell me. You see the boys will be here before dark, and of course they will see, and what in the world shall I say to them?"

"What, indeed?" said her poor mother. "Terrible it is, dear child, because your father is so wretched. I have just come from him. He would not let me stay, and yet for the minute I was there, I saw that no one else could come in to goad him. Dear, dear papa, he is so resolute and brave, and yet any minute I was afraid that he would break a blood-vessel and fall dead before me. Oh, Matty, Matty, my darling, it is terrible!"

And this time the poor woman could not control herself longer, but gave way to her sobs, and her voice fairly broke, so that she was inarticulate, as she laid her cheek against her daughter's on the sofa.

"What is terrible? Dear mamma, you must tell me!"

"I think I must tell you, Matty, my darling. I believe if I cannot tell some one, I shall die."

Then Mrs. Molyneux told the whole horror to Matty. Here was her husband charged with the grossest plunder of the treasury, and now charged even in the House of Representatives. It had been whispered about before, and had been hinted at in some of the lower newspapers, but now even a committee of Congress had noticed it, and had "given him an opportunity to clear himself." There was no less a sum than forty-seven thousand dollars, in three separate payments, charged to him at the Navy Department as long ago as the second and third years of the Civil War. At the Navy they had his receipts for it. Not that he had been in that department then any more than he was now. He was then chief clerk in the Bureau of Internal Improvement, as he was now Commissioner there. But this was when the second Rio Grande expedition was fitted out; and from Mr. Molyneux's knowledge of Spanish, and his old connection with the Santa Fé trade, this particular matter had been intrusted to him.

"Yes, dear mamma!"

"Well, papa has it all down on his own cash-book; that book he carries in his breast-pocket. There are the three payments, and then all the transfers he made to the different people. One was that old white-haired Spaniard with the hare-lip, who used to come here at the back door, so that he should not be seen at the Department. But it was before you remember. The others were in smaller sums. But the whole thing was done in three weeks, and then the expedition sailed, and papa had enough else to think of, and has never thought of it since, till ten or fifteen days ago, when somebody in the Eleventh Auditor's office discovered this charge, and his receipt for this money."

"Well, dear mamma?"

"Well, dear child, that is all, but that now the newspapers have got hold of it, and the Committee on Retrenchment, who are all new men, with their reputations to make, have got hold of it, and some of them really think, you know, that papa has stolen the money!" And she broke down crying again.

"But he can show his accounts, mamma!"

"What are his accounts worth? He must show the vouchers, as they are called. He must show these people's receipts, and what has become of these people; what they did with the money. He must show everything. Well, when the 'Copperhead' first spoke of it — that was a fortnight ago — papa was really pleased. For he said it would be a good chance to bring out a piece of war history. He said that in our Bureau we had never had any credit for the Rio Grande successes, that they were all our thunder; because *then* he could laugh about this horrid thing. He said the Navy had taken all the honors, while we deserved them all. And he said if these horrid 'Copperhead' and 'Argus' and 'Scorpion' people would only publish the vouchers half as freely as they published the charges, we should get a little of the credit that was our due."

"Well, mamma, and what is the trouble now?"

"Why, papa was so sure that he would do nothing until an official call came. But on Monday it got into Congress. That hairy man from the Yellowstone brought in a resolution or something, and the Committee was ordered to inquire. And when the order came down, papa told Mr. Waltsingham to bring him the papers, and, Matty, the papers were not there!"

"Stolen!" cried Matty, understanding the crisis for the first time.

"Yes — perhaps — or lost — hidden somewhere. You have no idea of the work of those days — night work and all that. Many a time your father did not undress for a week."

"And now he must remember where he put a horrid pile of papers, eleven, twelve years ago. Mamma, that pile is stolen. That odious Greenhithe stole it. He lives in Philadelphia now, and he has put up these newspapers to this lie."

Mr. Greenhithe was an underclerk in the Internal Improvement Bureau, who had shown an amount of attention to Miss Matty, which she had disliked and had refused to receive. She had always said he was bad and would come to a bad end, and when he was detected in a low trick, selling stationery which he had stolen from the supply room, and was discharged in disgrace, Matty had said it was good enough for him.

These were her reasons for pronouncing at once

that he had stolen the vouchers and had started the rumors.

"I do not know. Papa does not know. He hardly tries to guess. He says either way it is bad. If the vouchers are stolen, he is in fault, for he is responsible for the archives; if he cannot produce the vouchers, then all the country is down on him for stealing. I only hope," said poor Mrs. Molyneux, "that they won't say our poor old wagon is a coach and six;" and this time she tried to smile.

And now she had told her story. All last night, while the children were asleep, Mr. Molyneux had been at the office, even till four o'clock in the morning, taking old dusty piles from their lairs and searching for those wretched vouchers. And mamma had been waiting — shall one not say, had been weeping? — here at home. That was the reason poor papa had looked so haggard at breakfast this morning.

This was all mamma had to tell. She had been to the office this morning, but papa would not let her stay. He must see all comers, just as if nothing had happened, was happening, or was going to happen.

Well! Matty did make her mother take off her jacket and her hat and her gloves. She even made her drink a glass of wine and lie down. And then the poor girl retired to her own room, with such appetite as she might for taking the last stitches in worsted work, for stippling in the lights into drawings, for writing the presentation lines in books, and for doing the thousand little niceties in the way of finishing touches which she had promised the children to do for them.

Her dominant feeling — yes, it was a dominant passion, as she knew — was simply rage against this miserable Greenhithe, this cowardly sneak who was thus taking his revenge upon her, because she had been so cold to him. Or was it that he made up to her because he was already in trouble at the Office and hoped she would clear him with her father? Either way he was a snake and a scorpion, but he had worked out for himself a terrible revenge. Poor Matty! She tried to think what she could do, how she could help, for that was the habit of her life. But this was now hard indeed. Her mind would not now take that turn. All that it would turn to was to the wretched and worse than worthless question, what punishment might fall on him for such utter baseness and wickedncss.

All the same the children must have their lunch, and they must not know that anything was the matter. Oh dear! this concealment was the worst of all!

So they had their lunch. And poor Matty counselled again, and helped again, and took the last stitches, and mended the last breaks, and waited and wondered, and tried to hope, till at five o'clock an office messenger came up with this message.

4.45 P. M.

DEAR MATTY, — I shall not come up to dinner. There is pressing work here. Tell mamma not to sit up for me. I have my key.

I have no chance to get my things for the children. Will you see to it? Here is twenty dollars, and if you need more let them send in the bill. I had only thought of that jig-saw — was it? — that Horace wants. See that the dear fellow has a good one.

Love to all and ever yours,

PAPA.

"Poor, dear papa," said Matty aloud, shedding tears in spite of herself. "To be thinking of jig-saws and children in all this horrid hunt! As if hunting for anything was not the worst trial of all, always." And at once the brave girl took down her wraps and put on her walking-shoes, that her father's commissions might be met before their six-o'clock dinner. And she determined that first of all shc would meet Tom at the station.

At the station she met Tom; that was well. Matty had not been charged to secrecy; that was well. She told him all the story, not without adding her suspicions, and giving him some notion of her rage.

And Tom was angry enough, — there was a crumb of comfort there. But Tom went off on another track. Tom distrusted the Navy Department. He had been long enough at Annapolis to doubt the red tape of the bureaus with which his chiefs had to do. "If the navy had the money, the navy had the vouchers," that was Tom's theory. He knew a chief clerk in the navy, and Tom was going at once round there.

But Matty held him in check at least for the moment. Whatever else he did, he must come home first; he must see mamma and he must see the children, and he must have dinner. She had not told him yet how well he looked, and how handsome he was.

But after Tom had seen them he slipped off, pretended he had unfinished preparations to make, and went right to the Department, forced his way in because he was Mr. Molyneux's son, and found his poor father with Zeigler, the chief clerk, still on this wretched and fruitless overhaul of the old files. Tom stated frankly, in his off-hand, business-like way, what his theory was. Neither Zeigler nor Tom's father believed in it in the least. Tom knew nothing, they said; the Navy paid the money, but the Navy was satisfied with our receipt, and should be.

Tom continued to say, "If the Navy paid the money the Navy must have the vouchers;" and at last, more to be rid of him than with any hope of the result, Mr. Molyneux let the eager fellow go round to his friend, Eben Ricketts, and see if Eben would not give an hour or two of his Christmas to looking up the thing. Mr. Molyneux even went so far as to write a frank line to Mr. Ricketts, and enclosed a letter which he had had that day from the chairman of the House Committee, — a letter which was smooth enough in the language, but horrible enough in the thing.

Ah me! Had not Ricketts read it all already in the evening "Argus"? He was willing, if he could, to serve. So he with Tom went round and found the Navy Department messenger, and opened and lighted up the necessary rooms, and they spent three hours of their Christmas there. Meanwhile Beverly had arrived from Norfolk. He had a frolic with the children, and then called his mother and Matty away from them.

"What in thunder is the matter?" said the poor boy.

And they told him. How could they help telling him? And so soon as the story was finished, the boy had his coat on and was putting on his boots. He went right down to his father's office, he made old Stratton admit him, and told his father he too had reported for duty.

CHAPTER II

CHRISTMAS MORNING

AND at last Christmas morning dawned, — gray enough and grim enough.

In that house the general presenting was reserved for evening after dinner, — when in olden days there had always been a large Christmas-tree lighted and dressed for the children and their little friends. As the children had grown older, and the trees at the Sunday-school and elsewhere had grown larger, the family tree had grown smaller, and on this day was to be simply a typical tree, a little suggestion of a tree, between the front windows; while most of the presents of every sort and kind were to be dispersed — where room could be made for them — in any part of the front parlors. All the grand ceremonial of present-giving was thus reserved to the afternoon of Christmas, because then it was certain papa would be at home, Tom and Beverly would both be ready, and, indeed, as the little people confessed, they themselves would have more chance to be quite prepared.

But none the less was the myth of Santa Claus and the stockings kept up, although that was a business of less account, and one in which the children themselves had no share, except to wonder, to enjoy, and to receive. You will observe that there is a duality in most of the enjoyments of life, — that if you have a long-expected letter from your brother who is in Yokohama, by the same mail or the next mail there comes a letter from your sister who is in Cawnpore. And so it was of Christmas at this Molyneux house. Besides the great wonders, like those wrought out by Aladdin's slave of the lamp, there were the wonders, less gigantic but not less exquisite, of the morning hours, wrought out by the slave of the ring. How this series of wonders came about, the youngest of the children did not know, and were still imaginative enough and truly wise enough not to inquire.

While, then, the two young men and their father were at one or the other Department, now on step-ladders, handing down dusty old paste-board boxes, now under gaslights, running down long indexes with inquiring fingers and unwinking eyes, Matty and her mother watched and waited till eleven o'clock came, not saying much of what was on the hearts of both, but sometimes just recurring to it, as by some invisible influence, — an influence which would overcome both of them at the same moment. For the mother and daughter were as two sisters, not parted far, even in age, and not parted at all in sympathy. For occupation, they were wrapping up in thin paper a hundred barley dogs, cats, eagles, locomotives, suns, moons, and stars, — with little parcels of nuts, raisins, and figs, large red apples, and bright Florida oranges, — all of which were destined to be dragged out of different stockings at daybreak.

"And now, dear, dear mamma," said Matty, "you will go to bed, — please do, dear mamma." This was said as she compelled the last obstinate eagle to accept his fate and stay in his wrapping-paper, from which he had more than once struggled out, with the instincts of freedom.

"Please do, dear mamma; I will sort these all

out, and will be quite sure that each has his own. At least, let us come upstairs together. I will comb your hair for you; that is one of the little comforts. And you shall get into bed and see me arrange them, and if I do it wrong you can tell me."

Poor mamma, she yielded to her — as who does not yield, and because it was easier to go upstairs than to stay. And the girl led her up and made herself a toilet woman indeed, and did put her worn-out mamma into bed, and then hurried to the laundry, where she was sure she could find what Diana had been bidden to reserve there — a pair of clean stockings belonging to each member of the family. The youngest children, alas, who would need the most room for their spread-eagles and sugar locomotives, had the smallest feet and legs. But nature compensates for all things, and Matty did not fail to provide an extra pair of her mother's longest stockings for each of "the three," as the youngest were called in the councils of their elders. So a name was printed by Santa Claus on a large red card and pinned upon each receptacle, FLOSSY or LAURA, while all were willing to accept of his bounties contained within, even if they did not recognize yarn or knitting as familiar. Matty hurried back with their treasures. She brought from her own room the large red tickets, already prepared, and then, on the floor by her mother's bedside, assorted the innumerable parcels, and filled each stocking full.

Dear girl! she had not wrongly guessed. There was just occupation enough, and just little enough, for the poor mother's anxious, tired thought. Matty was wise. She asked fewer and fewer questions; fewer and fewer she made her journeys to the great high fender, where she pinned all these stiff models of gouty legs. And when the last hung there quietly, the girl had the exquisite satisfaction of seeing that her mother was fast asleep. She would not leave the room. She turned the gas-light down to a tiny bead. She slipped off her own frock, put on her mother's heavy dressing-gown, lay down quietly by her side without rousing her, and in a little while — for with those so young this resource is well-nigh sure — she slept too.

It was five o'clock when she was wakened by her father's hand. He led her out into his own dressing-room, and before she spoke she kissed him!

She knew what his answer would be. She knew that from his heavy face. But all the same she tried to smile, and she said, —

"Found?"

"Found? No, no, dear child, nor ever will be. How is mamma?"

And Matty told him, and begged him to come and sleep in her own little room, because the children would come in in a rout at daybreak. But no! he would not hear to that. "Whatever else is left, dear Matty, we have each other. And we will not begin — on what will be a new life to all of us — we will not begin by 'bating a jot of the dear children's joys. Matty, that is what I have been thinking of all the way as I walked home. But maybe I should not have said it, but that Beverly said it just now to me. Dear fellow! I cannot tell you the comfort it was to me to see him come in! I told him he should not have come, but he knew that he made me almost happy. He is a fine fellow, Matty, and all night long he has shown the temper and the sense of a man."

For a moment Matty could not say a word. Her eyes were all running over with tears. She kissed her father again, and then found out how to say, "I shall tell him what you say, papa, and there will be two happy children in this house, after all."

So she ran to Beverly's room, found him before he was undressed, and told him. And the boy who was just becoming a man, and the girl who, without knowing it, had become a woman, kissed each other; held each other for a minute, each by both hands, looked each other so lovingly in the eyes, comforted each other by the infinite comfort of love, and then said good-night and were asleep. Tom had stolen to bed without waking his mother or his sister, some hours before.

Yes! They all slept. The little ones slept, though they had been so certain that they should not sleep one wink from anxiety. This poor jaded man slept because he must sleep. His poor wife slept because she had not slept now for two nights before. And Matty and Tom and Beverly slept because they were young and brave and certain and pure, and because they were between seventeen and twenty-two years of age. This is all to say that they could seek God's help and find it. This is to say that they were well-nigh omnipotent over earthly ills, — so far, at the least, that sleep came when sleep was needed.

But not after seven o'clock! Venty and Diana had been retained by Flossy and Laura to call them at five minutes of seven, and Laura and Flossy had called the others. And at seven o'clock, precisely, a bugle-horn sounded in the children's quarters, and then four grotesque riders, each with a soldier hat made of newspaper, each with a bright sash girt round a dressing-gown, each with bare feet stuck into stout shoes, came storming down the stairs, and as soon as the lower floor was reached, each mounted on a hobby-horse or stick, and with riot not to be told came knocking at Matty's door, at Beverly's, and at Tom's. And these all appeared, also with paper soldier hats upon their heads, and girt in some very spontaneous costume, and so the whole troop proceeded with loud fanfaron and drumbeat to mamma's door and knocked for admission, and heard her cheery "Come in." And papa and mamma had heard the bugle-calls, and had wrapped some sort of shawls around their shoulders, and were sitting up in bed, they also with paper soldier hats upon them; and one scream of "Merry Christmas" resounded as the doors flew open, — and then a wild rampage of kissing and of hugging as the little ones rushed for the best places they could find on the bed — not to say in it. This was the Christmas custom.

And Tom rolled up a lounge on one side of the bed, which after a fashion widened it, and Beverly brought up his mother's easy-chair, which had earned the name of "Moses' seat," on the other side, and thus, in a minute, the great broad bed was peopled with the whole family, as jolly, if as absurd, a sight as the rising sun looked upon. And then Flossy and Beverly were deputed to go to the fender, and to bring the crowded, stiff stockings, whose crackle was so delicate and exquisite; and so, youngest by youngest, they brought forth their treasures, — not indeed gold, frankincense, and myrrh, but what answered the immediate purposes better, — barley cats, dogs, elephants and locomotives, figs, raisins, walnuts, and pecans.

Yes, and for one noisy half-hour not one person thought of the cloud which hung over the house only the night before!

But such happy forgetfulness cannot last forever. There was the Christmas breakfast. And Tom tried to tell of Academy times, and Beverly tried to tell stories of the University. But it was a hard pull. The lines under papa's eyes were only too dark. And all of a sudden he would start, and ask some question which showed that he did not know what they were talking of. Matty had taken care to have the newspapers out of the way; but everybody knew why they were out of the way, — and perhaps this made things worse. Poor blundering Laura must needs say, "That is the good of Christmas, that there are no horrid newspapers for people to bother with," when everybody above Horace's age knew that there *were* papers somewhere, and soon Horace was bright enough to see what he had not been told in words, — that something was going wrong.

And as soon as breakfast was done, Flossy cried out, "And now papa will tell us the story of the bear! Papa always tells us that on Christmas morning. Laura, you shall come; and, Horace, you shall sit there." And then her poor papa had to take her up and kiss her, and say that this morning he could not stop to tell stories, that he had to go to the Department. And then Flossy and Laura fairly cried. It was too bad. They hated the Department. There never could be any fun but what that horrid old Department came in. And when Horace found that Tom was going to the Department too, and that Bev meant to go with him, he was mad, and said he did not see what was the use of having Christmas. Here he had tin-foil and plaster upstairs, and little Watrous had lent him a set of government medals, and they should have such a real good time if Bev would only stay. He wished the Department was at the bottom of the Potomac. Matty fairly had to take the scolding boy out of the room.

Mr. Molyneux, poor fellow, undertook the soothing of Flossy. "Anyway, old girl, you shall meet me as you go to church, and we will go through the avenue together, and I will show you the new Topsy girl selling cigars at Pierre's tobacco shop. She is as big as Flossy. She has not got quite such golden hair, but she never says one word to her papa, because she is never cross to him."

"That 's because he is never kind to her," said the quick child, speaking wiser than she knew.

For Matty, she got a word with Tom, and he too promised that they would be away from the Department in time to meet the home party, and that all of them should go to church together.

CHAPTER III

CHURCH AND SERMON

AND, accordingly, as Mrs. Molyneux with her little troop crossed F Street, they met the gentlemen all coming toward them. They broke up into groups, and Tom and Matty got their first real chance for talk since they had parted the night before. No! Tom had found no clue at the Navy Department. And although Eben Ricketts had been good as gold, and had stayed and worked with Tom till long after midnight, Eben had only worked to show good-will, for Eben had not the least faith that there was any clue there. Eben had said that if old Mr. Whilthaugh, who knew the archive rooms through and through, had not been turned out, they could do in fifteen minutes what had cost them six hours, and that old Mr. Whilthaugh, without looking, could tell whether it was worth while to look. But old Mr. Whilthaugh had been turned out, and Eben, even, did not know precisely what had become of him. He thought he had gone back into Pennsylvania, where his wife came from, but he did not know.

"But, Matty, if nothing turns up to-day, I go to Pennsylvania to-morrow to find this old Mr. Whilthaugh. For I shall die if I stay here; and all the Eben Rickettses in the world will never persuade me that the vouchers are not in that archive-room. If the Navy did the work, the Navy must have the vouchers."

Then Matty ventured to ask what she and her mother had wondered about once and again, — why these particular bits of paper were so necessary. Surely other vouchers, or certified copies, or books of account could be found somewhere!

"Yes! I know; you would say so. And if it were all yesterday, and was all in these lazy times of peace, you would say true. But you see, in the first place, this is ever so long ago. Then, in the second place, it was in the heat of war, when everything was on a gigantic scale, and things had to be done in unheard-of ways. Then, chiefly, this particular business involved the buying up of I do not know who among the Rebels there in Texas, and among their allies on the other side the Rio Grande. This old Spaniard, whom mamma remembers, and whom I just remember, he was the chief captain among the turncoats, and there were two or three others, F. F. men in their places, — "First Family men," that means, you know; but after they did this work they did not stay in their places long. No! papa says he was mighty careful; that he had three of the scoundrels sworn before notaries, or rather before one notary, and had their receipts and acknowledgments stamped with his notary's seal. Still, it did not do to have a word said in public then. And after everything succeeded so perfectly, after the troops landed without a shot, and found all the base ready for them, corn and pork just where they wanted it, — why, then everybody was too gratified to think of imagining, as they do now, that papa had stolen that money that bought the pork and the corn."

"I wish they were only half as grateful now," he said, after a pause.

"Tom," said Matty, eagerly, "who was that notary?"

"I thought of that, too," said Tom. "There is no doubt who it was. It was old Gilbert; you must remember his sign, just below Faulkner's on the avenue. But in the first place, Gilbert died just after our taking Richmond. In the second place, he never knew what the papers were — and he executed twenty such sets of papers every day, very likely. All he could say, at the very best, would be that at such a time father brought in an old Spaniard and two or three other greasers, and that he took their acknowledgments of something."

"I do not know that, Tom," said the girl, without flinching at his mannish information. "If notaries in Washington are anything like notaries in novels, that man kept a record or register of his work. If he was not very unlike everybody else who lives and works here, he left a very destitute widow when he died. Tom, I shall go after church and hunt up the Widow Gilbert. I shall ask her for her husband's books, and shall tell her why I want them."

The girl dropped her voice and said: "Tom, I shall ask her IN HIS NAME."

"God grant it does any good, dear girl," said he. "Far be it from me to say that you shall not try — "

But here he stopped speaking, for he felt Matty's arm shake in his, and her whole frame trembled. Tom had only to keep his eyes before him to see why.

Mr. Greenhithe, Matty's old admirer, the clerk who had been dismissed for stealing, was just entering the church, and even touched his hat to her as she went by.

Tom resisted his temptation to thrash him then and there. He said, —

"Matty, I believe I will tackle that man!"

"Oh, Tom!"

"Yes, Matty, I can keep my temper, and he cannot keep his. He has one advantage over most knaves, that he is not only a knave of the first water, but he is sometimes a fool, too. If it were only decent and right to take him into Downing's saloon, and give him just one more glass of whiskey than the blackguard would care to pay for, I could get at his whole story."

"But, Tom, I thought you were so sure the Navy had the papers!"

"Well! well!" said Tom, a little annoyed, as eager people are when other eager people remember their words against them. "I was sure — I was wholly sure — till I left Eben Ricketts. But after that — well, of course, we ought to pull every string."

"Tom!" This with a terrible gulp.

"Tom, you don't think I ought to speak with him!"

"Matty!"

"Why, Tom, yes; if he does know — if he is holding this up in terror, Tom, I could make him do what I chose once, Tom. You don't think I ought to try?"

"Matty, if you ever speak to that snake again, I will thrash him within an inch of his life, and I will never say a word to you as long as you live."

"That 's my dear Tom!" And, hidden as they were, and crying as she was under her veil, she flung her arms around him and kissed him.

"All the same," said Tom, after he had kissed her again and again, — "all the same, I shall find out, after church, where the snake is staying. I shall go to the hotel and take a cigar. I shall offer him one, and he is so mean and stingy that he will take it. Perhaps this may be one of his fool days. Perhaps somebody else will treat him to the whiskey. No, Matty! honor bright, *I* will not, though that ten cents might give us all a Merry Christmas. Honor bright, I will not treat. But I am not a saint, Matty! If anybody else treats, I must not be expected to be far away."

Then he wiped her eyes with his own handkerchief and led her in to the service. Their own pew was already full. He had to take her back into Dr. Metcalf's pew.

So Matty was spared one annoyance which was prepared for her.

Directly in front of her father's pew, sitting in the most conspicuous seat on the other side of the aisle, was the hateful Mr. Greenhithe.

Had he put himself there to watch Matty's face?

If he did, he was disappointed. If he had

persuaded himself he was to see a pale cheek or tearful eyes, or that he was going to compel her to drop her veil, he had reckoned quite without his host. Whenever he did look that way, all he saw was the face of Master Horace. Horace was engaged in counting the large tassels on his side of the pulpit curtains; in counting, also, the number of small tassels between them, and from the data thus obtained, in calculating how many tassels there must be on all the curtains to the pulpit, and how many on the curtains behind the rail to the chancel. Mr. Greenhithe, therefore, had but little comfort in studying Horace's face.

Just as the Creed was finished, when the rest of the church was still, the sexton led up the aisle a grim-looking man, with a shaggy coat and a very dirty face, and brought him close to the door of Mr. Molyneux's pew — as if he would fain bring him in. Mr. Molyneux was at the end of the pew, but happened to be turning away from the aisle, and the sexton actually touched him. He turned round and looked at the stranger, — evidently did not know him, — but with the instinct of hospitality, stepped into the aisle and offered him his seat. The stranger was embarrassed; hesitated as if he would speak, then shook his head in refusal of the attention, and crossing the aisle, took a seat offered him there, in full sight of Mr. Molyneux, and, indeed, of Matty.

Poor girl! The trifle — of course it was a trifle — upset her sadly.

Was the man a marshal or a sheriff? Would they really arrest her father on Christmas Day, in church?

CHAPTER IV

IS THIS CHRISTMAS?

YES; it was, as you have said, a very curious Christmas service for all those people.

What Horace turned his mind to, at intervals, has been told.

Of the elder members of our little company who sat there near the head of the side aisle, it may be said, in general, that they did their best to keep their hearts and minds engaged in the service, and that sometimes they succeeded. They succeeded better while they could really join in the hymns and the prayers than they did when it came to the sermon. Good Dr. Gill, overruled by one of those lesser demons, whose work is so apparent though so inexplicable in this finite world, had selected for the text of his sermon of gladness the words, "Search and look." And so it happened — it was what did not often happen with him — he must needs repeat those words often, at the beginning and end, indeed, of every leading paragraph of the sermon. Now this duty of searching and looking had been just what all the elder members of the Molyneux family had been solidly doing — each in his way or hers, directly or by sympathy — in the last forty-eight hours. To get such relief as they might from it, they had come to church, to look rather higher if they could. So that it was to them more a misfortune than a matter of immediate spiritual relief that their dear old friend, who loved each one of them with an intimate and peculiar love, happened to enlarge on his text just as he did.

If poor Mr. Molyneux, by dint of severe self-command, had succeeded in abstracting his thoughts from disgrace almost certain, — from thinking over, in horrible variety, the several threads of inquiry and answer by which that disgrace was to be avoided or precipitated, — how was it possible to maintain such abstraction, while the worthy preacher, wholly unconscious of the blood he drew with every word, ground out his sentences in such words as these: —

"Search and look, my brethren. Time passes faster than we think. Our gray hairs gather apace above our foreheads. And the treasure which we prized beyond price in years bygone has, perhaps, amid the cares of this world, or in the deceitfulness of riches, been thrust on one side, neglected, at last forgotten. How is it with you, dear friends? Are you the man? Are you the woman? Have you put on one side the very treasure of your life, — as some careless housewife might lay aside on a forgotten shelf this parcel or that, once so precious to her? Dear friends, as the year draws to a close, awaken from such neglect! Brush away the dust from these forgotten caskets! Lift them from their hiding-places and set them forth, even in your Christmas festivities. Search and look!"

Poor Mrs. Molyneux had never wished before so earnestly that a sermon might be done. She dared not look round to see her husband for a while, but after one of these invocations — not quite so terrible as the rest, perhaps — she stole a glance that way, to find — that she might have spared her anxiety. Two nights of "searching and looking" had done their duty by the poor man, and though his head was firm braced against the column which rose from the side of their pew, his eyes were closed, and his wife was relieved by the certainty that he was listening, as those happy members of the human family listen who assure me that they hear when their lids are tight pressed over their eyeballs. As for Beverly, he was assuming the resolute aspect of a sailor under fire, and was imagining himself taking the whole storm of Fort Constantine as he led an American squadron into the Bay of Sevastopol. Tom did not know what the preacher said, but was devising the method of his interview with Greenhithe. Matty did know. Dear girl! she knew very well. And with every well-rounded sentence of the sermon she was more determined as to the method of her appeal to Mrs. Gilbert, the widow of the notary. She would search and look there.

Yes! and it was well for every one of them that they went to that service. The sermon at the worst was but twenty minutes. "Twenty minutes in length," said Beverly, wickedly, "and no depth at all." But that was not true nor fair; nor was that, either way, the thing that was essential. By the time they had all sung

"Praise God from whom all blessings flow,"

even before the good old Doctor had asked for Heaven's blessing upon them, it had come. To Mr. Molyneux it had come in an hour's rest of mind, body, and soul. To Matty it had come in an hour's calm determination. To Mrs. Molyneux it had come in the certainty that there is One Eye which sees through all hiding-places and behind all disguises. To the children it had come, because the hour had called up to them a hundred memories of Galilee and Nazareth, of Mary Mother, and of children made happy, to supplement and help out their legends of Santa Claus. Yes, and even Beverly the brave, and Tom the outraged, as they stood to receive the benediction of the preacher, were more of men and less of firebrands than they were. They all stood with reverence; they paused a moment, and then slowly walked down the aisle.

"Where is your father, Horace?" said Mrs. Molyneux, a little anxiously, as she came where she could speak aloud. Horace was waiting for her.

"Papa? He went away with the gentleman who came in after service began; they crossed the street and took a carriage together."

"And did papa leave no message?"

"Why, no; he did not turn round. The strange man — the man in the rough coat — just touched him and spoke to him half-way down the aisle. Then papa whispered to him and he whispered back. Then, as soon as they came into the vestibule here, papa led him out at that side door, and did not seem to remember me. They almost ran across the street, and took George Gibb's hack. I knew the horses."

"That's too bad," said Laura; "I thought papa would walk home with us and tell us the story of the bears."

Poor Mrs. Molyneux thought it was too bad, too; but she said nothing.

And Matty, when she joined her mother, said, —

"I shall feel a thousand times happier, mamma, if I go and see Mrs. Gilbert now." And she explained who Mrs. Gilbert was. "Perhaps it may do some good. Anyway, I shall feel as if I were doing something. I will be home in time to finish the tree and things, for Horace will like to help me."

And the poor girl looked her entreaties so eagerly that her mother could not but assent to her plan. So she made Beverly go up the avenue with her, — Beverly, who would have swum the Potomac and back for her, had she asked him, — as he was on his way to join his father at the Bureau.

As they came out upon the broad sidewalk, that odious Greenhithe, with some one whom Beverly called a blackguard of his crew, pushed by them, and he had the impudence to turn and touch his hat to Matty again.

Matty's hand trembled on Beverly's arm, but she would not speak for a minute, only she walked slower and slower.

Then she said: "I am so afraid, Bev, that Tom and he will get into a quarrel. Tom declares he will go into Willard's and find out whether he does know anything."

But Beverly, very mannish, tried to reassure her and make her believe that Tom would be very self-restrained and perfectly careful.

On Christmas Day the Jew's dry-goods store, which had taken the place of old Mr. Gilbert's notary's office, was closed — not perhaps so much from the Israelite's enthusiasm about Christmas as in deference to what in New England is called "the sense of the street." Matty, however, acting from a precise knowledge of Washington life, rang boldly at the green door adjacent, Beverly still waiting to see what might turn up; and when a brisk "colored girl" appeared, Matty inquired if Mrs. Munroe was at home.

Now all that Matty knew of Mrs. Munroe was that her name was on a well-scoured brass plate on the door.

Mrs. Munroe was in. Beverly said he would wait in the passage. Mrs. Munroe proved to be a nice, motherly sort of a person, who, as it need hardly be said, was stone-deaf. It required some time for Matty to adjust her speaking apparatus to the exigency, but when this was done, Mrs. Munroe explained that Mr. Gilbert was dead, — that an effort had been made to continue the business with the old sign and the old good will, under the direction of a certain Mr. Bundy, who had sometimes been called in as an assistant. But Mr. Bundy, after some years, paid more attention to whiskey than he did to notarying, and the law business had suffered. Finally, Mr. Bundy was brought home by the police one night with a broken head, and then Mrs. Gilbert had withdrawn the signs, cancelled the lease, turned Mr. Bundy out-of-doors, and retired to live with a step-sister of her brother's wife's father near the Arsenal; good Mrs. Munroe was not certain whether on Delaware Avenue, or whether on T Street, U Street, or V Street. And, indeed, whether the lady's name were Butman before she married her second husband, and Lichtenfels afterward — or whether his name were Butman and hers Lichtenfels, Mrs. Munroe was not quite sure. Nor could she say whether Mr. Gilbert took the account books and registers

— there were heaps on heaps of them, for Mr. Gilbert had been a notary ever since General Jackson's day — or whether Bundy did not take them, or whether they were not sold for old paper, Mrs. Munroe was not sure. For all this happened — all the break-up and removal — while Mrs. Munroe was on a visit to her sister not far from Brick Church above Little Falls, on your way to Frederic. And Mrs. Munroe offered this visit as a constant apology for her not knowing more precisely every detail of her old friend's business.

This explanation took a good deal of time, through all of which poor Beverly was fretting and fuming and stamping his cold feet in the passage, hearing the occasional questions of his sister, uttered with thunder tone in the "setting-room" above, but hearing no word of the placid widow's replies.

When Matty returned and held a consultation with him, the question was, whether to follow the books of account to Georgetown, where Mr. Bundy was understood to be still residing, or to the neighborhood of the Arsenal, in the hope of finding Mrs. Gilbert, Mrs. Lichtenfels, or Mrs. Butman, as the case might be. Readers should understand that these two points, both unknown to the young people, are some six miles asunder, the original notary's office being about half-way between them. Beverly was more disposed to advise following the man. He was of a mind to attack some one of his own sex. But the enterprise was, in truth, Matty's enterprise. Beverly had but little faith in it from the beginning, and Matty was minded to follow such clue as they had to Mrs. Gilbert, quite sure that, woman with woman, she should succeed better with her than, man with man, Beverly with Bundy. Beverly assented to this view the more willingly, because Matty was quite willing to undertake the quest alone. She was very brave about it indeed. "Plenty of nice people at the Arsenal," or near it, whom she could fall back upon for counsel or information. So they parted. Matty took a street car for the east and south, and Beverly went his ways to the Bureau of Internal Improvement to report for duty to his father.

This story must not follow the details of Matty's quest for the firm of "Gilbert, Lichtenfels, or Butman." Certain it is that she would never have succeeded had she rested simply on the directory or on such crude information as Mrs. Munroe had so freely given. But Matty had an English tongue in her head, — a courteous, which is to say a confiding, address with strangers; she seemed almost to be conferring a favor at the moment when she asked one, and she knew, in this business, that there was no such word as fail. After one or two false starts — some very stupid answers, and some very blunt refusals — she found her quarry at last, by as simple a process as walking into a Sunday-school of colored children, where she heard singing in the basement of a little chapel.

In a few words Matty explained her errand to the Superintendent, and that it was necessary that she should find Mrs. Gilbert before dark.

"Ting!" one stroke of the bell called hundreds of eager voices to silence.

"Who knows where Mrs. Gilbert lives? Is it at Mrs. Butman's house or Mrs. Lichtenfels'?"

Twenty eager hands contended with each other for the honor of giving the information, and in three minutes more, Matty, all encouraged by her success, was on her way.

And Mrs. Gilbert was at home. Good fortune number two! Matty's star was surely in the ascendant! Matty sent in her card, and the nice old lady presented herself at once, remembered who Matty was, remembered how much business Mr. Molyneux used to bring to the office, and how grateful Mr. Gilbert always was. She was so glad to see Matty, and she hoped Mr. Molyneux was well, and Mrs. Molyneux and all those little ones! She used to see them every Sunday as they went to church, if they went on the avenue.

Thus encouraged, Matty opened on her sad story, and was fairly helped from stage to stage by the wonder, indignation, and exclamations of the kind old lady. When Matty came to the end, and made her understand how much depended on the day-book, register, and ledger of her husband, it was a fair minute before she spoke.

"We will see, my dear, we will see. I wish it may be so, but I 'm all afeard. It would not be like him, my dear. It would not be like any of them. But come with me, my dear, we will see — we will see."

Then, as Matty followed her, through devious ways, out through the kitchen, across a queer bricked yard, into a half stable, half woodshed, which the good woman unlocked, she went on talking: —

"You see, my dear child, that though notaries are called notaries, as if it were their business to give notice, the most important part of their business is keeping secrets. Now, when a man's note goes to protest, the notary tells him what has happened, which he knew very well before; and then he comes to the notary and begs him not to tell anybody else, and of course he does not. And the business of a notary's account books, as my husband used to say, is to tell just enough, and not to tell any more.

"Why, my dear child, he would not use blotting-paper in the office, — he would always use sand. 'Blotting-paper! Never!' he would say; 'Blotting-paper tells secrets!'"

With such chatter they came to the little chilly room, which was shelved all around, and to Matty's glad eyes presented rows of green and blue and blue and red boxes, — and folio and quarto books of every date, from 1829 to 1869, forty years in which the late Mr. Gilbert had been confirming history, keeping secret what he knew, but making sure what, but for him, might have been doubted by a sceptic world.

Things were in good order. Mrs. Gilbert was proud to show that they were in good order. The day-book for 1863 was at hand. Matty knew the fatal dates only too well. And the fatal entries were here!

How her heart beat as she began to read!

Cr.

To Thomas Molyneux Esq., (B. I. I.) official authentication of signature of Felipe Gazza . .	$1.25
Same, authentication of signature of Jose B. Du Camara	1.25
Same, authentication of signature of Jacob H. Cole	1.25

And this was all! Poor Matty copied it all, but all the time she begged Mrs. Gilbert to tell her if there was not some note-book or journal that would tell more. And kind Mrs. Gilbert looked eagerly for what she called the "Diry." At the proper dates on the cash-book, at intervals of a week or two, Matty found similar entries — the names of the two Spaniards appearing in all these — but other names in place of Cole's just as Tom had told her already. By the time she had copied all of these, Mrs. Gilbert had found the "Diry." Eager, and yet heart-sick, Matty turned it over with her old friend.

This was all: —

"Mr. Molyneux here. Very private. Papers

in R. G. E." And then followed a little burst of unintelligible short-hand.

Poor Matty! She could not but feel that here would not be evidence good for anything, even in a novel. But she copied every word carefully, as a chief clerk's daughter should do. She thanked the kind old lady, and even kissed her. She looked at her watch. Heavens! how fast time had gone! and the afternoons were so short!

"Yes, my dear Miss Molyneux; but they have turned, my dear, the day is a little longer and a little lighter."

Did the old lady mean it for an omen, or was it only one of those chattering remarks on meteors and weather change of which old age is so fond? Matty wondered, but did not know. Fast as she could, she tripped bravely on to the avenue for her street car.

"The day is longer and lighter."

Meanwhile Tom was following his clue in the public rooms at Willard's, to which, as he prophesied, Mr. Greenhithe had returned after the unusual variation in his life of a morning spent in the sanctuary. Tom bought a copy of the Baltimore "The Sun," and went into one of the larger rooms resorted to by travellers and loafers, and sat down. But Mr. Greenhithe did not appear there. Tom walked up and down through the passages a little uneasily, for he was sure the ex-clerk had come into the hotel. He went up and looked in at the ladies' sitting-rooms, to see if perhaps some Duchess of Devonshire, of high political circles, had found it worth while to drag Mr. Greenhithe up there by a single hair. No Mr. Greenhithe! Tom was forced to go down and drink a glass of beer to see if Mr. Greenhithe was not thirsty. But at that moment, though Mr. Greenhithe was generally thirsty in the middle of the day, and although many men were thirsty at the time Tom hung over his glass of lager, Mr. Greenhithe was not thirsty there. It was only as Tom passed the billiard-room that he saw Mr. Greenhithe was playing a game of billiards, by way of celebrating the new birth of a regenerated world.

What to do now! Tom could not, in common decency, go in to look on at the game of a man he wanted to choke. Yet Tom would have given all his chances for rank in the Academy to know what Greenhithe was talking about. Tom slowly withdrew.

As he withdrew, whom should he meet but one of his kindest friends, Commodore Benbow? When the boys made their "experimental cruise" the year before, they had found Commodore Benbow's ship at Lisbon. The Commodore had taken a particular fancy to Tom, because he had known his mother when they were boy and girl. Tom had even been invited personally to the flag-ship, and was to have been presented at Court, but that they sailed too soon.

To tell the whole truth, the Commodore was not overpleased to see his *protégé* hanging about the bar and billiard-room on Christmas Day. For himself, his whole family were living at Willard's, but he knew Tom's father was not living there, and he thought Tom might be better employed.

Perhaps Tom guessed this. Perhaps he was in despair. Anyway he knew "Old Benbow," as the boys called him, would be a good counsellor. In point of statistics "Old Benbow" was just turned forty, had not a gray hair in his head, could have beaten any one of Tom's class, whether in gunning or at billiards, could have demonstrated every problem in Euclid while they were fiddling over the forty-seventh proposition. He was at the very prime of well-preserved power, but young nineteen called him "Old Benbow," as young nineteen will, in such cases.

Bold with despair, or with love for his father, Tom stopped "Old Benbow" and asked him if he would come into one of the sitting-rooms with him. Then he made this venerable man his confidant. The Commodore had seen the slurs in the "Scorpion" and the "Argus" and the "Evening Journal." "A pity," said he, "that Newspaper Row, that can do so much good, should do so much harm. What is Newspaper Row? Three or four men of honor, three or four dreamers, three or four schoolboys, three or four fools, and three or four scamps. And the public, Molyneux,—which is to say you and I,—accept the trumpet blast of one of these heralds precisely as we do that of another. Practically," said he, pensively, "when we were detached to serve with the 33d Corps in Mobile Bay, I found I liked the talk of those light-infantry men who had been in every scrimmage of the war, quite as much as I did that of the bandmen who played the trumpets on parade. But this is neither here nor there. I thought of coming round to see your father, but I knew I should bother him. What can I do, my boy?"

Then Tom told him, rather doubtfully, that he had reason to fear that Mr. Greenhithe was at the bottom of the whole scandal. He said he wished he did not think that Mr. Greenhithe had himself stolen the papers. "If I am wrong, I want to know it," said he; "if I am right, I want to know it. I do not want to be doing any man injustice. But I do not want to keep old Eben Ricketts down at the department hunting for a file of papers which Greenhithe has hidden in his trunk or put into the fire."

"No! — no! — no, indeed," said "old Benbow," musing. "No! — No! — No! —"

Then after a pause, "Tom," said he, "come round here in an hour. I know that young fellow your friend is playing with, and I wish he were in better company than he is. I think I know enough of the usages of modern society to 'interview' him and his companion, though times have changed since I was of your age in that regard. Come here in an hour, or give me rather more, come here at half-past two, and we will see what we will see."

So Tom went round to the Navy Department, and here he found the faithful Eben — faithful to him, though utterly faithless as to any success in the special quest which was making the entertainment of the Christmas holiday. Vainly did Tom repeat to him his formula, —

"If the Navy did the work, the Navy has the vouchers."

"My dear boy," Eben Ricketts repeated a hundred times, "though the Navy did the work, the Navy did not provide the pork and beans; it did not arrange in advance for the landing, least of all did it buy the greasers. I will look where you like, for love of your father and you; but that file of vouchers is not here, never was here, and never will be found here."

An assistant like this is not an encouraging companion or adviser.

And, in short, the vouchers were not found in the Navy Department, in that particular midday search. At twenty-five minutes past two Tom gave it up unwillingly, bade Eben Ricketts good-by, washed from his hands the accretions of coal-dust, which will gather even on letter-boxes in Navy Departments, and ran across in front of the President's House, to Willard's. He looked up at the White House, and wondered how the people there were spending their Christmas Day.

Commodore Benbow was waiting for him. He took him up into his own parlor.

"Molyneux, your Mr. Greenhithe is either the most ingenious liar and the best actor on God's earth, or he knows no more of your lost papers than a child in heaven.

"I went back to the billiard-room, after you left me. I walked up to Millet — that was Lieutenant Millet playing with Greenhithe — and I shook hands. He had to introduce me to your friend. Then I asked them both to come here, told Millet I had some papers from Montevideo that he would be glad to see, and that I should be glad of a call when they had done their game. Well, they came. I am sorry to say your friend — "

"Oh, don't, my dear Commodore Benbow, don't call him my friend, even in a joke; it makes me feel awfully."

"I am glad it does," said the Commodore, laughing. "Well, I am very sorry to say that the black sheep had been drinking more of the whisky downstairs than was good for him; and, no fault of mine, he drank more of my Madeira than he should have done, and, Tom, I do not believe he was in any condition to keep secrets. Well, first of all, it appeared that he had been in Bremen and Vienna for six months. He only arrived in New York yesterday morning."

Tom's face fell.

"And, next — you may take this for what it is worth — but I believe he spoke the truth for once;

he certainly did if there is any truth in liquor or in swearing. For when I asked Millet what all this stuff about your father meant, Greenhithe interrupted, very unnecessarily and very rudely, and said, with more oaths than I will trouble you with, that the whole was a damned lie of the newspaper men; that they had lied about him (Greenhithe) and now were lying about old Molyneux; that Molyneux had been very hard on him and very unjust to him, but he would say that he was honest as the clock — honest enough to be mean. And that he would say that to the committee, if they would call on him, and so on and so on."

"Much good would he do before the committee," said poor Tom.

And thus ended Tom's branch of the investigation. "Come to me, if I can help you, my boy," said Old Benbow. "It is always the darkest, old fellow, the hour before day."

Tom was astronomer enough to know that this old saw was as false as most old saws. But with this for his only comfort, he returned to the bureau to seek Beverly and his father.

Neither Beverly nor his father was there!

Tom went directly home. His mother was eager to see him.

She had come home alone, and, save Horace and Laura and Flossy and Brick, she had seen nobody but a messenger from the bureau.

Brick was the family name for Robert, one of the youngest of this household.

Of Beverly's movements the story must be more briefly told. They took more time than Tom's; as much indeed as his sister's, after they parted. But they were conducted by means of that marvel of marvels, the telegraph, — the chief of whose marvels is that it compels even a long-winded generation like ours to speak in very short metre.

Beverly began with Mr. Bundy at Georgetown. Georgetown is but a quiet place on the most active of days. On Christmas Day Beverly found but little stirring out of doors.

Still, with the directory, with the advice of a saloon-keeper and the information of a police officer, Beverly tracked Mr. Bundy to his lair.

It was not a notary's office, it was a liquor shop of the lowest grade, with many badly painted signs, which explained that this was "Our House," and that here Mr. Bundy made and sold with proper license — let us be grateful — Tom and Jerry, Smashes, Cocktails, and did other "deeds without a name." On this occasion, however, even the door of "Our House" was closed. Mr. Bundy had gone to a turkey-shooting match at Fairfax Court House. The period of his return was very doubtful. He had never done anything but keep this drinking-room since old Mrs. Gilbert turned him out of doors.

With this information Master Beverly returned to town. He then began on his own line of search. Relying on Tom's news, he went to the office of the Western Union Telegraph and concocted this despatch, which he thought a masterpiece.

GREENSBURG, Westmoreland Co., Pa.

TO ROBERT JOHN WHILTHAUGH:

When and where can I see you on important business? Answer.

BEVERLY MOLYNEUX, for THOMAS MOLYNEUX.

Then he took a walk, and after half an hour called at the office again. The office was still engaged in calling Greensburg. Greensburg was eating its Christmas dinner. But at last Greensburg was called. Then Beverly received this answer: —

Whilthaugh has been dead more than a year.

GREENSBURG.

To which Beverly replied: —

Where does his wife live, or his administrator?

To which Greensburg, having been called a second time with difficulty, replied: —

His wife is crazy, and we never heard of any property. GREENSBURG.

With this result of his investment as a non-dividend member of the great Western Union Mutual Information Club, Beverly returned home, chewing the cud of sweet and bitter fancies.

"There is no speech nor language," sang the choir in St. Matthews as he passed, "where their voice is not heard. Their line is gone out through all the earth —" And Tom heard no more, as he passed on.

As he walked, almost unwillingly, up the street to the high steps of his father's house, Matty, out of breath, overtook him.

"What have you found, Bev?"

"Nothing," said the boy, moodily. And poor Matty had to confess that she had hardly more to tell.

They came into the house by the lower entrance, that they need not attract their mother's attention. But she was on the alert. Even Horace and the younger children knew by this time that something was wrong.

Horace's story about the strange man and papa was the last news of papa. Papa had not been at the bureau. The bureau people waited for him till two, and he did not come. Then Stratton had come round to see if he was to keep open any longer. Stratton had told Mrs. Molyneux that her husband had not been there since church.

Where in the world was he?

Poor Mrs. Molyneux had not known where to send or to go. She had just looked in at the Doctor's, but he was not there.

Tom had appeared first to her tedious waiting. Tom would not tell her, but he even went and looked in on Newspaper Row, which he had been abusing so. For Tom's first thought was that a formal information had been lodged somewhere, and that his father was arrested.

But Newspaper Row evidently was unsuspicious of any arrest.

Tom even walked down to the old jail, and made an absurd errand to see the Deputy-Marshal. But the Deputy-Marshal was at his Christmas dinner.

Tom told all this in the hall to Beverly and to Matty.

Everything had failed, and papa was gone. Who could the man in the shaggy coat be?

The three went together into the parlor.

For a little, Matty and Horace and Tom and Beverly then made a pretence of arranging the tree. But, in truth, Mrs. Molyneux, in the midst of all her care, had done that, while they were all away.

Dinner was postponed half an hour, and they gathered, all in the darkness, looking at the sickliest blaze that ever rambled over half-burned Cumberland coal.

The Brick came climbing up on Tom's knees and bade him tell a story; but even Laura saw that something was wrong, and hushed the child, and said she and Flossy would sing one of their carols. And they sang it, and were praised; and they sang another, and were praised. But then it was quite dark, and nobody had any heart to say one word.

"Where is papa?" said the Brick.

"Where indeed?" everybody wanted to say, and no one did.

But then the door-bell rang, and Chloe brought in a note.

"He 's waiting for an answer, mum."

And Tom lighted the gas. It popped up so bright that little Flossy said, —

"The people that sat in darkness saw a great light — "

This was just as Mrs. Molyneux tore open the note. For the instant she could not speak. She handed it to the three.

"*Found*

"Home in half an hour!

"All right! thank God! T. M."

"Saw a great light, indeed!" said Horace, who, for once, felt awed.

CHAPTER V

THIS IS CHRISTMAS

FOR half a minute, as it seemed afterwards, no one spoke. Then Matty flew to her mother, and flung her arms around her neck, and kissed her again and again.

Tom hardly knew what he was doing; but he recovered self-command enough to know that he must try to be manly and businesslike, — and so he rushed downstairs to find the man who brought the note. It proved to be a man he did not know. Not a messenger from the bureau, not one from the Navy Department, least of all, an aid of the Assistant Marshal's. He was an innocent waiter from the Seaton House, who said a gentleman called him and gave him the note, told him to lose no time, and gave him half a dollar for coming. He had asked for an answer, though the gentleman had not told him to do so.

Tom wrote: "Hurrah! All's well! All at home. — T." and gave this note to the man.

They all talked at once, and then they sat still without talking. The children — must it be confessed? — asked all sorts of inopportune questions. At last Tom was even fain to tell the story of the bear himself, by way of silencing the Brick and Laura; and with much correction from Horace, had got the bear well advanced in smelling at the almond-candy and the figs, when a carriage was heard on the street, evidently coming rapidly towards them. It stopped at the door. The bear was forgotten, as all the elders in this free-and-easy family rushed out of the parlor into the hall.

Papa was there, and was as happy as they. With papa, or just behind him, came in the man with the rough coat, whose face at church had been so dirty, whose face now was clean. To think that papa should have brought the Deputy-Marshal with him! For by the name of "the Deputy-Marshal" had this mysterious stranger been spoken of in private by the two young men since the fatal theory had been advanced that he had come into the church to arrest Mr. Molyneux.

The unknown, with great tact, managed to keep in the background, while Mrs. Molyneux kissed her husband, and while Matty kissed him, and while among them they pulled off his coat. But Mr. Molyneux did not forget. He made a chance in a moment for saying, "You must speak to our friend who has brought me here; no one was ever so welcome at a Christmas dinner. Mr. Kuypers, my dear, Mr. Kuypers, Matty dear; these are my boys, Mr. Kuypers."

Then the ladies welcomed the stranger, and the boys shook hands with him. Mr. Molyneux added, what hardly any one understood: "It is not every friend that travels two thousand miles to jog a friend's memory."

And they all huddled into the parlor. But in a moment more, Mrs. Molyneux had invited Mr. Kuypers to go upstairs to wash himself, and he, with good feeling, which he showed all the evening, gladly took himself out of the way, and so, as Tom returned from showing him to his room, the parlor was filled with "those God made there," as the little boy used to say, and with none beside.

"Now tell us all about it, dear papa," cried Tom.

"I was trying to tell your mother. But there is not much to tell. Poor Mr. Kuypers had travelled all the way from Colorado, the minute he heard I was in trouble. Yesterday he bought the 'Scorpion' in the train, and found the Committee was down on us. He drove here from the station as soon as the train came in. He missed you here, and drove by mistake to Trinity. That made him late with us, and so, as the service had begun, he waited till it was done."

"Well!" said Bev, perhaps a little impatiently.

"But so soon as we were going out he touched me, and said he had come to find me, in the matter of the Rio Grande vouchers. Do you know, Eliza, I can afford to laugh at it now, but at the moment I thought he was a deputy of the Sergeant-at-Arms?"

"There!" screamed Tom, "I said he was a deputy-marshal!"

"I said, 'Certainly;' and I laughed, and said they seemed to interest all my friends. Then he said, 'Then you have them? If I had known that, I would have spared my journey.' This threw me off guard, and I said I supposed I had them, but I could not find them. And he said eagerly — this was just on the church steps — 'But I can.'

"Then he said he had a carriage waiting, and he bade me jump in.

"So soon as we were in the carriage he explained, what I ought to have remembered, but could not then recollect for the life of me, that after General Trebou returned from Texas, there was a Court of Inquiry, and that there was some question about these very supplies, the beans and the coffee particularly; they had nothing to do with the landing nor with the Mexicans. And the Court of Inquiry sent over one day from the War Department, where they were sitting, to our office for an account, because we were said to have it.

Mr. Kuypers was their messenger to us, and because we had bound them all together, the whole file was sent as it was. He took them, and as it happened, he looked them over, and what was better, he remembered them. Where our receipt is, Heaven knows!

"Well, that Court of Inquiry was endless, as those army inquiries always are. Mr. Kuypers was in attendance all the time. He says he never shall forget it, if other people do.

"So, as soon as he saw that we were in trouble at the bureau — that I was in trouble, I mean," said Mr. Molyneux, stoutly, "he knew that he knew what nobody else knew, — that the vouchers were in the papers of that Court of Inquiry."

"And he came all the way to tell? What a good fellow!"

"Yes, he came on purpose. He says he could not help coming. He says he made two or three telegrams; but every time he tried to telegraph, he felt as if he were shirking. And I believe he was right. I believe we should never have pulled through without him. 'Personal presence moves the world,' as Eli Thayer used to say."

"And you found them?" asked Mrs. Molyneux, faintly essaying to get back to the story.

"Oh yes, we found them; but not in one minute. You see, first of all, I had to go to the chief clerk at the War Department and get the department opened on a holiday. Then we had no end of clerks to disturb at their Christmas dinners, and at last we found a good fellow named Breen who was willing to take hold with Mr. Kuypers. And Mr. Kuypers himself," here he dropped his voice, "why, we have not three men in all the departments who know the history of this government or the system of its records as he does.

"Once in the office, he went to work like a master. Breen was amazed. Why! We found those documents in less than half an hour!

"Then I sent Breen with a note to the Secretary. He was good as gold; came down in his own carriage, congratulated me as heartily — well almost as heartily as you do, Tom — and took us both round, with the files, to Mr. McDermot, the Chairman of the House Committee. He was dining with his mess, at the Seaton House, but we called him out, and I declare, I believe he was as much pleased as we were.

"I only stopped to make him give me a receipt for the papers, because they all said it was idle to take copies, and here we are!"

On the hush that followed, the Brick made his way up on his father's knee and said, —

"And now, papa, will you tell us the story of the bear? Tom does not tell it very well."

They all laughed, — they could afford to laugh now; and Mr. Molyneux was just beginning upon the story of the bear, when Mr. Kuypers reappeared. He had in this short time revised his toilet, and looked, Mr. Molyneux said in an aside, like the angel of light that he was. "Bears!" said he, "are there any bears in Washington? Why, it was only last Monday that I killed a bear, and I ate him on Tuesday."

"Did you eat him all?" asked the Brick, whose reverence for Mr. Kuypers was much more increased by this story than by any of the unintelligible conversation which had gone before. But just as Mr. Kuypers began on the story of the bear, Chloe appeared with beaming face, and announced that dinner was ready.

That dinner, which this morning every one who had any sense had so dreaded, and which now seemed a festival indeed!

Well! there was great pretence in fun and form in marshalling. And Mr. Kuypers gave his arm to Matty, and Horace his to Laura, and Beverly his to Flossy, and Tom brought up the rear with the Brick on his shoulders. And Mr. Molyneux returned thanks and asked a blessing all together. And then they fell to, on the turkey and on the chicken pie. And they tried to talk about Colorado and mining; about Gold Hill and Hale-and-Norcross, and Uncle Sam and Overman and Yellow Jacket. But in spite of them all, the talk would drift back to Bundy and his various signs, "Our House" and Tom and Jerry; to the wife of Mr. Whilthaugh; to Commodore Benbow; to old Mrs. Gilbert and Delaware Avenue. And this was really quite as much the fault of Mr. Kuypers as it was of any of the Molyneux family. He seemed as much one of them as did Tom himself. This anecdote of failure and that of success kept cropping out. Walsingham's high-bred and dignified enthusiasm for the triumph of the office, and the satisfaction that Eben Ricketts would feel when he was told that the Navy never had the vouchers, — all were commented on. Then Mr. Molyneux would start and say, "We are talking shop again. You say the autumn has been mild in the mountains;" and then in two minutes they would be on the trail of "Search and Look" again.

It was in one of these false starts that Mr. Kuypers explained why he came, which in Horace's mind and perhaps in the minds of the others had been the question most puzzling of all.

"Why," said Horace, bluntly, "had you ever heard of papa before!"

"Had I heard of him?" said Mr. Kuypers. "I think so. Why, my dear boy, your father is my oldest and kindest friend!" At this exclamation even Mrs. Molyneux showed amazement. Tom laid down his fork and looked to see if the man was crazy, and Mr. Molyneux himself was thrown off his balance.

Mr. Kuypers was a well-bred man, but this time he could not conceal his amazement. He laid down knife and fork both, looked up and almost laughed, as he said with wonder, —

"Don't you know who I am?"

"We know you are our good angel to-day," said Mrs. Molyneux, bravely; "and that is enough to know."

"But don't you know why I am here, or what sent me?"

Mr. Molyneux said that he understood very well that his friend wanted to see justice done, and that he had preferred to see to this in person.

"I thought you looked queer," said Mr. Kuypers, frankly; "but still, I did not know I was changed. Why, don't you remember Bruce? You remember Mrs. Chappell, surely."

"Are you Bruce?" cried Mr. Molyneux; and he fairly left his chair and went round the table to the young man. "Why, I can see it now. But then —why, you were a boy, you know, and this black beard — "

"But pray explain, pray explain," cried Tom. "The mysteries increase on us. Who is Mrs. Chappell, and, for that matter, who is Bruce, if his real name be not Kuypers?"

And they all laughed heartily. People got back their self-possession a little, and Mr. Kuypers explained.

"I am Bruce Kuypers," said he, "though your father does not seem to remember the Kuypers part."

"No," said Mr. Molyneux, "I cannot remember the Kuypers part, but the Bruce part I remember very well."

"My mother was Mrs. Kuypers before she married Mr. Chappell, and Mr. Chappell died when my brother Ben was six years old, and little Lizzy was a baby."

"Lizzy was my godchild," said Mrs. Molyneux, who now remembered everything.

"Certainly she was, Mrs. Molyneux, and last month Lizzy was married to as good a fellow as ever presided over the melting of ingots. We marry them earlier at the West than you do here."

"Where Lizzie would have been," he said more gravely, addressing Tom again, "where my mother would have been, or where I should have been but for your father and mother here, it would be hard to tell. And all to-day I have taken it for granted that to him, as to me, this has been one part of that old Christmas! Surely you remember?" he turned to Mrs. Molyneux.

Yes, Mrs. Molyneux did remember, but her eyes were all running over with tears and she did not say so.

"Mr. Molyneux," said Bruce Kuypers, again addressing Tom, "seventeen years ago this blessed day, there was a Christmas morning in the poor old tenement above Massachusetts Avenue such as you never saw, and such as I hope you never may see.

"There was fire in the stove because your father had sent the coal. There was oatmeal mush on the table because your father paid my mother's scot at your father's grocer.

"But there was not much jollity in that house, and there were no Christmas presents, but what your mother had sent to Bruce and Ben and Flora, and even to the baby. Still we kept up such courage as we could. It was a terribly cold day, and there was a wet storm.

"All of a sudden a carriage stopped at the door, and in came your father here. He came to say that that day's mail had brought a letter from Dr. Wilder of the navy, conveying the full certificate that William Chappell's death was caused by exposure in the service. That certificate was what my mother needed for her pension. She never could get it, but your father here had sifted and worried and worked. The 'Macedonian' arrived Thursday at New York, and had Dr. Wilder on board, and Friday afternoon your father had Wilder's letter, and he left his own Christmas dinner to make light my mother's and mine. That was not all. Your father, as he came, had stopped to see Mr. Birdsall, who was the Speaker of the House. He had seen the Speaker before, and had said kind things about me. And that day the Speaker told him to tell me to come and see him at his room at the Capitol next day. Oh! how my mother dressed me up! Was there ever such a page seen before! What with your father's kind words and my dear mother's extra buttons, the Speaker made me his own page the next day, and there I served for four years. It was then that I was big enough to go into the War Department, and Mr. Goodsell — he was the next Speaker, if you remember — recommended me there.

"After that," said Bruce Kuypers, modestly, "I did not see you so often, but I used to see you sometimes, and I did not think" — this with a roguish twinkling of the eye — "that you forgot your young friends so soon."

"I remember you," said Tom. "I used to think you were the grandest man in Washington. You gave me the first ride on a sled I ever had, when there was some exceptional fall of snow."

"I think we all remember Mr. Kuypers now," said Matty, and she laughed while she blushed; "he always bought things for our stockings. I have a Noah's Ark upstairs now, that he gave me. In my youngest days I had a queer mixture of the name Bruce and the name Santa Claus. I believe I thought Santa Claus' name was Nicholas Bruce. I am sure I did not know that Mr. Bruce had any other name."

"If you had said you were Mr. Chappell," said Mr. Molyneux, "I should have known you in a minute."

"But I was not," said the young man, laughing.

"Well, if you had said you were 'Bruce,' I should have known."

"Dear me, yes; but I have been a man so long, and at Gem City nobody calls me Bruce, but my mother and Lizzy. So I said 'Mr. Kuypers,' forgetting that I had ever been a boy. But now I am in Washington again, I shall remember that things change here very fast in ten years. And yet not so fast as they change at the mines."

And now everybody was at ease. How well Mrs. Molyneux recalled to herself what she would not speak of that Christmas Day of which Mr. Kuypers told his story! It was in their young married life. She had her father and mother to dine with her, and the event was really a trial in her young experience. And then, just as the old folks were expected, her husband came dashing in and had asked her to put dinner a little later because he had had this good news for the poor Widow Chappell, and she had to tell her father and mother, when they came, that they must all wait for his return.

The Widow Chappell was one of those waifs who seem attracted to Washington by some fatal law. It had been two or three months before that Mr. Molyneux had been asked to hunt her up and help her. A letter had come, asking him to do this, from Mrs. Fales, in Roxbury, and Mrs. Fales had sent money for the Chappells. But the money had gone in back rent, and shoes, and the rest, and the wolf was very near the Chappells' door, when the telegraph announced the "Macedonian." Mr. Molyneux had telegraphed instanter to this Dr. Wilder. Dr. Wilder had some sense of Christmas promptness. He remembered poor Chappell perfectly, and mailed that night a thorough certificate. This certificate it was which Mr. Molyneux had carried to the poor old tenement of Massachusetts Avenue, and this had made happy that Christmas Day — and this.

"Why," said Mr. Bruce Kuypers, almost as if he were speaking aloud, "it seems so queer that

Christmas comes and goes with you, and you have forgotten all about that stormy day, and your ride to Mrs. Chappell's!

"Why, at our place, we drink Mr. Molyneux's health every Christmas Day, and I am afraid the little ones used to think that you had a red nose, a gray beard, and came down the chimney!"

"As, at another place," said Matty, "they thought of Mr. Bruce — of Noah's Ark memory."

"Anyway," said Mr. Molyneux, "any crumbs of comfort we scattered that day were BREAD UPON THE WATERS."

Of Mr. Kuypers's quick journey the main points have been told. Six days before, by some good luck, which could hardly have been expected, the "Gem City Medium's" despatch from Washington was full enough to be intelligible. It was headed, "ANOTHER SWINDLER NAILED." It said that Mr. Molyneux, of the Internal Improvement office, had feathered his nest with $500,000 during the war, in a pretended expedition to the Rio Grande. It had now been discovered that there never was any such expedition, and the correspondent of the Associated Press hoped that justice would be done.

The moment Bruce Kuypers read this he was anxious. Before an hour passed he had determined to cross to the Pacific train eastward. Before night he was in a sleeping-car. Day by day as he met Eastern papers, he searched for news of the investigation. Day by day he met it, but thanks to his promptness he had arrived in time.

It was pathetic to hear him describe his anxiety from point to point, and they were all hushed to silence when he told how glad he was when he found he should certainly appear on Christmas Day.

After the dinner, another procession, not wholly unlike the rabble rout of the morning, moved from the dining-room to the great front parlor, where the tree was lighted, and parcels of gray and white and brown lay round on mantel, on piano, on chairs, on tables, and on the floor.

No; this tale is too long already. We will not tell what all the presents were to all the ten, — to Venty, Chloe, Diana, and all of their color. Only let it tell that all the ten had presents. To Mr. Kuypers's surprise, and to every one's surprise, indeed, there were careful presents for him as for the rest, but it must be confessed that Horace and Laura had spelled *Chipah* a little wildly. The truth was that each separate person had feared that he would feel a little left on one side, — he to whom so much was due on that day. And each person, severally, down to the Brick himself, had gone secretly, without consulting the others, to select from his own possessions something very dear, and had wrapped it up and marked it for the stranger. When Mr. Kuypers opened a pretty paper, to find Matty's own illustrated Browning, he was touched indeed. When in a rough brown paper he found the Brick's jack-knife labelled "FOR THE MAN," the tears stood in his eyes.

The next day the "Evening Lantern" contained this editorial article: —

"The absurd fiasco regarding the accounts of Mr. Molyneux, which has occupied the correspondents of the periodical press for some days, and has even been adverted to in New York journals claiming the title of metropolitan, came to a fit end at the Capitol yesterday. The wiseacre owls who started it did not see fit to put in an appearance before the committee. Mr. Molyneux himself sent to the Chairman a most interesting volume of manuscript, which is, indeed, a valuable historical memorial of times that tried men's souls. The committee and other gentlemen present examined this curious record with great interest. Not to speak of the minor details, an autograph letter of the lamented Gen. Trebou gives full credit to the Bureau of Internal Improvement for the skill with which they executed the commission given them in a department quite out of their line. Our brethren of the 'Argus' will be pleased to know that every grain of oats and every spear of straw paid for by the now famous $47,000, are accounted for in detail. The authenticated signatures of the somewhat celebrated Camara and Gazza and the mythical Captain Cole appear. Very valuable letters, throwing interesting light on our relations with the Government of Mexico, from the pens of the lamented Adams and Prigg, show what were the services of those Spanish turncoats and their allies.

"We cannot say that we regret the attention which has thus been given to a very important piece of history, too long neglected in the rush of more petty affairs.

We take the occasion, however, to enter our protest once more against this preposterous system of 'Resolutions,' in which, as it were in echo to every *niaiserie* of every hired pen in the country, the House degrades itself to the work of the common scavenger, orders at immense expense an investigation into some subject where all well informed persons are fully advised, and at a cost of the national treasure, 'etc., etc., etc. to the end of that chapter.'"

But I fear no one at the Molyneux mansion had "the lantern." They had "found a man," and did not need a lantern to look farther.

It was as Mr. Molyneux had said: he had cast his Bread upon the Waters, and he had found it after many days.

THE LOST PALACE

THE LOST PALACE

[From the Ingham Papers.]

"PASSENGERS for Philadelphia and New York will change cars."

This annoying and astonishing cry was loudly made in the palace-car "City of Thebes," at Pittsburg, just as the babies were well asleep, and all the passengers adapting themselves to a quiet evening.

"Impossible!" said I, mildly, to the "gentlemanly conductor," who beamed before me in the majesty of gilt lace on his cap, and the embroidered letters P. P. C. These letters do not mean, as in French, "to take leave," for the peculiarity of this man is, that he does not leave you till your journey's end: they mean, in American, "Pullman's Palace Car." "Impossible!" said I; "I bought my ticket at Chicago through to Philadelphia, with the assurance that the palace-car would go through. This lady has done the same for herself and her children. Nay, if you remember, you told me yourself that the 'City of Thebes' was built for the Philadelphia service, and that I need not move my hat, unless I wished, till we were there."

The man did not blush, but answered, in the well-mannered tone of a subordinate used to obey, "Here are my orders, sir; telegram just received here from headquarters: '"City of Thebes" is to go to Baltimore.' Another palace here, sir, waiting for you." And so we were trans-shipped into such chairs and berths as might have been left in this other palace, as not wanted by anybody in the great law of natural selection; and the "City of Thebes" went to Baltimore, I suppose. The promises which had been made to us when we bought our tickets went to their place, and the people who made them went to theirs.

Except for this little incident, of which all my readers have probably experienced the like in these days of travel, the story I am now to tell would have seemed to me essentially improbable. But so soon as I reflected, that, in truth, these palaces go hither, go thither, controlled or not, as it may be, by some distant bureau, the story recurred to me as having elements of *vraisemblance* which I had not noticed before. Having occasion, nearly at the same time, to inquire at the Metropolitan station in Boston for a lost shawl which had been left in a certain Brookline car, the gentlemanly official told me that he did not know where that car was; he had not heard of it for several days. This again reminded me of "The Lost Palace." Why should not one palace, more or less, go astray, when there are thousands to care for? Indeed, had not Mr. Firth told me, at the Albany, that the worst difficulty in the administration of a strong railway is, that they cannot call their freight-cars home? They go astray on the line of some weaker sister, which finds it convenient to use them till they begin to show a need for paint or repairs. If freight-cars disappear, why not palaces? So the story seems to me of more worth, and I put it upon paper.

It was on my second visit to Melbourne that I heard it. It was late at night, in the coffee-room of the Auckland Arms, rather an indifferent third-class house, in a by-street in that city, to which, in truth, I should not have gone had my finances been on a better scale than they were. I laid down, at last, an old New York "Herald," which the captain of the "Osprey" had given me that morning, and which, in the hope of home-news, I had read and read again to the last syllable of the "personals." I put down the paper as one always puts down an American paper in a foreign land, saying to myself, "Happy is that nation whose history is unwritten." At that moment Sir Roger Tichborne, who had been talking with an intelligent-looking American on the other side of the table, stretched his giant form, and said he believed he would play a game of billiards before he went to bed. He left us alone; and the American crossed the room, and addressed me.

"You are from Massachusetts, are you not?" said he. I said I had lived in that State.

"Good State to come from," said he. "I was

there myself for three or four months, — four months and ten days precisely. Did not like it very well; did not like it. At least I liked it well enough: my wife did not like it; she could not get acquainted."

"Does she get acquainted here?" said I, acting on a principle which I learned from Scipio Africanus at the Latin School, and so carrying the war into the enemy's regions promptly. That is to say, I saw I must talk with this man, and I preferred to have him talk of his own concerns rather than of mine.

"O sir, I lost her, — I lost her ten years ago! Lived in New Altoona then. I married this woman the next autumn, in Vandalia. Yes, Mrs. Joslyn is very well satisfied here. She sees a good deal of society, and enjoys very good health."

I said that most people did who were fortunate enough to have it to enjoy. But Mr. Joslyn did not understand this bitter sarcasm, far less resent it. He went on, with sufficient volubility, to give to me his impressions of the colony, — of the advantages it would derive from declaring its independence, and then from annexing itself to the United States. At the end of one of his periods, goaded again to say something, I asked why he left his own country for a "colony," if he so greatly preferred the independent order of government.

Mr. Joslyn looked round somewhat carefully, shut the door of the room in which we were now alone, — and were likely, at that hour of the night, to be alone, — and answered my question at length, as the reader will see.

"Did you ever hear of the lost palace?" said he a little anxiously.

I said, no; that, with every year or two, I heard that Mr. Layard had found a palace at Nineveh, but that I had never heard of one's being lost.

"They don't tell of it, sir. Sometimes I think they do not know themselves. Does not that seem possible?" And the poor man repeated this question with such eagerness, that, in spite of my anger at being bored by him, my heart really warmed toward him. "I really think they do not know. I have never seen one word in the papers about it. Now, they would have put something in the papers, — do you not think they would? If they knew it themselves, they would."

"Knew what?" said I, really startled out of my determination to snub him.

"Knew where the palace is, — knew how it was lost."

By this time, of course, I supposed he was crazy. But a minute more dispelled that notion; and I beg the reader to relieve his mind from it. This man knew perfectly well what he was talking about, and never, in the whole narration, showed any symptom of mania, — a matter on which I affect to speak with the intelligence of the "experts" indeed.

After a little of this fencing with each other, in which he satisfied himself that my ignorance was not affected, he took a sudden resolution, as if it were a relief to him to tell me the whole story.

"It was years on years ago," said he. "It was when they first had palaces."

Still thinking of Nimrod's palace and Priam's, I said that must have been a great while ago.

"Yes, indeed," said he. "You would not call them palaces now, since you have seen Pullman's and Wagner's. But we called them palaces then. So many looking-glasses, you know, and tapestry carpets and gold spit-boxes. Ours was the first line that run palaces."

I asked myself, mentally, of what metal were the spit-boxes in Semiramis's palace; but I said nothing.

"Our line was the first line that had them. We were running our lightning express on the 'Great Alleghanian.' We were in opposition to everybody, made close connections, served supper on board, and our passengers only were sure of the night-boat at St. Louis. Those were the days of river-boats, you know. We introduced the palace feature on the railroad; and very successful it was. I was an engineer. I had a first-rate character, and the best wages of any man on the line. Never put me on a dirt-dragger or a lazy freight loafer, I tell you. No, sir! I ran the expresses, and nothing else, and lay off two days in the week, besides. I don't think I should have thought of it but for Todhunter, who was my palace conductor."

Again this IT, which had appeared so mysteriously in what the man said before. I asked no question, but listened, really interested now, in the hope I should find out what IT was; and this the reader will learn. He went on, in a hurried way:—

"Todhunter was my palace conductor. One night he was full, and his palace was hot, and smelled bad of whale-oil. We did not burn petroleum then. Well, it was a splendid full moon in August; and we were coming down grade, making up the time we had lost at the Brentford Junction. Seventy miles an hour she ran if she ran one. Todhunter had brought his cigar out on the tender, and was sitting by me. Good Lord! it seems like last week.

"Todhunter says to me, 'Joslyn,' says he, 'what 's the use of crooking all round these valleys, when it would be so easy to go across?'

"You see, we were just beginning to crook round, so as to make that long bend there is at Chamoguin; but right across the valley we could see the stern lights of Fisher's train: it was not more than half a mile away, but we should run eleven miles before we came there."

I knew what Mr. Joslyn meant. To cross the mountain ranges by rail, the engineers are obliged to wind up one side of a valley, and then, boldly crossing the head of the ravine on a high arch, to wind up the other side still, so that perhaps half an hour's journey is consumed, while not a mile of real distance is made. Joslyn took out his pencil, and on the back of an envelope drew a little sketch of the country; which, as it happened, I still preserve, and which, with his com-

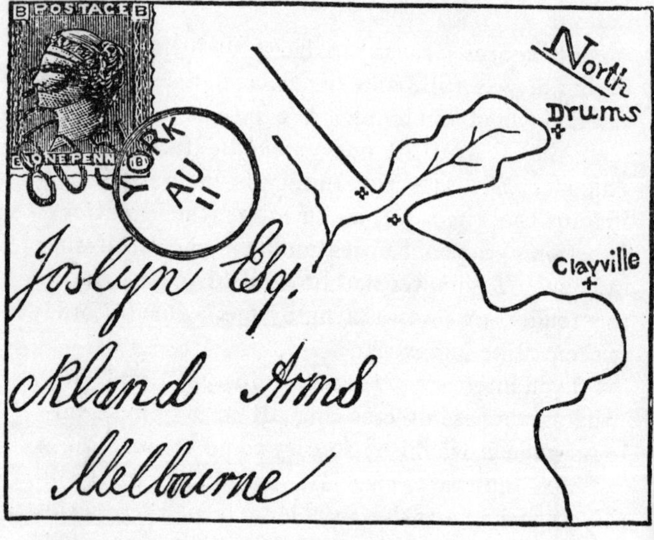

ments, explains his whole story completely. "Here we are," said he. "This black line is the Great Alleghanian, — double track, seventy pounds to the yard; no figuring off there, I tell you. This was a good straight run, down grade a hundred and seventy-two feet on the mile. There, where I make this ×, we came on the

Chamoguin Valley, and turned short, nearly north. So we ran wriggling about till Drums here, where we stopped if they showed lanterns, — what we call a flag-station. But there we got across the valley, and worked south again to this other ×, which was, as I say, not five-eighths of a mile from this × above, though it had taken us eleven miles to get there."

He had said it was not more than half a mile; but this half-mile grew to five-eighths as he became more accurate and serious.

"Well," said he, now resuming the thread of his story, "it was Todhunter put it into my head. He owns he did. Todhunter says, says he, 'Joslyn, what 's the use of crooking round all these valleys, when it would be so easy to go across?'

"Well, sir, I saw it then, as clear as I see it now. When that trip was done, I had two days to myself, — one was Sunday, — and Todhunter had the same; and he came round to my house. His wife knew mine, and we liked them. Well, we fell talking about it; and I got down the Cyclopædia, and we found out there about the speed of cannon-balls, and the direction they had to give them. You know this was only talk then; we never thought what would come of it; but very curious it all was."

And here Mr. Joslyn went into a long mathematical talk, with which I will not harass the reader, perfectly sure, from other experiments which I have tried with other readers, that this reader would skip it all if it were written down. Stated very briefly, it amounted to this: In the old-fashioned experiments of those days, a cannon-ball travelled four thousand and one hundred feet in nine seconds. Now, Joslyn was convinced, like every other engineman I ever talked to, that on a steep down-grade he could drive a train at the rate of a hundred miles an hour. This is thirteen hundred and fourteen feet in nine seconds, — almost exactly one-third of the cannon-ball's velocity. At those rates, if the valley at Chamoguin were really but five-eighths of a mile wide, the cannon-ball would cross it in seven or eight seconds, and the train in about twenty-three seconds. Both Todhunter and Joslyn were good enough mechanics and machinists to know that the rate for thirty-three hundred feet, the width of the valley, was not quite the same as that for four thousand feet; for which, in their book, they had the calculations and formulas; but they also knew that the difference was to their advantage, or the advantage of the bold experiment which had occurred to both of them when Todhunter had made on the tender his very critical suggestion.

The reader has already conceived the idea of this experiment. These rash men were wondering already whether it were not possible to leap an engine flying over the Chamoguin ravine, as Eclipse or Flying Childers might have leaped the brook at the bottom of it. Joslyn believed implicitly, as I found in talk with him, the received statement of conversation, that Eclipse, at a single bound, sprang forty feet. "If Eclipse, who weighed perhaps one thousand two hundred, would spring forty feet, could not my train, weighing two hundred tons, spring a hundred times as far?" asked he triumphantly. At least, he said that he said this to Todhunter. They went into more careful studies of projectiles, to see if it could or could not.

The article on "Gunnery" gave them just one of those convenient tables which are the blessing of wise men and learned men, and which lead half-trained men to their ruin. They found that for their "range," which was, as they supposed, eleven hundred yards, the elevation of a forty-two pounder was one degree and a third; of a nine-pounder, three degrees. The elevation for a railway train, alas! no man had calculated. But this had occurred to both of them from the beginning. In descending the grade, at the spot where, on his little map, Joslyn made the more westerly ×, they were more than eleven hundred feet above the spot where he had made his second, or easterly ×. All this descent was to the advantage of the experiment. A gunner would have said that the first × "commanded" the second ×, and that a battery there would inevitably silence a battery at the point below.

"We need not figure on it," said Todhunter, as Mrs. Joslyn called them in to supper. "If we did, we should make a mistake. Give me your papers. When I go up, Monday night, I 'll give them to my brother Bill. I shall pass him at Faber's Mills. He has studied all these things, of course; and he will like the fun of making it out for us." So they sat down to Mrs. Joslyn's waffles; and, but for Bill Todhunter, this story would never have been told to me, nor would John Joslyn and "this woman" ever have gone to Australia.

But Bill Todhunter was one of those acute men of whom the new civilization of this country is raising thousands with every year; who, in the midst of hard hand-work, and a daily duty which to collegians and to the ignorant men among their professors seems repulsive, carry on careful scientific study, read the best results of the latest inquiry, manage to bring together a first-rate library of reference, never spend a cent for liquor or tobacco, never waste an hour at a circus or a ball, but make their wives happy by sitting all the evening, "figuring," one side of the table, while the wife is hemming napkins on the other. All of a sudden, when such a man is wanted, he steps out, and bridges the Gulf of Bothnia; and people wonder, who forget that for two centuries and a half the foresighted men and women of this country have been building up, in the face of the Devil of Selfishness on the one hand, and of the Pope of Rome on the other, a system of popular education, improving every hour.

At this moment Bill Todhunter was foreman of Repair Section No. 11 on the "Great Alleghanian," — a position which needed a man of first-rate promptness, of great resource, of good education in engineering. Such a man had the "Great Alleghanian" found in him, by good luck; and they had promoted him to their hardest-worked and best-paid section, — the section on which, as it happened, was this Chamoguin run, and the long bend which I have described, by which the road "headed" that stream.

The younger Todhunter did meet his brother at Faber's Mills, where the repair-train had hauled out of the way of the express, and where the express took wood. The brothers always looked for each other on such occasions; and Bill promised to examine the paper which Joslyn had carefully written out, and which his brother brought to him.

I have never repeated in detail the mass of calculations which Bill Todhunter made on the suggestion thus given to him. If I had, I would not repeat them here, for a reason which has been suggested already. He became fascinated with the problem presented to him. Stated in the language of the craft, it was this: —

"Given a moving body, with a velocity eight thousand eight hundred feet in a minute, what should be its elevation that it may fall eleven hundred feet in the transit of five-eighths of a mile?" He had not only to work up the parabola, comparatively simple, but he had to allow for the resistance of the air, on the supposition of a calm, according to the really admirable formulas of Robins and Coulomb, which were the best he had access to. Joslyn brought me, one day, a letter from Bill Todhunter, which shows how carefully he went into this intricate inquiry.

Unfortunately for them all, it took possession of this spirited and accomplished young man. You see, he not only had the mathematical ability for the calculation of the fatal curve, but, as had been ordered without any effort of his, he was in precisely the situation of the whole world for trying in practice his own great experiment. At each of the two ×× of Joslyn's map, the company had, as it happened, switches for repair-trains or wood-trains. Had it not, Bill Todhunter had ample power to make them.

For the "experiment," all that was necessary was, that under the pretext of re-adjusting these switches, he should lay out that at the upper × so that it should run, on the exact grade which he required, to the western edge of the ravine, in a line which should be the direct continuation of the long, straight run with which the little map begins.

An engine, then, running down that grade at the immense rapidity practicable there, would take the switch with its full speed, would fly the ravine at precisely the proper slopes, and, if the switch had been rightly aligned, would land on the similar switch at the lower X. It would come down exactly right on the track, as you sit precisely on a chair when you know exactly how high it is.

"If." And why should it not be rightly aligned, if Bill Todhunter himself aligned it? This he was well disposed to do. He also would align the lower switch, that at the lower X, that it might receive into its willing embrace the engine on its arrival.

When the bold engineer had conceived this plan, it was he who pushed the others on to it, not they who urged him. They were at work on their daily duty, sometimes did not meet each other for a day or two. Bill Todhunter did not see them more than once in a fortnight. But whenever they did meet, the thing seemed to be taken more and more for granted. At last Joslyn observed one day, as he ran down, that there was a large working-party at the switch above Drums, and he could see Bill Todhunter, in his broad sombrero, directing them all. Joslyn was not surprised, somehow, when he came to the lower switch, to find another working-party there. The next time they all three met, Bill Todhunter told them that all was ready if they were. He said that he had left a few birches to screen the line of the upper switch, for fear some nervous bungler, driving an engine down, might be frightened, and "blow" about the switch. But he said that any night when the others were ready to make the fly, he was; that there would be a full moon the next Wednesday, and, if there was no wind, he hoped they would do it then.

"You know," said poor Joslyn, describing it to me, "I should never have done it alone; August would never have done it alone; no, I do not think that Bill Todhunter himself would have done it alone. But our heads were full of it. We had thought of it and thought of it till we did not think of much else; and here was everything ready, and neither of us was afraid, and neither of us chose to have the others think he was afraid. I did say, what was the truth, that I had never meant to try it with a train. I had only thought that we should apply to the supe, and that he would get up a little excursion party of gentlemen, — editors, you know, and stockholders, — who would like to do it together, and that I should have the pleasure and honor of taking them over. But Todhunter poohed at that. He said all the calculations were made for the inertia of a full train, that that was what the switch was graded for, and that everything would have to be altered if any part of the plan were altered. Besides, he said the superintendent would never agree, that he would insist on consulting the board and the chief engineer, and that they would fiddle over it till Christmas.

"'No,' said Bill, 'next Wednesday, or never! If you will not do it then, I will put the tracks back again.' August Todhunter said nothing; but I knew he would do what we agreed to, and he did.

"So at last I said I would jump it on Wednesday night, if the night was fine. But I had just as lief own to you that I hoped it would not be fine. Todhunter — Bill Todhunter, I mean — was to leave the switch open after the freight had passed, and to drive up to the Widow Jones's Cross Road. There he would have a lantern, and I would stop and take him up. He had a right to stop us, as chief of repairs. Then we should have seven miles down-grade to get up our speed, and then — we should see!

"Mr. Ingham, I might have spared myself the hoping for foul weather. It was the finest moonlight night that you ever knew in October. And if Bill Todhunter had weighed that train himself, he could not have been better pleased, — one baggage-car, one smoking-car, two regular first-class, and two palaces: she run just as steady as an old cow! We came to the Widow Jones's, square on time; and there was Bill's lantern waving. I slowed the train: he jumped on the tender without stopping it. I 'up brakes' again, and then I told Flanagan, my fireman, to go back to the baggage-car, and see if they would lend me some tobacco. You see, we wanted to talk, and we did n't want him to see. 'Mr. Todhunter and I will feed her till you come back,' says I to

Flanagan. In a minute after he had gone, August Todhunter came forward on the engine; and, I tell you, she did fly!

"'Not too fast,' said Bill, 'not too fast: too fast is as bad as too slow.'

"'Never you fear me,' says I. 'I guess I know this road and this engine. Take out your watch, and time the mile-posts,' says I; and he timed them. 'Thirty-eight seconds,' says he; 'thirty-seven and a half, thirty-six, thirty-six, thirty-six,' — three times thirty-six, as we passed the posts, just as regular as an old clock! And then we came right on the mile-post you know at Old Flander's. 'Thirty-six,' says Bill again. And then she took the switch, — I can hear that switch-rod ring under us now Mr. Ingham, — and then — we were clear!

"Was n't it grand? The range was a little bit up, you see, at first; but it seemed as if we were flying just straight across. All the rattle of the rail stopped, you know, though the pistons worked just as true as ever; neither of us said one word, you know; and she just flew — well, as you see a hawk fly sometimes, when he pounces, you know, only she flew so straight and true! I think you may have dreamed of such things. I have; and now, — now I dream it very often. It was not half a minute, you know, but it seemed a good long time. I said nothing and they said nothing; only Bill just squeezed my hand. And just as I knew we must be half over, — for I could see by the star I was watching ahead that we were not going up, but were falling again, — do you think the rope by my side tightened quick, and the old bell on the engine gave one savage bang, turned right over as far as the catch would let it, and stuck where it turned! Just that one sound, everything else was still; and then she landed on the rails, perhaps seventy feet inside the ravine, took the rails as true and sweet as you ever saw a ship take the water, hardly touched them, you know, skimmed — well, as I have seen a swallow skim on the sea; the prettiest, well, the tenderest touch, Mr. Ingham, that ever I did see! And I could just hear the connecting rods tighten the least bit in the world behind me, and we went right on.

"We just looked at each other in the faces, and we could not speak; no, I do not believe we spoke for three quarters of a minute. Then August said, 'Was not that grand? Will they let us do it always, Bill?' But we could not talk then. Flanagan came back with the tobacco, and I had just the wit to ask him why he had been gone so long. Poor fellow! he was frightened enough when we pulled up at Clayville, and he thought it was Drums. Drums, you see, was way up the bend, a dozen miles above Clayville. Poor Flanagan thought we must have passed there while he was skylarking in the baggage-car, and that he had not minded it. We never stopped at Drums unless we had passengers, or they. It was what we call a flag-station. So I blew Flanagan up, and told him he was gone too long.

"Well, sir, at Clayville we did stop, — always stopped there for wood. August Todhunter, he was the palace conductor; he went back to look to his passengers. Bill stayed with me. But in a minute August came running back, and called me off the engine. He led me forward, where it was dark; but I could see, as we went, that something was to pay. The minute we were alone he says, —

"'John, we've lost the rear palace.'

"'Don't fool me, August,' says I.

"'No fooling, John,' says he. 'The shackle parted. The cord parted, and is flying loose behind now. If you want to see, come and count the cars. The "General Fremont" is here all right; but I tell you the "James Buchanan" is at the bottom of the Chamoguin Creek.'

"I walked back to the other end of the platform, as fast as I could go and not be minded. Todhunter was there before me, tying up the loose end of the bell-cord. There was a bit of the broken end of the shackle twisted in with the bolt. I pulled the bolt and threw the iron into the swamp far as I could fling her. Then I nodded to Todhunter and walked forward just as that old goose at Clayville had got his trousers on, so he could come out, and ask me if we were not ahead of time. I tell you, sir, I did not stop to talk with him. I just rang 'All aboard!'

and started her again; and this time I run slow enough to save the time before we came down to Steuben. We were on time, all right, there."

Here poor Joslyn stopped a while in his story; and I could see that he was so wrought up with excitement that I had better not interrupt, either with questions or with sympathy. He rallied in a minute or two, and said, —

"I thought — we all thought — that there would be a despatch somewhere waiting us. But no; all was as regular as the clock. One palace more or less, — what did they know, and what did they care? So daylight came. We could not say a word, you know, with Flanagan there; and we only stopped, you know, a minute or two every hour; and just then was when August Todhunter had to be with his passengers, you know. Was not I glad when we came into Pemaquid, — our road ran from Pemaquid across the mountains to Eden, you know, — when we came into Pemaquid, and nobody had asked any questions?

"I reported my time at the office of the master of trains, and I went home. I tell you, Mr. Ingham, I have never seen Pemaquid Station since that day.

"I had done nothing wrong, of course. I had obeyed every order, and minded every signal. But still I knew public opinion might be against me when they heard of the loss of the palace. I did not feel very well about it, and I wrote a note to say I was not well enough to take my train the next night; and I and Mrs. Joslyn went to New York, and I went aboard a Collins steamer as fireman; and Mrs. Joslyn, she went as stewardess; and I wrote to Pemaquid, and gave up my place. It was a good place, too; but I gave it up, and I left America.

"Bill Todhunter, he resigned his place too, that same day, though that was a good place. He is in the Russian service now. He is running their line from Archangel to Astrachan; good pay, he says, but lonely. August would not stay in America after his brother left; and he is now captain's clerk on the Harkaway steamers between Bangkok and Cochbang; good place he says, but hot. So we are all parted.

"And do you know, sir, never one of us ever heard of the lost palace!"

Sure enough, under that very curious system of responsibility, by which one corporation owns the carriages which another corporation uses, nobody in the world has to this moment ever missed "The Lost Palace." On each connecting line, everybody knew that "she" was not there; but no one knew or asked where she was. The descent into the rocky bottom of the Chamoguin, more than fifteen hundred feet below the line of flight, had of course been rapid, — slow at first, but in the end rapid. In the first second, the lost palace had fallen sixteen feet; in the second, sixty-four; in the third, one hundred and forty-four; in the fourth, two hundred and fifty-six; in the fifth, four hundred feet; so that it must have been near the end of the sixth second of its fall, that, with a velocity now of more than six hundred feet in a second, the falling palace, with its unconscious passengers, fell upon the rocks at the bottom of the Chamoguin ravine. In the dead of night, wholly without jar or parting, those passengers must have been sleeping soundly; and it is impossible, therefore, on any calculation of human probability, that any one of them can have been waked an instant before the complete destruction of the palace, by the sudden shock of its fall upon the bed of the stream. To them the accident, if it is fair to call it so, must have been wholly free from pain.

The tangles of that ravine, and the swamp below it, are such that I suppose that even the most adventurous huntsman never finds his way there. On the only occasion when I ever met Mr. Jules Verne he expressed a desire to descend there from one of his balloons, to learn whether the inhabitants of "The Lost Palace" might not still survive, and be living in a happy republican colony there, — a place without railroads, without telegrams, without mails, and certainly without palaces. But at the moment when these sheets go to press, no account of such an adventure has appeared from his rapid pen.

99 LINWOOD STREET

A CHRISTMAS STORY

99 LINWOOD STREET

A GRAY cold morning, the deck wet, the iron all beaded with frost, all the longshoremen in heavy pea-jackets or cardigans, the whole ship in a bustle, and the favored first-class passengers just leaving.

One sad-looking Irish girl stands with her knit hood already spotted with the rime, and you cannot tell whether those are tears which hang from her black eyelashes or whether the fog is beginning to freeze there. What you see is that the poor thing looks right and left and up the pier and down the pier, and that in the whole crowd — they all seem so selfish — she sees nobody. Hundreds of people going and coming, pushing and hauling, and Nora's big brother is not there, as he promised to be and should be.

Mrs. Ohstrom, the motherly Swedish woman, who has four children and ten tin cups and a great bed and five trunks and a fatuous, feckless husband, makes time, between cousins and uncles and custom-house men and sharpers, to run up every now and then to say that Nora must not cry, that she must be easy, that she has spoken to the master and the master has said they are three hours earlier than they were expected. And all this was so kindly meant and so kindly said that poor Nora brushed the tears away, if they were tears, and thanked her, though she did not understand one word that dear Mrs. Ohstrom said to her. What is language, or what are words, after all?

And the bright-buttoned, daintily dressed little ship's doctor, whom poor Nora hardly knew in his shore finery, — he made time to stop and tell her that the ship was too early, and that she must not worry. Father, was it, she was waiting for? "Oh, brother! Oh, he will be sure to be here! Better sit down. Here is a chair. Don't cry. I am afraid you had no breakfast. Take this orange. It will cheer you up. I shall see you again."

Alas! the little doctor was swept away and forgot Nora for a week, and she "was left lamenting."

For one hour went by, and two, and three. The Swedish woman went, and the doctor went, and the girl could see the captain go, and the mate that gave them their orders every morning. The custom-house people began to go. The cabs and other carriages for the gentry had gone long before.

And poor Nora was left lamenting.

Then was it that that queer Salvation Army girl, with a coal-scuttle for a bonnet, came up again. She had smiled pleasantly two or three times before, and had asked Nora to eat a bun.

Poor Nora broke down and cried heartily this time. But the other was patient and kind, and said just what the others had said. Only she did not go away. And she had the sense to ask if Nora knew where the brother lived.

"Fwhy, of course I do, miss. See, here is the paper."

And the little soldier lass read it: "99 Linwood Street, Boston."

"My poor child, what a pity you did not let us see it before!"

Alas and alas! Nora's box was of the biggest. But the army lass flinched at nothing.

An immense wagon, with two giant horses, loaded with the most extraordinary chests which have been seen since the days of the Vikings. Piled on the top were many feather-beds, and on the top of the feather-beds a Scandinavian matron. With Mike, the good-natured teamster, who was at once captain and pilot of this craft, the army lass had easily made her treaty, when he was told the story. He was to carry Nora and her outfit to the Linwood Street house after he had taken these Swedes to theirs. "And indade it will not be farr, miss. There 's a shorrt cut behind Egan's, if indade he did not put up a tinimint house since I was that way." And with new explanations to Nora that all was right, that indeed it was better this way than it would have been had her brother been called from his work, she was lifted, without much consent of her own, to the driver's seat, and her precious "box" was so placed that she could rest her little feet upon it.

Nora had proudly confided to the friendly lass the assurance that she had money, had even shown a crisp $2 bill which had been sent to her for exigencies.

But when the lass made the contract with Mike Dermott, the good fellow said he should take Nora and her box for the love of County Cork. "Indade, indade, I don't take money from the like of her."

And so they started, with the Swedish men walking on one side of the cart with their rifles, keeping a good lookout for buffaloes and red Indians and grizzly bears, as men landing in a new country which they were to civilize. More sailing, for there was the ferry to cross to old Boston. Much waiting, for there was a broken-down coal-wagon in Salutation Alley. Long conference between Nora and Mike, in which he did all the talking and she all the listening, as to home rule and Mr. McCarthy, and what O'Brien thought of this, and what Cunniff thought of that. Then an occasional question came in Swedish from the matron above their heads, and was followed by a reply in Celtic English from Mike, each wholly ignorant of the views or wishes of the others. And occasionally the escort of riflemen, after some particular attack of chaff, in words which they fortunately did not understand, looked up to their matron, controller, and director, exchanged words with her, and then studied the pavement again for tracks of buffalo. A long hour of all this, the stone and brick of the city giving way to green trees between the houses as they come to Dorchester.

Poor Nora looks right and looks left, hoping to meet her big brother. She begins to think she shall remember him. Everybody else looks so different from Fermoy that he must look like home.

But there is no brother.

There is at last a joyful cry as the Swedish matron and the riflemen recognize familiar faces. And Mike smiles gladly, and brings round the stout bays with a twitch, so that the end of the cart comes square to the sidewalk. Somebody produces a step-ladder, and the Swedish matron, with her bird-cage in her hand, descends in triumph. Much kissing, much shaking of hands, much thanking of God, more or less reverent. Then the cords are cut, beds flung down, the giant boxes lifted, the sons of Anak only know how. The money covenanted for is produced and paid, and Mike mounts lightly to Nora's side.

"And now, Nora, my child, wherr is the paper? For in two minutes we 'll soon be therr, now that this rubbish is landed."

And he read on the precious paper, "John McLaughlin, 99 Linwood Street."

Strange to say, the paper said just what it had said two hours before.

"And now, my dear child, we will be therr

in ten minutes, if only we can cross back of Egan's."

And although they could not cross back of Egan's, for Egan had put up a "tinimint" house since Mike had passed that way, yet in ten minutes Linwood Street had been found. No. 99 at last revealed itself, between Nos. 7 and 2,—a great six-story wooden tinder-box, with clothes-lines mysterious behind, open doors in front, long passages running through, three doors on each side of a passage, and the wondering heads of eleven women who belonged to five different races and spoke in six different languages appearing from their eleven windows, as Mike and Nora and the two bays all stopped at one and the same moment at the door.

Mike was already anxious about his time, for he was to be at the custom-house an hour away or more at eleven sharp. But he selected a certain Widow Flynn from the eleven white-capped women; he explained to her briefly that John McLaughlin was to be found; he told Nora for the thirty-seventh time that all was right and that she must not cry; he looked at his watch again, rather anxiously, mounted his box, and drove swiftly away.

He was the one thread which bound Nora to this world. And this thread broke before her eyes.

Mrs. Flynn affected to be cheerful. But she was not cheerful. Mrs. Flynn was a prominent person in her sodality. And well she knew that if any John McLaughlin in those parts were expecting any sister from home, she should know him and where he lived. Well she knew, also, that John McLaughlin, the mason, was born in Glasgow; that John McLaughlin, who is on the city work, had all his family around him, and, most distinct of all, she knew that no McLaughlin, sisterless or many-sistered, lived in this beehive which she lived in, though it were 99 Linwood Street. Into her own cell of that beehive, however, she took poor, sad, desolate Nora. Into the hallway she bade the loafing neighbor boys bring Nora's trunk; in a language Nora could hardly understand she explained to her that all would be well as soon as the policeman passed by. She sent Mary Murphy, who happened to be at home from school, for a pint of milk, and so compelled Nora to drink a cup of tea and to eat a biscuit and a dropped egg, while they waited for the policeman.

Of course he knew of seven John McLaughlins. He even went to the drug-store and looked in the Boston Directory to find that there were there the names of sixty-one more. But not one of them lived in Linwood Street, as they all knew already. All the same Nora was charged not to cry, to drink more tea and eat more bread and butter. The "cop" said he would look in on three of the Johns whom he knew, and intelligent boys now returning from school were sent to the homes of the other four to interrogate them as to any expected sister. Within an hour, now nearly one o'clock, answers were received from all the seven. No one of them expected chick or child from Fermoy.

But the "cop" had a suggestion to make. His pocket list of names of streets revealed another Linwood Street — in Roxbury; not this one in Dorchester. Be it known to unlearned readers, who in snug shelter in Montana follow along this little tale, that Roxbury and Dorchester are both parts of that large municipality called Boston. Though no John McLaughlin was in the directory for 99 Linwood Street, Roxbury, was not that the objective? Poor Nora was questioned as to Roxbury. She was sure she never heard of it.

But the clue was too good to be lost, and the authority of the friendly "cop" was too great to be resisted. He telephoned to the central office that Nora McLaughlin, just from Ireland, had been found, in a fashion, but that no one knew where to put her. Then he stopped a milkman from Braintree, who delivered afternoon milk for invalids.

Was he not going through Roxbury?

Of course he was.

Would he not take this lost child to 99 Linwood Street?

Of course he would. Milkmen, from their profession, have hearts warm toward children.

Well, if he were to take her, he had better take her trunk too.

To which illogical proposal the milkman acceded — on the afternoon route there is so much less milk to take than there is in the morning.

So Nora was lifted into the milk-wagon. In tears she kissed good Mrs. Flynn. The boys and girls assembled to bid her good-by, and even she had a hope for a few moments that her troubles were at an end.

At 99 Linwood Street, Roxbury, they were preparing for the Review Club.

The Review Club met once a fortnight at half-past two o'clock at the house of one or another of the members. They first arranged the little details of the business. Then the hostess read, or made some one read, the scraps which seemed most worthy in the reviews and magazines of the last issues, and at four the husbands and brothers and neighbors generally dropped in, and there was afternoon tea.

"You are sure you have cream enough, Ellen?"

"Oh, yes, mum."

"All kinds of tea, you know, that which the Chinese gentlemen sent, and be sure of the chocolate for Mrs. Bunce."

"Indeed yes, mum."

"And let me know just before you bring up the hot water." Doorbell rings. "There is Mrs. Walter now!"

No, it was n't Mrs. Walter. She came three minutes after. But before she came, Howells, the milkman, had lifted Nora from her seat. As the snow fell fast on the doorsteps, he carried her carefully up to the door, and even by the time Ellen answered the bell he had the heavy chest, dragging it over the snow by the stout rope at one end.

Ellen was amazed to find this group instead of Mrs. Walter. She called her mistress, who heard Howells's realistic story with amazement, not to say amusement.

"You poor dear child!" she cried at once. "Come in where it is dry! John McLaughlin? No, indeed! Who can John McLaughlin be? Ellen, what is Mike's last name?"

Mike was the choreman, who made the furnace fire and kept the sidewalk.

"Mike's name, mum? I don't know, mum. Mary will know, mum."

And for the moment Ellen disappeared to find Mary.

"Never mind, never mind. Come in, you poor child. You are very good to bring her, Mr. Howells, very good indeed. We will take care of her. Is it going to storm?"

Mr. Howells thought it was going to storm, and turned to go away. At that moment Mrs. Walter arrived, the first comer of the Review Club. And Nora's new hostess had to turn to her guests, while Ellen in the last cares for the afternoon table had to comfort Nora by spasms. It was left for Margaret the chambermaid to pump out — or to screw out, as you choose — the details of the story from the poor frightened waif, who seemed more astray than ever.

John McLaughlin? No. Nobody knew anything about him. The last choreman was named McManus, but he went to Ottawa three years ago!

And while the different facts and doubts were canvassed in the kitchen, upstairs they settled the Bulgarian question, the origin of the natives of Tasmania, and the last questions about realism.

Only the mind of the lady of the house returned again and again to questions as to the present residence of John McLaughlin.

For in spite of the gathering snow and the prospect of more, the members of the Review Club had followed fast on Mrs. Walters and gathered in full force.

The hostess, though somewhat preoccupied, was courteous and ready.

Only the functions of the club, as they went forward, would be occasionally interrupted. Thus she would read aloud "as in her private duty bound"—

"'The peasantry were excited, but were held in check by promises from Stambuloff. The emissaries of the Czar—'

"Mrs. Goodspeed, would you mind reading on? Here is the place. I see my postman pass the window."

And so, moving quickly to the front door, she interviewed the faithful Harrington, dressed, heaven knows why, in Confederate uniform of gray. For Harrington had served his four years on the loyal side. Four times a day did Harrington with his letter-bag renew the connection of this household with the world and other worlds.

"Dear Mr. Harrington, I thought you could tell us. Here is a girl named Nora McLaughlin, and here is her trunk, both left at the door by the milkman, and we do not know anything about where she belongs."

"Insufficient address?" asked Harrington, professionally.

"Exactly. All she knows is that her brother is named John."

"A great many of them are," said Harrington, already writing on his memorandum book, and in his memory fixing the fact that a large, two-legged living parcel, insufficiently addressed, had been left at the wrong door for John McLaughlin; also a trunk, too large for delivery by the penny post.

"I will tell the other men, and if I was you I would send to the police."

"Would you mind telling the first officer you meet? I hate to send my girls out." And so she returned to Bulgaria.

But Bulgaria was ended, and Mrs. Conover handed her an article on "Antarctic Discovery." She was again reading: —

"Under these circumstances Captain Wilkes, who had collected a boatload of stones from the front of the glacier," when she gave back the "Forum" to Mrs. Conover. "Would you mind going on just a minute?" she said, and ran out to meet the icecream man. So soon as he had left his tins she said, —

"Mr. Fridge, would you mind stopping at the Dudley School as you go home and telling Miss Lougee that there is a lost girl here?" etc.

Good Mr. Fridge was most eager to help, and the hostess returned, took the book again and read on with "the temperature, as they observed it, was 99 degrees C.; but, as the alcohol in their tins was frozen at the moment, there seemed reason to suspect the correctness of this observation."

And a shiver passed over the Review Club.

Thus far the powers of confusion and error seemed to have been triumphant over poor Nora, or such was the success of that power who uses these agencies, if the reader prefer to personify him.

But the time had come to turn his left flank and to attack his forces in the rear, for the postman now took the field, — that is to say, Harrington, good fellow, finished his third delivery, four good miles and nine-tenths of a furlong, snow two inches deep, three, four, six, before he was done, and then returned to his branch office to report.

"Two-legged parcel; insufficient address; 99 Linwood Street! Jim, what ever come to that letter that went to 99 Linwood Street with insufficient address six weeks ago?"

"Linwood Street? Insufficient address? Foreign letter? Why, of course, you know, went back to the central office."

"I guess it did," said Harrington, grimly; "so I must go there too."

This meant that after Harrington had gone his rounds again on delivery route No. 6, four more miles and nine-tenths more of a furlong, 313 door-bells and only 73 slit boxes, snow now ranging from 6 inches to 12 on the sidewalks, and breast-deep where there was a chance for drifting,— when all this was well done, so that Harrington had no more duties to Uncle Sam, he could take Nora McLaughlin's work in hand, and thus defeat the prince of evil.

To the central office by a horse-car. Blocked once or twice, but well at the office at 7.30 in the evening.

Christmas work heavy, so the whole home staff is on duty. That is well. Enemy of souls loses one point there.

Blind-letter clerks all here. Insufficient-delivery men both here. Chief of returned bureau here. All summoned to the foreign office as Harrington tells his story. Indexes produced, ledgers, journals, day-books, and private passbooks. John McLaughlin's biography followed out on 67 of the different avatars in which his personality has been manifested under that name. False trail here — clue breaks there — scent fails here, but at last — a joyful cry from Will Search: —

"Here you are! Insufficient address. November 1. Queenstown letter — 'Linwood, to John McLaughlin. Try Dorchester. Try Roxbury. Try East Boston. Try Somerville'—and there it stops, and was not returned."

"Try Somerville!"

In these words great light fell over the eager circle. Not because Somerville is the seat of an insane hospital. No! But because it is not in the Boston Directory.

If you please, Somerville is an independent city, and so, unless John McLaughlin worked in Boston, if he lived in Somerville, he would not be in the Boston Directory.

Not much! Somerville has its own seven John McLaughlins besides those Boston ones.

"I say, Harry, Tom, Dick—somebody fetch Somerville Directory!"

Dick flew and returned with the book.

"Here you be! 'John McLaughlin, laborer, 99 Linwood Street!'"

"Victory!"

Satan's forces tremble, and as the different officers return to their desks "even the ranks of Tuscany" in that well-bred office "can scarce forbear to cheer."

As for Harrington, he bids good-by, wraps his tartan around him, and is out in the snow again. Where Linwood Street is he "knows no more than the dead." But somebody will know.

Somerville car. Draw of bridge open. Man falls into the river and has to be rescued. Draw closes. Snow-drift at Margin Street. Shovels. Drift open. Centre of Somerville. Apothecary's shop open. "Please, where is Linwood Street?"

"Take your second left, cross three or four streets, turn to the right by the water-pipe, take the third right, go down hill by the schoolhouse and take second left, and you come out at 11 Linwood Street."

All which Harrington does. He experiences one continual burst of joy that his route does not take him through these detours daily. But his professional experience is good for him. We have no need to describe his false turns. Even aniseed would have been useless in that snow. At last, just as the Somerville bells ring for nine o'clock, Harrington also rings triumphant at the door of the little five-roomed cottage, where his lantern has already revealed the magic number 99.

Ring! as for a gilt-edged special delivery!

Door thrown open by a solid man with curly red hair, unshaven since Sunday, in his shirt-sleeves and with kerosene lamp in his hand.

"Are you John McLaughlin?"

"Indade I am; the same."

"And where's your sister Nora?"

The good fellow, who had been stern before, broke down. "And indade I was saying to Ellen it's an awful night for 'em all in the gale off the coast in the ship. The holy Virgin and the good God take care of 'em!"

"They have taken care of them," said Harrington, reverently. "The ship is safe in dock, and your sister Nora is in Roxbury, at 99 Linwood Street!"

And a broad grin lighted his face as he spoke the words.

There was joy in every bed and at every door of the five rooms. Then John hastily donned coat, cardigan, and ulster. He persuaded Harrington to drink a cup of red-hot tea which was brewing on the stove. While the good fellow did so, and ate a St. Anne's bun, which Mrs. McLaughlin produced in triumph, John was persuading Hermann Gross, the expressman next door, to put the gray into a light pung he had for special delivery. By the time Harrington went to the door two lanterns were flitting about in the snow-piled yard behind the two houses.

Harrington assisted in yoking the gray. In five minutes he and John were defying the gale as they sped across the silent bridge, bound south to Roxbury. Poor little Nora was asleep in the parlor on the sofa. She had begged and begged that she need not be put to bed, and by her side her protector sat reading about the antarctic. But of a sudden Harrington reappeared!

Is it Santa Claus?

Indeed it is! Beard, hat, coat, all white with snow!

And Santa Claus has come for the best present he will deliver that evening!

Dear little Nora is wrapped in sealskins and other skins, mauds and astrakhan rugs. She has a hot brick at her feet, and Pompey, the dog, is made to lie over them, so John McLaughlin

No. 68 takes her in triumph to 99 Linwood Street.

That was a Christmas to be remembered! And Christmas morning, after church, the Brothers of St. Patrick, which was the men's society, and the Sodality of St. Anne's, which was the women's, determined on a great Twelfth-night feast to celebrate Nora's return.

It was to show "how these brethren love one another."

They proposed to take the rink. People did n't use it for skating in winter as much as in summer.

Nora was to receive, with John McLaughlin and his wife to assist. The other 74 John McLaughlins were to act as ushers.

The Salvation Army came first, led by the lass who found Michael.

Procession No. 2 was Mike and the teamsters who "don't take nothing for such as she."

Third, in special horse-cars, which went through from Dorchester to Somerville by a vermilion edict from the West End Company, the eleven families of that No. 99. They stopped in Roxbury to pick up Ellen and the hostess of the Review Club.

Fourth, all the patrolmen who had helped and all who tried to help, led by "cop" No. 47.

Fifth, all the school children who had told the story and had made inquiries.

Sixth, the man who made the Somerville Directory.

Seventh and last, in two barouches, Harrington and the chiefs of staff at the general post-office. And the boys asked Father McElroy to make a speech to all just before the dancing began.

And he said: "The lost sheep was never lost. She thought she was lost in the wilderness, but she was at home, for she was met by the Christmas greeting of the world into which the dear Lord was born!"

NOTE. — It may interest the reader to know that the important part of this story is true.

IDEALS

CHAPTER I

IN ACCOUNT

I HAVE a little circle of friends, among all my other friends quite distinct, though of them. They are four men and four women; the husbands more in love with their wives than on the days when they married them, and the wives with their husbands. These people live for the good of the world, to a fair extent, but much, very much, of their lives is passed together. Perhaps the happiest period they ever knew was when, in different subordinate capacities, they were all on the staff of the same magazine. Then they met daily at the office, lunched together perforce, and could make arrangements for the evening. But, to say true, things differ little with them now, though that magazine long since took wings and went to a better world.

Their names are Felix and Fausta Carter, Frederic and Mary Ingham, George and Anna Haliburton, George and Julia Hackmatack.

I get the children's names wrong to their faces — except that in general their name is Legion, for they are many — so I will not attempt them here.

These people live in very different houses, with very different "advantages," as the world says. Haliburton has grown very rich in the rag and paper business, rich enough to discard rag money and believe in gold. He even spits at silver, which I am glad to get when I can. Frederic Ingham will never be rich. His regular income consists in his half-pay as a retired brevet officer in the patriot service of Garibaldi of the year 1859. For the rest, he invested his money in the Brick Moon, and, as I need hardly add, insured his life in the late Continental Insurance Company. But the Inghams find just as much in life as the Haliburtons, and Anna Haliburton consults Polly Ingham about the shade of a flounce just as readily and as eagerly as Polly consults her about the children's dentistry. They are all very fond of each other.

They get a great deal out of life, these eight, partly because they are so closely allied together. Just two whist-parties, you see; or, if they go to ride, they just fill two carriages. Eight is such a good number — makes such a nice dinner-party. Perhaps they see a little too much of each other. That we shall never know.

They got a great deal of life, and yet they were not satisfied. They found that out very queerly. They have not many standards. Ingham does take the "Spectator;" Hackmatack condescends to read the "Evening Post;" Haliburton, who used to be in the insurance business, and keeps his old extravagant habits, reads the "Advertiser" and the "Transcript;" all of them have the "Christian Union," and all of them buy "Harper's Weekly." Every separate week of their lives they buy of the boys, instead of subscribing; they think they may not want the next number, but they always do. Not one of them has read the "Nation" for five years, for they like to keep good-natured. In fact, they do not take much stock in the general organs of opinion, and the standard books you find about are scandalously few. The Bible, Shakespeare, John Milton; Polly has Dante; Julia has "Barclay's Apology," with ever so many marks in it; one George has "Owen Felltham," and the other is strong on Marcus Aurelius. Well, no matter about these separate things; the uniform books besides those I named, in different editions but in every house, are the "Arabian Nights" and "Robinson Crusoe." Hackmatack has the priceless first edition. Haliburton has Grandville's (the English Grandville). Ingham has a proof copy of the Stothard. Carter has a good copy of the Cruikshank.

If you ask me which of these four I should like best, I should say as the Laureate did when they gave him his choice of two kinds of cake, —

"Both 's as good as one."

Well, "Robinson Crusoe" being their lay gospel and creed, not to say epistle and psalter, it was not queer that one night, when the election had gone awfully, and the men were as blue as that little porcelain Osiris of mine yonder, who is so blue that he cannot stand on his feet — it was not queer, I say, that they turned instinctively to "Robinson Crusoe" for relief.

Now, Robinson Crusoe was once in a very bad box indeed, and to comfort himself as well as he could, and to set the good against the evil, that he might have something to distinguish his case from worse, he stated impartially, like debtor and creditor, the comforts and miseries, thus: —

EVIL.	GOOD.
I am cast upon a horrible desolate island, void of all hope of recovery.	But I am alive, and not drowned as all my ship's company were.
I am singled out and separated, as it were, from all the world, to be miserable.	But I am singled out, too, from the ship's crew to be spared from death.

And so the debtor and creditor account goes on.

Julia Hackmatack read this aloud to them — the whole of it — and they agreed, as Robinson says, not so much for their posterity as to keep their thoughts from daily poring on their trials, that for each family they would make such a balance. What might not come of it? Perhaps a partial — nay, perhaps a perfect cure!

So they determined that on the instant they would go to work, and two in the smoking-room, two in the dining-room, two in George's study, and two in the parlor, they should in the next half-hour make up their lists of good and evil. Here are the results: —

FREDERIC AND MARY INGHAM.

GOOD.	EVIL.
We have three nice boys and three nice girls.	But the door-bell rings all the time.
We have enough to eat, drink, and wear.	But the coal bill is awful, and the Larrabee furnace has given out. The firm that made it has gone up, and no castings can be got to mend it.
We have more books than we can read, and do not care to read many newspapers.	But our friends borrow our books, and only return odd volumes.
We have many very dear friends — enough.	But we are behindhand 143 names on our lists of calls.
We have health in our family.	But the children may be sick. The Lowndes children are.
We seem to be of some use in the world.	But Mrs. Hogarth has left Fred $200 for the poor, and he is afraid he shall spend it wrong.
	The country has gone to the dogs.

GEORGE AND ANNA HALIBURTON.

GOOD.	EVIL.
We have a nice home in town, and one in Sharon, and a sea-shore place at Little Gau, and we have friends enough to fill them.	You cannot give a cup of coffee to a beggar but he sends five hundred million tramps to the door.

GOOD.	EVIL.
We have some of the nicest children in the world.	A great many people call whose names we have forgotten.
We have enough to do, and not too much.	We have to give a party to all our acquaintance every year, which is horrid.
Business is good enough, though complaining.	We do not do anything we want to do, and we do a great deal that we do not want to do. George had added, "And there is no health in us." But Anna marked that out as wicked.
The children are all well.	People vote as if they were possessed.

GEORGE AND JULIA HACKMATACK

GOOD.	EVIL.
We have eight splendid children.	The plumbers' work always gives way at the wrong time, and the plumbers' bills are awful.
We have money enough, though we know what to do with more.	The furnace will not heat the house unless the wind is at the southwest. None of the chimneys draw well.
George will not have to go to Bahia next year.	We hate the Kydd School. The master drinks and the first assistant lies. But we live in that district; so the boys have to go there.
Tom got through with scarlet fever without being deaf.	Lucy said "commence" yesterday, Jane said "gent," Walter said "Bully for you," and Alice said "nobby." And what is coming we do not know.

GOOD.	EVIL.
Dr. Witherspoon has accepted the presidency of Tiberias College in Alaska.	How long any man can live under this government I do not know.

FELIX AND FAUSTA CARTER

GOOD.	EVIL.
Governments are stronger every year. Money goes farther than it did.	But as the children grow bigger, their clothes cost more.
All the boys are good and well. So are the girls. They are splendid children.	But the children get no good at school, except measles, whooping-cough, and scarlet fever.
Old Mr. Porter died last week, and Felix gets promotion in the office.	But the gas-meter lies; and the gas company wants to have it lie.
The lost volume of Fichte was left on the door-step last night by some one who rang the bell and ran away. It is rather wet, but when it is bound will look nicely.	But the Athenæum is always calling in its books to examine them, and making us say where Mr. Fred Curtis's books are. As if we cared.
The mistress of the Arbella School is dead.	But our drains smell awfully, though the Board of Health says they do not.
	We have to go to evening parties among our friends, or seem stuck up. We hate to go, and wish there were none. We had rather come here.
	The increasing worthlessness of the franchise.

With these papers they gathered all in the study just as the clock struck nine, and, in good old Boston fashion, Silas was bringing in some hot oysters. They ate the oysters, which were good — trust Anna for that — and then the women read the papers, while the smoking men smoked and pondered.

They all recognized the gravity of the situation. Still, as Julia said, they felt better already. It was like having the doctor come: you knew the worst, and could make ready for it.

They did not discuss the statements much. They had discussed them too much in severalty. They did agree that they should be left to Felix to report upon the next evening. He was, so to speak, to post them, to strike out from each side the quantities which could be eliminated, and leave the equations so simplified that the eight might determine what they should do about it — indeed, what they could do about it.

The visitors put on their "things" — how strange that that word should once have meant "parliaments!" — kissed good-by so far as they were womanly, and went home. George Haliburton screwed down the gas, and they went to bed.

CHAPTER II

STRIKING THE BALANCE

THE next night they went to see Warren at the Museum. That probably helped them. After the play they met by appointment at the Carters'. Felix read his

REPORT.

1. NUMBER. — There are twenty-one reasons for congratulation, twenty-four for regret. But of the twenty-four, four are the same; namely, the cursed political prospect of the country. Counting that as one only, there are twenty-one on each side.

2. EVIL. — The twenty-one evils may be classified thus: political, 1; social, 12; physical, 5; terrors, 3.

All the physical evils would be relieved by living in a temperate climate, instead of this abomination, which is not a climate, to which our ancestors were sold by the cupidity of the Dutch.

The political evil would be ended by leaving the jurisdiction of the United States.

The social evils, which are a majority of all, would be reduced by residence in any place where there were not so many people.

The terrors properly belong to all the classes. In a decent climate, in a country not governed by its vices, and a community not crowded, the three terrors would be materially abated, if not put to an end.

Respectfully submitted, FELIX CARTER.

How they discussed it now! Talk? I think so! They all talked awhile, and no one listened. But they had to stop when Phenice brought in the Welsh rare-bit (good before bed, but a little indigestible, unless your conscience is stainless), and Felix then put in a word.

"Now I tell you, this is not nonsense. Why not do what Winslow and Standish and those fellows thought they were doing when they sailed? Why not go to a climate like France, with milder winters and cooler summers than here? You want some winter, you want some summer."

"I hate centipedes and scorpions," said Anna.

"There's no need of them. There's a place in Mexico, not a hundred miles from the sea, where you can have your temperature just as you like."

"Stuff!"

"No, it is not stuff at all," said poor Felix, eagerly. "I do not mean just one spot. But you live in this valley, you know. If you find it is growing hot, you move about a quarter of a mile to another place higher up. If you find that hot, why you have another house a little higher. Don't you see? Then, when winter comes, you move down."

"Are there many people there?" asked Haliburton; "and do they make many calls?"

"There are a good many people, but they are a gentle set. They never quarrel. They are a little too high up for the revolutions, and there is something tranquillizing about the place; they seldom die, none are sick, need no aguardiente, do what the head of the village tells them to do — only he never has any occasion to tell them. They never make calls."

"I like that," said Ingham. "That patriarchal system is the true system of government."

"Where is this place?" said Anna, incredulously.

"I have been trying to remember all day, but I can't. It is in Mexico, I know. It is on this side of Mexico. It tells all about it in an old 'Harper' — oh, a good many years ago — but I never bound mine; there are always one or two missing every year. I asked Fausta to look for it, but she was busy. I thought," continued poor Felix, a little crestfallen, "one of you might remember."

No, nobody remembered; and nobody felt much like going to the public library to look, on Carter's rather vague indications. In fact, it was a suggestion of Haliburton's that proved more popular.

Haliburton said he had not laid in his coal. They all said the same. "Now," said he, "the coal of this crowd for this winter will cost a thousand dollars, if you add in the kindling and the matches, and patching the furnace pots and sweeping the chimneys."

To this they agreed.

"It is now Wednesday. Let us start Saturday for Memphis, take a cheap boat to New Orleans, go thence to Vera Cruz by steamer, explore the ground, buy the houses if we like, and return by the time we can do without fires next spring. Our board will cost less than it would here, for it is there the beef comes from. And the thousand dollars will pay the fares both ways."

The women, with one voice, cried, "And the children?"

"Oh yes," cried the eager adventurer. "I had forgotten the children. Well, they are all well, are they not?"

Yes; all were well.

"Then we will take them with us as far as Yellow Springs, in Ohio, and leave them for the fall and winter terms at Antioch College. They will be enough better taught than they are at the Kydd School, and they will get no scarlet fever. Nobody is ever sick there. They will be better cared for than my children are when they are left to me, and they will be seven hundred miles nearer to us than if they were here. The little ones can go to the Model School, the middling ones to the Academy, and the oldest can go to college. How many are there, Felix?"

Felix said there were twenty-nine.

"Well," said the arithmetical George, "it is the cheapest place I ever knew. Why, their Seniors get along for three hundred dollars a year, and squeeze more out of life than I do out of twenty thousand. The little ones won't cost at that rate. A hundred and fifty dollars for twenty-nine children; how much is that, Polly?"

"Forty-three hundred and fifty dollars, of course," said she.

"I thought so. Well, don't you see, we shall save that in wages to these servants we are boarding here, of whom there are eleven, who cost us, say, six dollars a week; that is, sixty-six dollars for twenty weeks is thirteen hundred and twenty dollars. We won't buy any clothes, but live on the old ones, and make the children wear their big brothers' and sisters'. There 's a saving of thirty-seven hundred dollars for thirty-seven of us. Why, we shall make money! I tell you what, if you 'll do it, I 'll pay all the bills till we come home. If you like, you shall then each pay me three-quarters of your last winter's accounts, and I 'll charge any difference to profit and loss. But I shall make by the bargain."

The women doubted if they could be ready. But it proved they could. Still they did not start Saturday; they started Monday, in two palace-cars. They left the children, all delighted with the change, at Antioch on Wednesday — a little tempted to spend the winter there themselves; but, this temptation well resisted, they sped on to Mexico.

CHAPTER III

FULFILMENT

SUCH a tranquil three days on the Mississippi, which was as an autumn flood, and revealed himself as indeed King of Waters! Such delightful three days in hospitable New Orleans! Might it not be possible to tarry even here? "No," cried the inexorable George. "We have put our hand to the plough. Who will turn back?" Two days of abject wretchedness on the Gulf of Mexico. "Why were we born? Why did we not die before we left solid land?" And then the light-house at Vera Cruz.

"Lo, land! and all was well."

What a splendid city! Why had nobody told them of this queen on the sea-shore? Red and white towers, cupolas, battlements! It was all like a story-book. When they landed, to be sure, it was not quite so big a place as they had fancied from all this show; but for this they did not care. To land — that was enough. Had they landed on a sand-spit, they would have been in heaven. No more swaying to and fro as they lay in bed, no more stumbling to and fro as they walked. They refused the amazed Mexicans who wanted them to ride to the hotel. To walk steadily was in itself a luxury.

And then it was not long before the men had selected the little caravan of horses and mules which were to carry them on their expedition of discovery. Some valley of paradise, where a man could change his climate from midwinter to midsummer by a journey of a mile. Did the consul happen to have heard of any such valley?

Had he heard of them? He had heard of fifty.

He had not, indeed, heard of much else. How could he help hearing of them?

Could the consul, then, recommend one or two valleys which might be for sale? Or was it, perhaps, impossible to buy a foothold in such an Eden?

For sale! There was nothing in the country, so far as the friend knew to whom the consul presented them, which was not for sale. Anywhere in Queretaro; or why should they not go to the Baxio? No; that was too flat and too far off. There were pretty places round Xalapa. Oh, plenty of plantations for sale. But they need not go so far. Anywhere on the rise of Chiquihiti.

Was the friend quite sure that there were no plumbers in the regions he named?

"Never a plumber in Mexico."

Any life-insurance men?

"Not one." The prudent friend did not add, "Risk too high."

Were the public schools graded schools or district schools?

"Not a public school in six provinces."

Would the neighbors be offended if we do not call?

"Cut your throats if you did."

Did the friend think there would be many tramps?

The friend seemed more doubtful here, but suggested that the occasional use of a six-shooter reduced the number, and gave a certain reputation to the premises where it was employed which diminished much tramping afterward, and said that the law did not object to this method.

They returned to a dinner of fish, for which Vera Cruz is celebrated. "If what the man says be true," said Ingham, "we must be very near heaven."

It was now in November. Oh, the glory of that ride, as they left Vera Cruz and through a wilderness of color jogged slowly on to their new paradise!

"Through Eden four glad couples took their way."

Higher and higher. This wonder and that. Not a blade of grass such as they ever saw before, not a chirping cricket such as they ever heard before; a hundred bright-winged birds, and not one that they had ever seen before. Higher and higher. Trees, skies, clouds, flowers, beasts, birds, insects, all new and all lovely.

The final purchase was of one small plantation, with a house large enough for a little army, yet without a stair. Oranges, lemons, pomegranates, mangoes, bananas, pine-apples, coffee, sugar — what did not ripen in those perennial gardens? Half a mile above there were two smaller houses belonging to the same estate; half a mile above, another was purchased easily. This was too cold to stay in in November, but in June and July and August the temperature would be sixty-six, without change.

They sent back the mules. A telegram from Vera Cruz brought from Boston, in fifteen days, the best books in the world, the best piano in the world, a few boxes of colors for the artists, a few reams of paper, and a few dozen of pencils for the men. And then began four months of blessed life. Never a gas-bill nor a water-leak, never a crack in the furnace nor a man to put in coal, never a request to speak for the benefit of the Fenians, never the necessity of attending at a primary meeting. The ladies found in their walks these gentle Mexican children, simple, happy, civil, and with the strange idea that the object for which life is given is that men may live. They came home with new wealth untold every day — of ipomœa, convolvulus, passion-flowers, and orchids. The gentlemen brought back every day a new species, even a new genus, — a new illustration of evolution, or a new mystery to be accounted for by the law of natural selection. Night was all sleep; day was all life. Digestion waited upon appetite; appetite waited upon exercise; exercise waited upon study; study waited upon conversation; conversation waited upon love. Could it be that November was over? Can life run by so fast? Can it be that Christmas has come? Can we let life go by so fast? Is it possible that it is the end of January? We cannot let life go so fast. Really, is this St. Valentine's Day! When ever did life go so fast?

And with the 1st of March the mules were ordered, and they moved to the next higher level. The men and women walked. And there, on the grade of a new climate, they began on a new botany, on new discoveries, and happy life found new forms as they began again.

So sped April and so sped May. Life had its battles, — oh yes, because it was life. But they were not the pettiest of battles. They were not the battles of prisoners shut up, to keep out the weather, in cells fifteen feet square. They fought, if they fought, with God's air in their veins, and God's warm sunshine around them, and God's blue sky above them. So they did what they could, as they wrote and read and drew and painted, as they walked and ran and swam and rode and drove, as they encouraged this peon boy and taught that peon girl, smoothed this old woman's pillow and listened to that old man's story, as they analyzed these wonderful flowers, as they tasted these wonderful fruits, as they climbed these wonderful mountains, or, at night, as they pointed the telescope through this cloudless and stainless sky.

With all their might they lived. And they were so many, and there were so many round them to whom their coming was a new life, that they lived in love, and every day drank in of the infinite elixir.

But June came. The mules are sent for again. Again they walked a quarter of a mile. And here in the little whitewashed cottage, with only a selection from the books below, with two guitars and a flute in place of the piano, — here they made ready for three weeks of June. Only three weeks; for on the 29th was the Commencement at Antioch, and Jane and Walter and Florence were to take their degrees. There would need five days from Vera Cruz to reach them. And so this summer was to be spent in the North with them, before October should bring all the children and the parents to the land of the open sky. Three busy weeks between the 1st and the 22d, in which all the pictures must be finished, Ingham's novel must be revised, Haliburton's articles completed, the new invention for measuring power must be gauged and tested, the dried flowers must be mounted and packed, the preserved fruits must be divided for the Northern friends. Three happy weeks of life eventful, but life without crowding, and, above all, without interruption. "Think of it," cried Felix, as they took their last walk among the lava crags, "the door-bell has not rung all this last winter.'"

"'This happy old king
On his gate he did swing,
Because there was never a door-bell to ring.'"

This was Julia's impromptu reply.

CHAPTER IV

HOME AGAIN

SO came one more journey. Why can we not go and come without this musty steamer, these odious smells, this food for dogs, and this surge — ah, how remorseless! — of the cruel sea?

But even this will end. Once more the Stars and Stripes! A land of furnaces and of water-pipes, a land of beggars and of caucuses, a land of gas-meters and of liars, a land of pasteboard and of cards, a land of etiquettes and of bad spelling, but still their country! A land of telegraphs, which told in an instant, as they landed on the levee, that all the twenty-nine were well, and begged them to be at the college on Tuesday evening, so as to see "Much Ado about Nothing." For at Antioch they act a play the night before Commencement. A land of Pullman's palace-cars. And lo! they secured sections 5 and 6, 7 and 8, in the "Mayflower." Just time to kiss the baby of one friend, and to give a basket of guavas to another, and then whir for Cincinnati and Xenia and Yellow Springs!

How beautiful were the live-oaks and the magnolias! How fresh the green of the cotton! How black the faces of the little negroes, and how beyond dispute the perfume of the baked peanuts at the stations where sometimes they had to stop for wood and water! Even the heavy pile of smoke above Cincinnati was golden with the hopes of a new-born day as they rushed up to the Ohio River, and as they crossed it. And then, the land of happy homes! It was Kapnist who said to me that the most favored places in the world were the larger villages in Ohio. He had gone everywhere, too. Xenia, and a perfect breakfast at the station, then the towers of Antioch, then the twenty-nine children waving their handkerchiefs as the train rushes in!

How much there was to tell, to show, to ask for, and to see! How much pleasure they gave with their cochineal, their mangoes, their bananas, their hat-bands for the boys, and their fans for the girls! Yes; and how much more they took from nut-brown faces, from smiles beaming from ear to ear, from the boy so tall that he looked down upon his father, from the girl so womanly that you asked if her mother were not masquerading. "You rascal Ozro, you do not pretend that those trousers were made for you? Why, my boy, you disgrace the family." "I hope not, papa; I had ninety-eight in the botany examination, passed with honors in Greek, and we beat the Buckeye Club to nothing in the return match yesterday." "You did, you little beggar?" the proud papa replied. "You ran all the better, I suppose, because you had nothing to trip you." And so on, and so on. The children did not live in paradise, perhaps, but this seems very like the kingdom come!

And after commencements and the president's party, up to the Yellow Springs platform came two unusual palaces, specially engaged. And one was named the "Valparaiso," and the other, as it happened, the "Bethlehem." And they took all the children, and by good luck Mrs. Tucker was going also, and three or four of the college girls, and they took them. So there were forty-two in all. And they sped and sped, without change of cars, save as Bethlehem visited Paradise and Paradise visited Bethlehem, till they came to New Salem, which is the station men buy tickets for when they would go to the beach below Quonochontaug, where the eight and the twenty-nine were to make their summer home before the final emigration.

They do not live at Quonochontaug, but to that post-office are their letters sent. They live in a hamlet of their own, known to the neighbors as the Little Gau. Four large houses, whitewashed without and within, with deep piazzas all around, the roofs of which join the roofs of the houses themselves, and run up on all sides to one point above the centre. In each house a hall some twenty feet by fifty, and in the hall — what is not in the hall? — maybe a piano, maybe a fish-rod, maybe a rifle or a telescope, a volume of sermons or a volume of songs, a spinning-wheel, or a guitar, or a battledore. You might ask widely for what you needed, for study or for play, and you would find it, though it were a deep divan of Osiût or a chibouque from Stamboul — you would find it in one of these simple whitewashed halls.

Little Gau is so near the sea-shore that every day they go down to the beach to bathe, and the beach is so near the Gulf Stream that the swim is — well, perfection. Still, the first day the ladies would not swim. They had the trunks to open, they said, and the closets to arrange. And the four men and the fourteen boys went to that bath of baths alone. And as Felix, the cynic grumbler, ran races naked on the beach with his boy and the boy beat him, even Felix was heard to say, "How little man needs here below to be perfectly happy!"

And at the Little Gau they spent the months from the Fourth of July to the 13th of October — two great days in history — getting ready for Mexico. New sewing-machines were bought, and the fall of the stream from the lake was taught to run the treadles. No end of clothing was got ready for a country which needs none; no end of memoranda made for the last purchases; no end of lists of books prepared, which they could read in that land of leisure. And on the 14th of October, with a passing sigh, they bade good-by to boats and dogs and cows and horses and neighbors and beaches — almost to sun and moon, which had smiled on so much happiness, and went back to Boston to make the last bargains, to pay the last bills, and to say the last good-byes.

After one day of bill-paying and house-advertising and farewelling, they met at Ingham's to "tell their times." And Julia told of her farewell call on dear Mrs Blake.

"The saint!" said she; "she does not see as well as she did. But it was just lovely there. There was the great bronze Japanese stork, which seemed so friendly, and the great vases, and her flowers as fresh as ever, and her books everywhere. She found something for Tom and Maud to play with, just as she used to for Ben and Horace. And we sat and talked of Mexico and Antioch and everything. I asked her if her eyes troubled her, and I was delighted because it seems they do not trouble her at all. She told all about Swampscott and her grandchildren. I asked her if the dust never troubled them on Gladstone Street, but she says it does not at all; and she told all about her son's family in Hong-Kong. I asked her if the failure of Rupee & Lac annoyed them, and she said not at all, and I was so glad, for I had been so afraid for them; and then she told about how much they were enjoying Macaulay. Then I asked her if the new anvil factory on the other side of the street did not trouble her, and she said not at all. And when I said, 'How can that be?' she said, 'Why, Julia dear, we do not let these things trouble us, don't you see. If I were you, I would not let such things trouble me.'"

George Haliburton laid down his knife as Julia told the story. "Do you remember Rabia at Mecca?"

Yes, they all remembered Rabia at Mecca: —

> "Oh heart, weak follower of the weak,
> That thou shouldst traverse land and sea;
> In this far place that God to seek
> Who long ago had come to thee!"

"Why should we not stay here, and not let these things trouble us?"

Why not, indeed?

And they stayed.

ONE CENT

A CHRISTMAS STORY

ONE CENT

SCENE I

DOWN

MR. STARR rose very early that day. The sun was not up. Yet, certainly, it was too light to strike a match. Ah, Mr. Starr, a match may be an economy!

So it was that when, as always, the keys jingled out from his trousers pockets upon the floor, and the money as well, one cent rolled under the bureau unseen by Mr. Starr. He went down to his work now, after he had gathered up the rest of the money and the keys, and answered yesterday's letters.

Then, of course, he could loiter over his breakfast.

But not too long. Clara, his wife, was in good spirits, and the boys were very jolly, but Mr. Starr, all the same, did the duty next his hand. He "kissed her good-by," and started down-town. Edgar stopped him to ask for fifty cents for his lunch; the postman wanted fifteen for an underpaid parcel; Susan, the maid, asked for ten for some extra milk; and then he kissed his hand to the parlor window, and was off.

No! He was not off.

For Clara threw up the window and waved her lily hand. Mr. Starr ran back to the door. She flung it open.

"My dear John, here is your best coat. That coat you have on has a frayed button. I saw it yesterday, and I cannot bear to have you wear it at the Board."

"Dear Clara, what a saint you are!" One more kiss, and Mr. Starr departed.

And loyally he did the duty next his hand. He stopped and signed the sewerage petition; he looked in on poor Colt and said a cheerful word to him; he bade Woolley, the fruit man, send a barrel of Nonesuches to old Mrs. Cowen; he was on time at the Board meeting, took the chair, and they changed the constitution. He looked in at the office and told Mr. Freemantle he should be late, but that he would look at the letters when he came back, and then, ho! for East Boston!

If only you knew, dear readers, that to East Boston you must go by a ferry-boat, as if it were named Greenbush, or Brooklyn, or Camden.

As Mr. Starr took the street car after he had crossed the ferry, to go into the unknown parts of East Boston, he did notice that he gave the conductor his last ticket. But what of that? "End of the route" came, and he girded his loins, trudged over to the pottery he was in search of, found it at last, found the foreman and gave his orders, and then, through mud unspeakable, waded back to the street car. He was the only passenger. No wonder! The only wonder was that there was a car.

"Ticket, sir," said the conductor, after half a mile.

·*Mr. Starr* (*smiling*). I have no ticket, but you may sell me a dollar's worth. (*Feels for pocketbook.*) Hello! I have not my pocketbook; changed my coat.

Conductor (*savagely*). They generally has changed their coats.

Mr. Starr (*with dignity, offering a five-cent nickel*). There 's your fare, man.

Conductor. That won't do, mud-hopper. Fare 's six cents.

Mr. Starr (*well remembering the cent, which is, alas! under the bureau, and grovelling for it in both pockets*). I have a cent somewhere.

Conductor (*stopping car and returning five-cent piece*). We 've had enough of you tramps who change your coats and cannot find your pennies. You step off — and step off mighty quick.

Mr. Starr declines; when they come to Maverick Square he will report the man to the superintendent, who knows him well. Slight scuffle. Mr. Starr resists. Conductor calls driver. Mr. Starr is ejected. Coat torn badly and hat thrown into mud. Car departs.

TABLEAU.

SCENE II

Up

(*Muddy street in East Boston.* Mr. Starr, *wiping his hat with his handkerchief, solus.*)

Mr. Starr. If only Clara had not been so anxious about the Board meeting! (*Eyes five-cent piece.*) Where can that penny be? (*Searches in pockets, is searching when*—)

(*Enter* R. H. U. E. *span of wild horses, swiftly dragging a carryall. In the carryall two children screaming. Speed of horses,* 2.41.)

Mr. Starr. Under the present circumstances life is worthless, or nearly so. Let me bravely throw it away!

(*Rushes upon the span. Catches each horse by the bit, and by sheer weight controls them. Horses on their mettle;* Mr. Starr *on his. Enter, running,* John Cradock.)

John Cradock. Whoa, whoa! Ha! they stop. How can I thank you, my man? You have saved my children's lives.

Mr. Starr (*still holding bits*). You had better take the reins.

John Cradock mounts the seat, seizes reins, but is eager to reward the poor, tattered wretch at their heads. Passes reins to right hand, and with left feels for a half eagle, which he throws, with grateful words, to Mr. Starr. Mr. Starr leaves the plunging horses, and they rush toward Prescott Street. (*Exeunt* JOHN CRADOCK, *horses and children.*)

Half amused, half ashamed, Mr. Starr picks up the coin, which he also supposes to be half an eagle.

It proves to be a bright penny, just from the mint.

Mr. Starr lays it with delight upon the five-cent nickel.

(*Enter a street car,* L. H. L. E. Mr. STARR *waves his hand with dignity, and enters car. Pays his fare, six cents, as he passes conductor.*)

In fifteen minutes they are at Maverick Square. Mr. Starr stops the car at the office of Siemens & Bessemer, and enters. Meets his friend Fothergill.

Fothergill. Bless me, Starr, you are covered with mud! Pottery, eh? Runaway horse, eh? No matter; we are just in time to see Wendell off. William, take Mr. Starr's hat to be pressed. Put on this light overcoat, Starr. Here is my tweed cap. Now, jump in, and we will go to the "Samaria" to bid Wendell good-by.

And indeed they both found Wendell. Mr. Starr bade him good-by, and advised him a little about the man he was to see in Dresden. He met Herr Birnebaum, and talked with him a little about the chemistry of enamels. Oddly enough, Fonseca was there, the attaché, the same whom Clara had taken to drive at Bethlehem. Mr. Starr talked a little Spanish with him. Then they were all rung on shore.

TABLEAU: *Departing steamer. Crowd waves handkerchiefs.*

SCENE III

CHRISTMAS — THE END

At Mr. Starr's Christmas dinner, beside their cousins from Harvard College and their second cousins from Wellesley College and their third cousins from Bradford Academy, they had young Clifford, the head book-keeper. As he came in, joining the party on their way home from church, he showed Mr. Starr a large parcel.

"It's the 'Alaska's' mail, and I thought you might like to see it."

"Ah, well!" said Mr. Starr, "it is Christmas, and I think the letters can wait, at least till after dinner."

And a jolly dinner it was. Turkey for those who wished, and goose for those who chose goose. And when the Washington pie and the Marlborough pudding came, the squash, the mince, the cranberry-tart, and the blazing plum-pudding, then the children were put through their genealogical catechism.

"Will, who is your mother's father's mother's father?"

"Lucy Pico, sir!" and then great shouting. Then was it that Mr. Starr told the story which the reader has read in scene one, — of the perils which may come when a man has not a penny. He did not speak hastily, nor cast reproach on

Clara for her care of the button. Over that part of the story he threw a cautious veil. But to boys and girls he pointed a terrible lesson of the value of one penny.

"How dangerous, papa, to drop it into a box for the heathen!"

But little Tom found this talk tiresome, and asked leave to slip away, teasing Clifford as he went about some postage-stamps Clifford had promised him.

"Go bring the parcel I left on the hall table, and your papa will give you some Spanish stamps."

So the boy brought the mail.

"What in the world is this?" cried Mr. Starr, as he cut open the great envelope; and more and more amazed he was as he ran down the lines: —

"'Much Esteemed and Respected Señor, Don JOHN STARR, Knight of the Order of the Golden Fleece:

"'SEÑOR, — It is with true yet inexpressible satisfaction that I write this private note, that I may be the first of your friends in Madrid to say to you that the order for your creation as a Knight Companion of the much esteemed and truly venerable Order of the Golden Fleece passed the seals of the Chancellerie yesterday. His Majesty is pleased to say that your views on the pacification of Porto Rico coincide precisely with his own; that the hands of the government will be strengthened as with the force of giants when he communicates them to the very excellent and much honored governor of the island, and that, as a mark of his confidence, he has the pleasure of sending to you the cordon of the order, and of asking your acceptance.'

"My dear Lady Dulcinea del Toboso, that is what came to you when that Cradock man threw a cent into the mud for me."

"But, papa, what are the other letters?"

"Oh, yes, what are they? Here is English; it's from Wendell. H'm — h'm — h'm. Short passage. Worcestershire — h'm — Wedgewood — h'm — Staffordshire — h'm. Why, Clara, George, listen:

"'I suppose you will not be surprised when I say that your suggestion made on the deck of the 'Samaria,' as to oxalate of strontium, was received with surprise by Herr Fernow and Herr Klee. But such is the respect in which suggestions from America are now held, that they ordered a trial at once in the Royal kilns, the result of which are memoranda A and B, enclosed. They are so much delighted with these results that they have formed a syndicate with the Winkels, of Potsdam, and the Schönhoffs, of Berlin, to undertake the manufacture in Germany; and I am instructed to ask you whether you will accept a round sum, say 150,000 marks, for the German patent, or join them, say as a partner, with twenty per cent of stock in their adventure.'

"I think so," said Mr. Starr. "That is what the bright penny comes to at compound interest. Let us try Birnebaum's letter."

"'GOTTFRIED BIRNEBAUM to JOHN STARR:

"'MY HONORED SIR, — I am at a loss to express to you the satisfaction with which I write. The eminently practical suggestions which you made to me so kindly and freely, as we parted, have, indeed, also proved themselves undoubtedly to be of even the first import. It has to me been also, indeed, of the very first pleasure to communicate them, as I said indeed, to the first director in charge at the works at Sèvres, as I passed through Paris, and now yet again, with equal precision also and readiness, to the Herr first fabricant at Dresden. Your statement regarding the action of the oxides of gold, in combination with the tungstate of bdellium, has more than in practice verified itself. I am requested by the authorities at Dresden to ask the acceptance, by your accomplished and highly respected lady, of a dinner-set of their recent manufacture, in token small of their appreciation, renewed daily, of your contribution so valuable to the resources of tint and color in their rooms of design; and M. Foudroyant, of Sèvres, tells me also, by telegraph of to-day, that to the same much esteemed and highly distinguished lady he has shipped by the 'San Laurent' a tea-service, made to the order of the Empress of China, and delayed only by the untoward state of hostilities, greatly to be regretted, on the Annamite frontier.'"

Mr. Starr read this long-winded letter with astonishment.

"Well, Dulcinea, you will be able to give a dinner-party to the King of Spain when he comes to visit you at Toboso.

"So much for Brother Cradock's penny."

"Dear John, till I die I will never be afraid to call you back when your buttons are tattered."

"And for me," said little Jack, "I will go now and look under the bureau for the lost cent, and will have it for my own."

(*Enter servants*, R. H. L. E., *with the Dresden china. They meet other servants*, L. H. L. E., *with the Sèvres china.*)

TABLEAU.

CURTAIN.

THANKSGIVING AT THE POLLS

A THANKSGIVING STORY

THANKSGIVING AT THE POLLS

I

FREDERICK DANE was on his way towards what he called his home. His home, alas, was but an indifferent attic in one of the southern suburbs of Boston. He had been walking; but he was now standing still, at the well-known corner of Massachusetts and Columbus Avenues.

As often happens, Frederick Dane had an opportunity to wait at this corner a quarter of an hour. As he looked around him on the silent houses, he could not but observe the polling-booth, which a watchful city government had placed in the street, a few days before, in preparation for the election which was to take place three weeks afterward. Dane is of an inquiring temper, and seeing that the polling-booth had a door and the door had a keyhole, he tried in the keyhole a steel key which he had picked up in Dock Square the day before. Almost to his surprise, the key governed the lock at once, and he found himself able to walk in.

He left the door wide open, and the gaslight streaming in revealed to him the aspect of the cells arranged for Australian voting. The rails were all in their places, and the election might take place the very next day. It instantly occurred to Dane that he might save the five cents which otherwise he would have given to his masters of the street railway, and be the next morning three miles nearer his work, if he spent the night in the polling-cabin. He looked around for a minute or two, and found some large rolls of street posters, which had been left there by some disappointed canvasser the year before, and which had accompanied one cell of the cabin in its travels. Dane is a prompt man, and, in a minute more, he had locked the door behind him, had struck a wax taper which he had in his cigar-box, had rolled the paper roll out on the floor, to serve as a pillow. In five minutes more, covered with his heavy coat, he lay on the floor, sleeping as soundly as he had slept the year before, when he found himself on the lee side of an iceberg under Peary's command.

This is perhaps unnecessary detail, by way of saying that this is the beginning of the arrangement which a city, not very intelligent, will make in the next century for unsettled people, whose own houses are not agreeable to them. There exist in Boston at this moment three or four hundred of the polling-booths, — nice little houses, enough better than most of the peasantry of most of Europe ever lived in. They are, alas, generally packed up in lavender and laid away for ten months of the year. But in the twentieth century we shall send them down to the shores of islands and other places where people like to spend the summer, and we shall utilize them, not for the few hours of an election only, but all the year round. This will not then be called "Nationalism," it will be called "Democracy;" and that is a very good name when it is applied to a very good thing.

Dane was an old soldier and an old seaman. He was not troubled by disagreeable dreams, and in the morning, when the street-cars began to travel, he was awaked a little after sunrise, by their clatter on the corner. He felt well satisfied with the success of his experiment, and began on a forecast, which the reader shall follow for a few weeks, which he thought, and thought rightly, would tend to his own convenience, possibly to that of his friends.

Dane telegraphed down to the office that he should be detained an hour that morning, went out to his home of the day before at Ashmont, paid his landlady her scot, brought in with him his little possessions in a valise to the office, and did not appear at his new home until after nightfall.

He was then able to establish himself on the basis which proved convenient afterwards, and which it is worth while to explain to a world which is not too well housed. The city had provided three or four chairs there, a stove, and two tables. Dane had little literature, but, as he was in the literary line himself, he did not care for this so much; men who write books are not commonly eager to read books which are worse than their own. At a nine-cent window of a neighboring tinman's he was able to buy himself the few little necessities which he wanted for housekeeping. And not to detain the reader too long upon merely fleshly arrangements, in the course of a couple of hours of Tuesday evening and Wednesday evening, he had fitted up his convenient if not pretty bower with all that man requires. It was easy to buy a mince pie or a cream cake, or a bit of boiled ham or roast chicken, according as payday was near or distant. One is glad to have a tablecloth. But if one have a large poster warning people, a year before, that they should vote the Prohibition ticket, one's conscience is not wounded if this poster, ink down, takes the place which a tablecloth would have taken under other circumstances. If there is not much crockery to use, there is but little to wash. And, in short, as well trained a man of the world as Dane had made himself thoroughly comfortable in his new quarters before the week was over.

II

At the beginning Frederick's views were purely personal, or, as the preachers say, selfish. Here was an empty house, three miles nearer his work than his hired attic was, and he had taken possession. But conscience always asserts itself, and it was not long before he felt that he ought to extend the benefits of this new discovery of his somewhat further. It really was a satisfaction to what the pulpits call a "felt want" when as he came through Massachusetts Avenue on Thursday evening, he met a boy and a girl, neither of them more than ten years old, crying on the sidewalk. Dane is sympathetic and fond of children. He stopped the little brats, and satisfied himself that neither had had any supper. He could not understand a word of the language in which they spoke, nor could they understand him. But kindness needs little spoken language; and accordingly Frederick led them along to his cabin, and after waiting, as he always did, a minute or two, to be sure that no one was in sight, he unlocked the door, and brought in his little companions.

It was clear enough that the children were such waifs and strays that nothing surprised them, and they readily accepted the modest hospitalities of the position. Like all masculine housekeepers, Frederick had provided three times as much food as he needed for his own physical wants, so that it was not difficult to make these children happy with the pieces of mince pie and lemon pie and cream cake and eclairs which were left from his unknown festivals of the day before. Poor little things, they were both cold and tired, and, before half an hour was over, they were snugly asleep on and under a pile of Prohibition posters.

III

FORTUNATELY for Frederick Dane, for the nine years before he joined Peary, he had lived in the city of Bagdad. He had there served as the English interpreter for the Caliph of that city. The Caliph did most of his business at night, and was in the habit of taking Mr. Dane with him on his evening excursions. In this way Mr. Dane had made the somewhat intimate acquaintance of Mr. Jaffrey, the private secretary of the Caliph; and he had indeed in his own employment for some time, a wide-awake black man, of the name of Mezrour, who, for his "other place," was engaged as a servant in the Caliph's household. Dane was thus not unfamiliar with the methods of unexpected evening visits; and it was fortunate for him that he was so. The little children whom he had picked up, explained to him, by pantomime which would have made the fortune of a ballet-girl, that they were much more comfortable in their new home than they had been in any other, and that they had no wish to leave it. But by various temptations addressed to them, in the form of barley horses and dogs, and sticks of barber's-candy, Dane, who was of a romantic and enterprising disposition, persuaded them to take him to some of their former haunts.

These were mostly at the North End of Boston,

and he soon found that he needed all his recollections of Bagdad for the purpose of conducting any conversation with any of the people they knew best. In a way, however, with a little broken Arabic, a little broken Hebrew, a great deal of broken China, and many gesticulations, he made acquaintance with two of their compatriots, who had, as it seemed, crossed the ocean with them in the same steerage. That is to say, they either had or had not; but for many months Mr. Dane was unable to discover which. Such as they were, however, they had been sleeping on the outside of the upper attic of the house in Salutation Alley where these children had lodged, or not lodged, as the case might be, during the last few days. When Mr. Dane saw what were called their lodgings, he did not wonder that they had accepted pot-luck with him.

It is necessary to explain all this, that the reader may understand why, on the first night after the arrival of these two children, the population of the polling-booth was enlarged by the presence of these two Hebrew compatriots. And, without further mystery, it may be as well to state that all four were from a village about nine hundred and twenty-three miles north of Odessa, in the southern part of Russia. They had emigrated in a compulsory manner from that province, first on account of the utter failure of anything to eat there; second, on account of a prejudice which the natives of that country had contracted against the Hebrew race.

The two North End friends of little Ezra and Sarah readily accepted the invitation of the two children to join in the College Settlement at the corner of the two avenues. The rules of the institution proved attractive, and before a second week was well advanced ten light excelsior mattresses were regularly rolled up every morning as the different inmates went to their duties; while, as evening closed in, eight cheerful companions told stories around the hospitable board.

IV

It is no part of this little tale to follow, with Mr. Stevenson's magic, or with that of the Arabian Nights, the fortunes from day to day of the little circle. Enough that men of Hebrew race do not prove lazy anywhere. Dane, certainly, gave them no bad example. The children were at once entered in a neighboring school, where they showed the quickness of their race. They had the advantage, when the week closed and began, that they could attend the Sabbath school provided for them by the Hebrews on Saturday and the several Sunday-schools of the Parker Memorial, the Berkeley Temple, and the other churches of the neighborhood. The day before the election, Frederick Dane asked Oleg and Vladimir to help him in bringing up some short boards, which they laid on the trusses in the roof above them. On the little attic thus prepared, they stored their mattresses and other personal effects before the great election of that year began. They had no intention of interfering, even by a cup of cold coffee, with the great wave of righteous indignation which, on that particular day of that particular year, "swept away, as by a great cosmic tidal flood, the pretences and ambitions, etc., etc., etc." These words are cited from Frederick Dane's editorial of the next morning, and were in fact used by him or by some of his friends, without variations, in all the cosmic changes of the elections of the next six years.

V

BUT so soon as this election was well over, the country and the city settled down, with what Ransom used to call "amazin'" readiness to the new order, such as it was. Only the people who "take up the streets" detached more men than ever to spoil the pavement. For now a city election was approaching. And it might be that the pavers and ditchers and shovellers and curbstone men and asphalt makers should vote wrong. Dane and his settlement were well aware that after this election they would all have to move out from their comfortable quarters. But, while they were in, they determined to prepare for a fit Thanksgiving to God, and the country which makes provision so generous for those in need. It is not every country, indeed, which provides four hundred empty houses, every autumn, for the convenience of any unlodged night-editor with a skeleton key, who comes along.

He explained to his companions that a great festival was near. They heard this with joy. He explained that no work would be done that day, — not in any cigar-shop or sweating-room. This also pleased them. He then, at some length, explained the necessity of the sacrifice of turkeys on the occasion. He told briefly how Josselyn and the fathers shot them as they passed through the sky. But he explained that now we shoot them, as one makes money, not directly but indirectly. We shoot our turkeys, say, at shooting-galleries. All this proved intelligible, and Frederick had no fear for turkeys.

As for Sarah and Ezra, he found that at Ezra's boys' club and at Sarah's girls' club, and each of her Sabbath-school classes and Sunday-school classes, and at each of his, it had been explained that on the day before Thanksgiving they must come with baskets to places named, and carry home a Thanksgiving dinner.

These announcements were hailed with satisfaction by all to whom Dane addressed them. Everything in the country was as strange to them as it would have been to an old friend of mine, an inhabitant of the planet Mars. And they accepted the custom of this holiday among the rest. Oddly enough, it proved that one or two of them were first-rate shots, and, by attendance at different shooting-galleries, they brought in more than a turkey apiece, as Governor Bradford's men did in 1621. Many of them were at work in large factories, where it was the custom of the house to give a roasted turkey and a pan of cranberry sauce to each person who had been on the pay-list for three months. One or two of them were errand men in the market, and it was the practice of the wholesale dealers there, who at this season become to a certain extent retailers, to encourage these errand men by presenting to each of them a turkey, which was promised in advance. As for Dane himself, the proprietors of his journal always presented a turkey to each man on their staff. And in looking forward to his Thanksgiving at the polls, he had expected to provide a twenty-two pound gobbler which a friend in Vermont was keeping for him. It may readily be imagined, then, that, when the day before Thanksgiving came, he was more oppressed by an embarrassment of riches than by any difficulty on the debtor side of his account. He had twelve people to feed, himself included. There were the two children, their eight friends, and a young Frenchman from Paris who, like all persons of that nationality who are six months in this country, had found many enemies here. Dane had invited him to dinner. He had arranged that there should be plates or saucers enough for each person to have two. And now there was to be a chicken-pie from Obed Shalom, some mince pies and Marlborough pies from the Union for Christian Work, a turkey at each end of the board; and he found he should have left over, after the largest computation for the appetites of the visitors, twenty-three pies of different structure, five dishes of cranberry sauce, three or four boxes of raisins, two or three drums of figs, two roasted geese and eleven turkeys. He counted all the turkeys as roasted, because he had the promise of the keeper of the Montgomery House that he would roast for him all the birds that were brought in to him before nine o'clock on Thanksgiving morning.

VI

HAVING stated all this on a list carefully written, first in the English language and second in the language of the Hebrews, Frederick called his fellow-lodgers together earlier than usual on the evening before Thanksgiving Day. He explained to them, in the patois which they used together, that it would be indecent for them to carry this supply of food farther than next Monday for their own purposes. He told them that the occasion was one of exuberant thanksgiving to the God of heaven. He showed them that they all had great reason for thanksgiving. And, in short, he made three heads of a discourse which might have been expanded by the most eloquent preacher in Boston the next day, and would have well covered the twenty-five minutes which the regulation would have required for a sermon. He then said that, as they had been favored with much more than they could use for their own appetites, they must look up those who were not so well off as themselves.

He was well pleased by finding that he was understood, and what he said was received with applause in the various forms in which Southern Russia applauds on such occasions. As for the two children, their eyes were wide open, and their mouths, and they looked their wonder.

Frederick then proposed that two of their number should volunteer to open a rival establishment at the polling-booth at the corner of Gates Street and Burgoyne Street, and that the company should on the next day invite guests enough to make another table of twelve. He proposed that the same course should be taken at the corner of Shapleigh and Bowditch Streets, and yet again at the booth which is at the corner of Curtis Avenue and Quincy Street. And he said that, as time would press upon them, they had better arrange to carry a part at least of the stores to these places that evening. To this there was a general assent. The company sat down to a hasty tea, administered much as the Israelites took their last meal in Egypt; for every man had on his long frieze coat and his heavy boots, and they were eager for the active work of Thanksgiving. For each the stewards packed two turkeys in a basket, filled in as far as they could with other stores, and Frederick headed his procession.

It was then that he was to learn, for the first time, that he was not the only person in Boston.

It was then that he found out that the revelation made to one man is frequently made to many.

He found out that he was as wise as the next fellow, but was no wiser; was as good as the next fellow, but was no better; and that, in short, he had no special patent upon his own undertaking.

The little procession soon arrived at the corner of Shapleigh and Bowditch Streets. Whoever had made the locks on the doors of the houses had been content to use the same pattern for all. It proved, therefore, that the key of No. 237 answered for No. 238, and it was not necessary to open the door with the "jimmy" which Simeon had under his ulster.

But on the other hand, to Frederick's amazement, as he threw the door open, he found a lighted room and a long table around which sat twelve men, guised or disguised in much the same way as those whom he had brought with him. A few moments showed that another leader of the people had discovered this vacant home a few weeks before, and had established there another settlement of the un-homed. As it proved, this gentleman was a Mashpee Indian. He was, in fact, the member of the House of Representatives from the town of Mashpee for the next winter. Arriving in

Boston to look for lodgings, he, not unnaturally, met with a Mohawk, two Dacotahs, and a Cherokee, who, for various errands, had come north and east. A similarity of color, not to say of racial relations, had established a warm friendship among the five, and they had brought together gradually twelve gentlemen of copper color, who had been residing in this polling-booth since the second day after the general election. Their fortune had not been unlike that of Frederick and his friends, and at this moment they were discussing the methods by which they might distribute several brace of ducks which had been sent up from Mashpee, a haunch of venison which had come down from above Machias, and some wild turkeys which had arrived by express from the St. Regis Indians of Northern New York. At the moment of the arrival of our friends, they were sending out two of their number to find how they might best distribute thus their extra provender.

These two gladly joined in the little procession, and all went together to the corner of Quincy Street and Curtis Avenue. There a similar revelation was made, only there was some difficulty at first in any real mutual understanding. For here they met a dozen, more or less, of French Canadians. These gentlemen had left their wives and their children in the province of Quebec, and, finding themselves in Boston, had taken possession of the polling-booth, where they were living much more comfortably than they would have lived at home. They too had been well provided for Thanksgiving, both by their friends at home and by their employers, and had been questioning as to the distribution which they could make of their supplies. Reinforced by four of their number, the delegation in search of hungry people was increased to fourteen in number, and with a certain curiosity, it must be confessed, they went together to try their respective keys on No. 311.

Opening this without so much as knocking at the door to know if here they might not provide the "annex" or "tender" which they wished to establish, they found, it must be confessed without any amazement or amusement, a company of Italians under the charge of one Antonio Fero, who had also worked out the problem of cheap lodgings, and had established themselves for some weeks here. These men also had been touched, either by some priest's voice or other divine word, with a sense of the duties of the occasion, and were just looking round to know where they might spread their second table. Five of them joined the fourteen, and the whole company, after a rapid conversation, agreed that they would try No. 277 on the other side of the Avenue. And here their fortunes changed.

For here it proved that the "cops" on that beat, finding nights growing somewhat cold, and that there was no provision made by the police commissioners for a club-room for gentlemen of their profession, had themselves arranged in the polling-booth a convenient place for the reading of the evening newspapers and for conference on their mutual affairs. These "cops" were unmarried men, and did not much know where was the home in which the governor requested them to spend their Thanksgiving. They had therefore determined to spread their own table in their club-room, and this evening had been making preparations for a picnic feast there at midnight on Thanksgiving Day, when they should be relieved from their more pressing duties. They also had found the liberality of each member of the force had brought in more than would be requisite, and were considering the same subject which had oppressed the consciences of the leaders of the other bands.

No one ever knew who made the great suggestion, but it is probable that it was one of these officials, well acquainted with the charter of the city of Boston and with its constitution and by-laws, who offered the proposal which was adopted. In the jealousy of the fierce democracy of Boston in the year 1820, when the present city charter was made, it reserved for itself permission to open Faneuil Hall at any time for a public meeting. It proves now that whenever fifty citizens unite to ask for the use of the hall for such a meeting, it must be given to them. At the time of which we are reading the mayor had to preside at every such meeting. At the "Cops'" club it was highly determined that the names of fifty citizens should at once be obtained, and that the Cradle of Liberty should be secured for the general Thanksgiving.

It was wisely resolved that no public notice should be given of this in the journals. It was well known that that many-eyed Argus called the press is very apt not to interfere with that which is none of its business.

VII

AND thus it happened that, when Thanksgiving Day came, the worthy Janitor of Faneuil Hall sent down his assistant to open it, and that the assistant, who meant to dine at home, found a good-natured friend from the country who took the keys and lighted the gas in his place. Before the sun had set, Frederick Dane and Antonio Fero and Michael Chevalier and the Honorable Mr. Walk-in-the-Water and Eben Kartschoff arrived with an express-wagon driven by a stepson of P. Nolan. There is no difficulty at Faneuil Hall in bringing out a few trestles and as many boards as one wants for tables, for Faneuil Hall is a place given to hospitality. And so, before six o'clock, the hour assigned for the extemporized dinner, the tables were set with turkeys, with geese, with venison, with mallards and plover, with quail and partridges, with cranberry and squash, and with dishes of Russia and Italy and Greece and Bohemia, such as have no names. The Greeks brought fruits, the Indians brought venison, the Italians brought red wine, the French brought walnuts and chestnuts, and the good God sent a blessing. Almost every man found up either a wife or a sweetheart or a daughter or a niece to come with him, and the feast went on to the small hours of Friday. The Mayor came down on time, and being an accomplished man, addressed them in English, in Latin, in Greek, in Hebrew, and in Tuscan. And it is to be hoped that they understood him.

But no record has ever been made of the feast in any account-book on this side the line. Yet there are those who have seen it, or something like it, with the eye of faith. And when, a hundred years hence, some antiquary reads this story in a number of the "Omaha Intelligencer," which has escaped the detrition of the thirty-six thousand days and nights, he will say, —

"Why, this was the beginning of what we do now! Only these people seem to have taken care of strangers only one month in the twelve. Why did they not welcome all strangers in like manner, until they had made them feel at home? These people, once a year, seem to have fed the hungry. Would it not have been simpler for them to provide that no man should ever be hungry? These people certainly thanked God to some purpose once a year; how happy is the nation which has learned to thank Him always!"

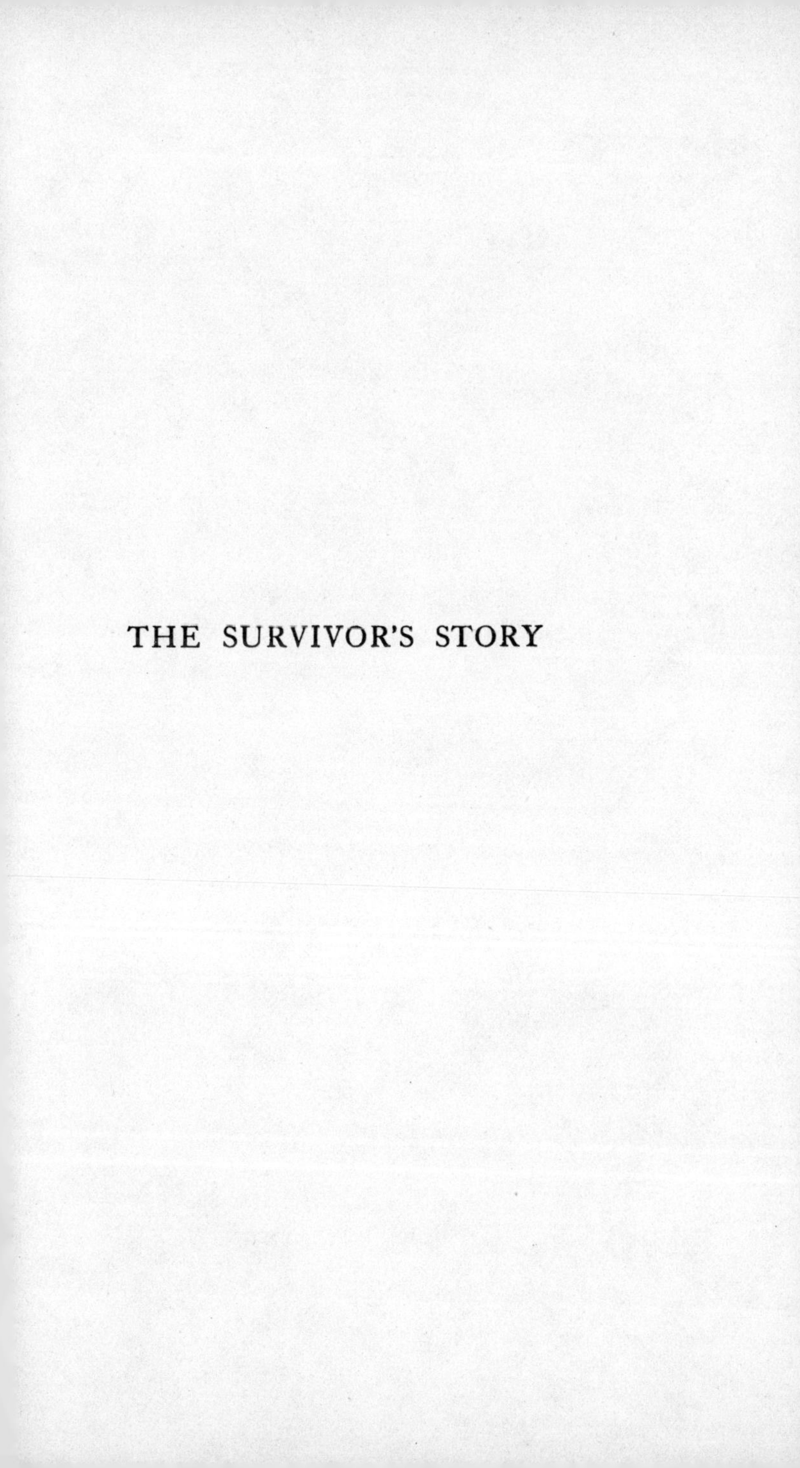

THE SURVIVOR'S STORY

THE SURVIVOR'S STORY

FORTUNATELY we were with our wives.

It is in general an excellent custom, as I will explain if opportunity is given.

First, you are thus sure of good company.

For four mortal hours we had ground along, and stopped and waited and started again, in the drifts between Westfield and Springfield. We had shrieked out our woes by the voices of five engines. Brave men had dug. Patient men had sat inside and waited for the results of the digging. At last, in triumph, at eleven and three quarters, as they say in "Cinderella," we entered the Springfield station.

It was Christmas Eve!

Leaving the train to its devices, Blatchford and his wife (her name was Sarah), and I with mine (her name was Phebe), walked quickly with our little sacks out of the station, ploughed and waded along the white street, not to the Massasoit — no, but to the old Eagle and Star, which was still standing, and was a favorite with us youngsters. Good waffles, maple syrup *ad lib.*, such fixings of other sorts as we preferred, and some liberty.

The amount of liberty in absolutely first-class hotels is but small. A drowsy boy waked, and turned up the gas. Blatchford entered our names on the register, and cried at once, "By George, Wolfgang is here, and Dick! What luck!" for Dick and Wolfgang also travel with their wives. The boy explained that they had come up the river in the New Haven train, were only nine hours behind time, had arrived at ten, and had just finished supper and gone to bed. We ordered rare beefsteak, waffles, dip-toast, omelettes with kidneys, and omelettes without; we toasted our feet at the open fire in the parlor; we ate the supper when it was ready; and we also went to bed; rejoicing that we had home with us, having travelled with our wives; and that we could keep our Merry Christmas here. If only Wolfgang and Dick and their wives would join us, all would be well. (Wolfgang's wife was named Bertha, and Dick's was named Hosanna, — a name I have never met with elsewhere.)

Bed followed; and I am a graceless dog that I do not write a sonnet here on the unbroken slumber that followed. Breakfast, by arrangement of us four, at nine. At 9.30, to us enter Bertha, Dick, Hosanna, and Wolfgang, to name them in alphabetical order. Four chairs had been turned down for them. Four chops, four omelettes, and four small oval dishes of fried potatoes had been ordered, and now appeared. Immense shouting, immense kissing among those who had that privilege, general wondering, and great congratulating that our wives were there. Solid resolution that we would advance no farther. Here, and here only, in Springfield itself, would we celebrate our Christmas Day.

It may be remarked in parenthesis that we had learned already that no train had entered the town since eleven and a quarter; and it was known by telegraph that none was within thirty-four miles and a half of the spot, at the moment the vow was made.

We waded and ploughed our way through the snow to church. I think Mr. Rumfry, if that is the gentleman's name who preached an admirable Christmas sermon in a beautiful church there, will remember the platoon of four men and four women who made perhaps a fifth of his congregation in that storm, — a storm which shut off most church-going. Home again: a jolly fire in the parlor, dry stockings, and dry slippers. Turkeys, and all things fitting for the dinner; and then a general assembly, not in a caravansary, not in a coffee-room, but in the regular guests' parlor of a New England second-class hotel, where, as it was ordered, there were no "transients" but ourselves that day; and whence all the "boarders" had gone either to their own rooms or to other homes.

For people who have their wives with them, it is not difficult to provide entertainment on such an occasion.

"Bertha," said Wolfgang, "could you not entertain us with one of your native dances?"

"Ho! slave," said Dick to Hosanna, "play upon the virginals." And Hosanna played a lively Arab air on the tavern piano, while the fair Bertha danced with a spirit unusual. Was it indeed in memory of the Christmas of her own dear home in Circassia?

All that, from "Bertha" to "Circassia," is not so. We did not do this at all. That was all a slip of the pen. What we did was this. John Blatchford pulled the bell-cord till it broke (they always break in novels, and sometimes they do in taverns). This bell-cord broke. The sleepy boy came; and John said, "Caitiff, is there never a barber in the house?" The frightened boy said there was; and John bade him send him. In a minute the barber appeared — black, as was expected — with a shining face, and white teeth, and in shirt-sleeves, and broad inquiry.

"Do you tell me, Cæsar," said John, "that in your country they do not wear their coats on Christmas Day?"

"Sartin, they do, sah, when they go outdoors."

"Do you tell me, Cæsar," said Dick, "that they have doors in your country?"

"Sartin, they do," said poor Cæsar, flurried.

"Boy," said I, "the gentlemen are making fun of you. They want to know if you ever keep Christmas in your country without a dance."

"Never, sah," said poor Cæsar.

"Do they dance without music?"

"No, sah; never."

"Go, then," I said, in my sternest accents,—"go fetch a zithern, or a banjo, or a kit, or a hurdy-gurdy, or a fiddle."

The black boy went, and returned with his violin. And as the light grew gray, and crept into the darkness, and as the darkness gathered more thick and more, he played for us, and he played for us, tune after tune; and we danced—first with precision, then in sport, then in wild holiday frenzy. We began with waltzes—so great is the convenience of travelling with your wives—where should we have been, had we been all sole alone, four men? Probably playing whist or euchre. And now we began with waltzes, which passed into polkas, which subsided into other round dances; and then in very exhaustion we fell back in a grave quadrille. I danced with Hosanna; Wolfgang and Sarah were our *vis-à-vis*. We went through the same set that Noah and his three boys danced in the ark with their four wives, and which has been danced ever since, in every moment, on one or another spot of the dry earth, going round it with the sun, like the drum-beat of England—right and left, first two forward, right hand across, *pastorale*—the whole series of them; we did them with as much spirit as if it had been on a flat on the side of Ararat, ground yet too muddy for croquet. Then Blatchford called for "Virginia Reel," and we raced and chased through that. Poor Cæsar began to get exhausted, but a little flip from downstairs helped him amazingly. And after the flip Dick cried, "Can you not dance 'Money-Musk'?" And in one wild frenzy of delight we danced "Money-Musk" and "Hull's Victory" and "Dusty Miller" and "Youth's Companion," and "Irish Jigs" on the closet-door lifted off for the occasion, till the men lay on the floor screaming with the fun, and the women fell back on the sofas, fairly faint with laughing.

All this last, since the sentence after "Circassia," is a mistake. There was not any bell, nor any barber, and we did not dance at all. This was all a slip of my memory.

What we really did was this:

John Blatchford said, "Let us all tell stories." It was growing dark and he put more logs on the fire.

Bertha said, —

> "Heap on more wood, the wind is chill;
> But let it whistle as it will,
> We'll keep our merry Christmas still."

She said that because it was in "Bertha's Visit," — a very stupid book, which she remembered.

Then Wolfgang told

THE PENNY-A-LINER'S STORY

[Wolfgang is a reporter, or was then, on the staff of the "Star."]

When I was on the "Tribune" [he never was on the "Tribune" an hour, unless he calls selling the "Tribune" at Fort Plains being on the "Tribune." But I tell the story as he told it. He said:] When I was on the "Tribune," I was despatched to report Mr. Webster's great reply to Hayne. This was in the days of stages. We had to ride from Baltimore to Washington early in the morning to get there in time. I found my boots were gone from my room when the stage-man called me, and I reported that speech in worsted slippers my wife had given me the week before. As we came into Bladensburg, it grew light, and I recognized my boots on the feet of my fellow-passenger, — there was but one other man in the stage. I turned to claim them, but stopped in a moment, for it was Webster himself. How serene his face looked as he slept there! He woke soon, passed the time of day, offered me a part of a sandwich, for we were old friends, — I was counsel against him in the Ogden case. Said Webster to me, "Steele, I am bothered about this speech; I have a paragraph in it which I cannot word up to my mind;" and he repeated it to me. "How would this do?" said he. "'Let us hope that the sense of unrestricted freedom may be so intertwined with the desire to preserve a connection of the several parts of the body politic, that some arrangement, more or less lasting, may prove in a measure satisfactory.' How would that do?"

I said I liked the idea, but the expression seemed involved.

"And it is involved," said Webster; "but I can't improve it."

"How would this do?" said I.

"'LIBERTY AND UNION, NOW AND FOREVER, ONE AND INSEPARABLE!'"

"Capital!" he said, "capital! write that down for me." At that moment we arrived at the Capitol steps. I wrote down the words for him, and from my notes he read them, when that place in the speech came along.

All of us applauded the story.

Phebe then told

THE SCHOOLMISTRESS'S STORY

You remind me of the impression that very speech made on me, as I heard Henry Chapin deliver it at an exhibition at Leicester Academy. I resolved then that I would free the slave, or perish in the attempt. But how? I, a woman — disfranchised by the law? Ha! I saw!

I went to Arkansas. I opened a "Normal College, or Academy for Teachers." We had balls every second night, to make it popular. Immense numbers came. Half the teachers of the Southern States were trained there. I had admirable instructors in oil painting and music — the most essential studies. The arithmetic I taught myself. I taught it well. I achieved fame. I achieved wealth; invested in Arkansas five per cents. Only one secret device I persevered in. To all — old and young, innocent girls and sturdy men — I so taught the multiplication table that one fatal error was hidden in its array of facts. The nine line is the difficult one. I buried the error there. "Nine times six," I taught them, "is fifty-six." The rhyme made it easy. The gilded falsehood passed from lip to lip, from State to State, — one little speck in a chain of golden verity. I retired from teaching. Slowly I watched the growth of the rebellion. At last the aloe blossom shot up — after its hundred years of waiting. The Southern heart was fired. I brooded over my revenge. I repaired to Richmond. I opened a first-class boarding-house, where all the Cabinet and most of the Senate came for their meals; and I had eight permanents. Soon their brows clouded. The first flush of victory passed away. Night after night they sat over their calculations, which all came wrong. I smiled — and was a villain! None of their sums would prove. None of their estimates matched the performance! Never a muster-roll that fitted as it should do! And I — the despised boarding-mistress — I alone knew why! Often and often, when Memminger has said to me, with an oath, "Why this discordancy in our totals?" have my lips burned to tell the secret! But no! I hid it in my bosom. And when at last I saw a black regiment march into Richmond, singing "John Brown," I cried, for the first time in twenty years, "Six times nine is fifty-four," and gloated in my sweet revenge.

Then was hushed the harp of Phebe, and Dick told his story.

THE INSPECTOR OF GAS-METERS' STORY

Mine is a tale of the ingratitude of republics. It is well-nigh thirty years since I was walking by the Owego and Ithaca Railroad, — a crooked road, not then adapted to high speed. Of a sudden I saw that a long cross timber, on a trestle, high above a swamp, had sprung up from its ties. I looked for a spike with which to secure it. I found a stone with which to hammer the spike. But at this moment a train approached, down hill. I screamed. They heard! But the engine had no power to stop the heavy train. With the presence of mind of a poet, and the courage of a hero, I flung my own weight on the fatal timber. I would hold it down, or perish. The engine came. The elasticity of the pine timber whirled me in the air! But I held on. The tender crossed. Again I was flung in wild gyrations. But I held on. "It is no bed of roses," I said; "but what act of Parliament was there that I should be happy?" Three passenger cars and ten freight cars, as was then the vicious custom of that road, passed me. But I held on, repeating to myself texts of Scripture to give me courage. As the last car passed, I was whirled into the air by the rebound of the rafter. "Heavens!" I said, "if my orbit is a hyperbola, I shall never return to earth." Hastily I estimated its ordinates, and calculated the curve. What bliss! It was a parabola! After a flight of a hundred and seventeen cubits, I landed, head down, in a soft mud-hole!

In that train was the young U. S. Grant, on his way to West Point for examination. But for me the armies of the Republic would have had no leader.

I pressed my claim, when I asked to be appointed Minister to England. Although no one else wished to go, I alone was forgotten. Such is gratitude with republics!

He ceased. Then Sarah Blatchford told

THE WHEELER AND WILSON'S OPERATIVE'S STORY

My father had left the anchorage of Sorrento for a short voyage, if voyage it may be called.

Life was young, and this world seemed heaven. The yacht bowled on under tight-reefed staysails, and all was happy. Suddenly the corsairs seized us; all were slain in my defence; but I — this fatal gift of beauty bade them spare my life!

Why linger on my tale? In the Zenana of the Shah of Persia I found my home. "How escape his eye?" I said; and, fortunately, I remembered that in my reticule I carried one box of F. Kidder's indelible ink. Instantly I applied the liquid in the large bottle to one cheek. Soon as it was dry, I applied that in the small bottle, and sat in the sun one hour. My head ached with the sunlight, but what of that? I was a fright, and I knew all would be well.

I was consigned, so soon as my hideous deficiencies were known, to the sewing-room. Then how I sighed for my machine! Alas! it was not there; but I constructed an imitation from a cannon-wheel, a coffee-mill, and two nut-crackers. And with this I made the underclothing for the palace and the Zenana.

I also vowed revenge. Nor did I doubt one instant how; for in my youth I had read Lucretia Borgia's memoirs, and I had a certain rule for slowly slaying a tyrant at a distance. I was in charge of the Shah's own linen. Every week I set back the buttons on his shirt collars by the width of one thread; or, by arts known to me, I shrunk the binding of the collar by a like proportion. Tighter and tighter with each week did the vice close around his larynx. Week by week, at the high religious festivals, I could see his face was blacker and blacker. At length the hated tyrant died. The leeches called it apoplexy. I did not undeceive them. His guards sacked the palace. I bagged the diamonds, fled with them to Trebizond, and sailed thence in a caïque to South Boston. No more! such memories oppress me.

Her voice was hushed. I told my tale in turn.

THE CONDUCTOR'S STORY

I was poor. Let this be my excuse, or rather my apology. I entered a Third Avenue car at Thirty-sixth Street, and saw the conductor sleeping. Satan tempted me, and I took from him his badge, 213. I see the hated figures now. When he woke, he knew not he had lost it. The car started, and he walked to the rear. With the badge on my coat I collected eight fares within, stepped forward, and sprang into the street. Poverty is my only apology for the crime. I concealed myself in a cellar where men were playing with props. Fear is my only excuse. Lest they should suspect me, I joined their game, and my forty cents were soon three dollars and seventy. With these ill-gotten gains I visited the gold exchange, then open evenings. My superior intelligence enabled me to place well my modest means, and at midnight I had a competence. Let me be a warning to all young men. Since that night I have never gambled more.

I threw the hated badge into the river. I bought a palace on Murray Hill, and led an upright and honorable life. But since that night of terror the sound of the horse-cars oppresses me. Always since, to go up town or down, I order my own coupé, with George to drive me; and never have I entered the cleanly, sweet, and airy carriage provided for the public. I cannot; conscience is too much for me. You see in me a monument of crime.

I said no more. A moment's pause, a few natural tears, and a single sigh hushed the assembly; then Bertha, with her siren voice, told

THE WIFE OF BIDDEFORD'S STORY

At the time you speak of I was the private governess of two lovely boys, Julius and Pompey — Pompey the senior of the two. The black-eyed darling! I see him now. I also see, hanging to his neck, his blue-eyed brother, who had given Pompey his black eye the day before. Pompey was generous to a fault; Julius parsimonious beyond virtue. I, therefore, instructed them in two different rooms. To Pompey I read the story of "Waste not, want not." To Julius, on the other hand, I spoke of the All-love of his great Mother Nature, and her profuse gifts to her children. Leaving him with grapes and oranges, I stepped back to Pompey, and taught him how to untie parcels so as to save the string. Leaving him winding the string neatly, I went back to Julius, and gave him ginger-cakes. The dear boys grew from year to year. They outgrew their knickerbockers, and had trousers. They outgrew their jackets, and became men; and I felt that I had not lived in vain. I had conquered nature. Pompey, the little spendthrift, was the honored cashier of a savings-bank, till he ran away with the capital. Julius, the miser, became the chief croupier at the New Crockford's. One of those boys is now in Botany Bay, and the other is in Sierra Leone!

"I thought you were going to say in a hotter place," said John Blatchford; and he told his story.

THE STOKER'S STORY

We were crossing the Atlantic in a Cunarder. I was second stoker on the starboard watch. In that horrible gale we spoke of before dinner, the coal was exhausted, and I, as the best-dressed man, was sent up to the captain to ask him what we should do. I found him himself at the wheel. He almost cursed me, and bade me say nothing of coal, at a moment when he must keep her head to the wind with her full power, or we were lost. He bade me slide my hand into his pocket, and take out the key of the after freight-room, open that, and use the contents for fuel. I returned hastily to the engine-room, and we did as we were bid. The room contained nothing but old account books, which made a hot and effective fire.

On the third day the captain came down himself into the engine-room, where I had never seen him before, called me aside, and told me that by mistake he had given me the wrong key; asking me if I had used it. I pointed to him the empty room; not a leaf was left. He turned pale with fright. As I saw his emotion, he confided to me the truth. The books were the evidences or accounts of the British national debt; of what is familiarly known as the Consolidated Fund, or the "Consols." They had been secretly sent to New York for the examination of James Fiske, who had been asked to advance a few millions on this security to the English Exchequer, and now all evidence of indebtedness was gone!

The captain was about to leap into the sea. But I dissuaded him. I told him to say nothing; I would keep his secret; no man else knew it. The government would never utter it. It was safe in our hands. He reconsidered his purpose. We came safe to port and did — nothing.

Only on the first quarter-day which followed, I obtained leave of absence, and visited the Bank of

England, to see what happened. At the door was this placard, "Applicants for dividends will file a written application, with name and amount, at desk A, and proceed in turn to the Paying Teller's Office." I saw their ingenuity. They were making out new books, certain that none would apply but those who were accustomed to. So skilfully do men of government study human nature.

I stepped lightly to one of the public desks. I took one of the blanks. I filled it out, "John Blatchford, £1747 6*s.* 8*d.*" and handed it in at the open trap. I took my place in the queue in the teller's room. After an agreeable hour, a pile, not thick, of Bank of England notes was given to me; and since that day I have quarterly drawn that amount from the maternal government of that country. As I left the teller's room, I observed the captain in the queue. He was the seventh man from the window, and I have never seen him more.

We then asked Hosanna for her story.

THE N. E. HISTORICAL GENEALOGIST'S STORY

"My story," said she, "will take us far back into the past. It will be necessary for me to dwell on some incidents in the first settlement of this country, and I propose that we first prepare and enjoy the Christmas tree. After this, if your courage holds, you shall hear an over-true tale."

Pretty· creature, how little she knew what was before us!

As we had sat listening to the stories, we had been preparing for the tree. Shopping being out of the question, we were fain from our own stores to make up our presents, while the women were arranging nuts, and blown egg-shells, and pop-corn strings from the stores of the Eagle and Star. The popping of corn in two corn-poppers had gone on through the whole of the story-telling. All being so nearly ready, I called the drowsy boy again, and, showing him a very large stick in the wood-box, asked him to bring me a hatchet. To my great joy he brought the axe of the establishment, and I bade him farewell. How little did he think what was before him! So soon as he had gone I went stealthily down the stairs, and stepping out into the deep snow, in front of the hotel, looked up into the lovely night. The storm had ceased, and I could see far back into the heavens. In the still evening my strokes might have been heard far and wide, as I cut down one of the two pretty Norways that shaded Mr. Pynchon's front walk, next the hotel. I dragged it over the snow. Blatchford and Steele lowered sheets to me from the large parlor window, which I attached to the larger end of the tree. With infinite difficulty they hauled it in. I joined them in the parlor, and soon we had as stately a tree growing there as was in any home of joy that night in the river counties.

With swift fingers did our wives adorn it. I should have said above, that we travelled with our wives, and that I would recommend that custom to others. It was impossible, under the circumstances, to maintain much secrecy; but it had been agreed that all who wished to turn their backs to the circle, in the preparation of presents, might do so without offence to the others. As the presents were wrapped, one by one, in paper of different colors, they were marked with the names of giver and receiver, and placed in a large clothes-basket. At last all was done. I had wrapped up my knife, my pencil-case, my letter-case, for Steele, Blatchford, and Dick. To my wife I gave my gold watch-key, which fortunately fits her watch; to Hosanna, a mere trifle, a seal ring I wore; to Bertha, my gold chain; and to Sarah Blatchford, the watch which generally hung from it. For a few moments we retired to our rooms while the pretty Hosanna arranged the forty-nine presents on the tree. Then she clapped her hands, and we rushed in. What a wondrous sight! What a shout of infantine laughter and charming prattle! for in that happy moment were we not all children again?

I see my story hurries to its close. Dick, who is the tallest, mounted a step-ladder, and called us by name to receive our presents. I had a nice gold watch-key from Hosanna, a knife from Steele, a letter-case from Phebe, and a pretty pencil-case from Bertha. Dick had given me his watch-chain, which he knew I fancied; Sarah Blatchford, a little toy of a Geneva watch she wore; and her husband, a handsome seal ring, — a present to him from the Czar, I believe; Phebe, that is my wife, — for we were travelling with our wives, — had a pencil-case from Steele, a pretty little letter-case from Dick, a watch-key from me, and a French repeater from Blatchford; Sarah Blatchford gave her the knife she carried, with some bright verses, saying that it was not to cut love; Bertha, a watch-chain; and Hosanna, a ring of turquoise and amethysts. The other presents were similar articles, and were received, as they were given, with much tender feeling. But at this moment, as Dick was on the top of the flight of steps, handing down a red apple from the tree, a slight catastrophe occurred.

The first thing I was conscious of was the angry hiss of steam. In a moment I perceived that the steam-boiler, from which the tavern was warmed, had exploded. The floor beneath us rose, and we were driven with it through the ceiling and the rooms above, — through an opening in the roof into the still night. Around us in the air were flying all the other contents and occupants of the Star and Eagle. How bitterly was I reminded of Dick's flight from the railroad track of the Ithaca and Owego Railroad! But I could not hope such an escape as his. Still my flight was in a parabola; and, in a period not longer than it has taken to describe it, I was thrown senseless, at last, into a deep snow-bank near the United States Arsenal.

Tender hands lifted me and assuaged me. Tender teams carried me to the City Hospital. Tender eyes brooded over me. Tender science cared for me. It proved necessary, before I recovered, to amputate my two legs at the hips. My right arm was wholly removed, by a delicate and curious operation, from the socket. We saved the stump of my left arm, which was amputated just below the shoulder. I am still in the hospital to recruit my strength. The doctor does not like to have me occupy my mind at all; but he says there is no harm in my compiling my memoirs, or writing magazine stories. My faithful nurse has laid me on my breast on a pillow, has put a camel's-hair pencil in my mouth, and, feeling almost personally acquainted with John Carter, the artist, I have written out for you, in his method, the story of my last Christmas.

I am sorry to say that the others have never been found.